KEPT

Books published by The Random House Publishing Group are available at quantity discounts on bulk purchases for premium, educational, fund-raising, and special sales use. For details, please call 1-800-733-3000.

KEPT

A Coveted Novel

SHAWNTELLE MADISON

BALLANTINE BOOKS • NEW YORK

Sale of this book without a front cover may be unauthorized. If this book is coverless, it may have been reported to the publisher as "unsold or destroyed," and neither the author nor the publisher may have received payment for it.

Kept is a work of fiction. Names, places, and incidents either are products of the author's imagination or are used fictitiously.

A Ballantine Mass Market Original

Copyright © 2012 by Shawntelle Madison

All rights reserved.

Published in the United States by Ballantine Books, an imprint of The Random House Publishing Group, a division of Random House, Inc., New York.

BALLANTINE and colophon are registered trademarks of Random House, Inc.

ISBN: 978-0-345-52917-6
eBook ISBN: 978-0-345-53601-3

Printed in the United States of America

www.ballantinebooks.com

Cover illustration: © Gene Mollica

9 8 7 6 5 4 3 2 1

Ballantine mass market edition: November 2012

To Ade, Deji, and Ronke,
I love you and thanks for
not burning the house down
while I wrote this book.

Acknowledgments

Coveted was a wild ride, but *Kept* even more so.

First of all, I have to thank my husband, Segun, and my kids. Your patience and willingness to eat out and take care of yourselves when I'm busy writing is appreciated. Also, I have to thank my mother as well as my extended family, who have offered their support and time. I'll never forget your kindness. To my critique partner-in-crime, Sarah Bromley, you're the best support system a gal could have. Huge thanks go to Amanda Bonilla for quickly reading *Kept* and offering critical feedback that helped make my manuscript shine.

To my critique partners Amanda Berry, Dawn Blankenship, Kristi Lea, and Jeannie Lin, you ladies rock! Thanks for supporting my work and keeping me in line.

I have to express my gratitude to my agent, Jim McCarthy. Jim, you make me want to work harder to be the best. I appreciate that. You ride the keep-it-real train and I value your advice.

Kept is such a great book thanks to my editorial team at Del Rey/Ballantine! First of all, an enthusiastic high five goes to my editor, Tricia Narwani. Tricia, you have a great eye for editing and I've learned *so* much from you! Thank you for having faith in me and my work. Thanks also goes to Mike Braff for his hard work.

My fabulous cover is astounding! Huge thanks go to Gene Mollica and the design team at Random House for such a mesmerizing cover. I'm still staring at it on most days.

Thanks to my Magic & Mayhem Writers blog sisters: Amanda Bonilla, Amanda Carlson, Nadia Lee, and Sandy Williams. You're a cheering squad that makes the journey a less bumpy one. Also, I'm so appreciative of the ladies of Missouri RWA for reading the opening of *Kept* and giving me wonderful feedback. Several authors have also given their valuable time to read *Coveted* and I want to thank them: Angie Fox, Michelle Rowen, and Ann Aguirre. Maggie Mae Gallagher, I will remember what you told me when we had our "talk." Thank you for your words. Another round of thanks goes to Tom Czuppon.

And finally, to the two laptops I've pretty much destroyed as I wrote my first two books, you were good while you lasted, but I guess not good enough. The 4-key that popped off had it coming and got what it deserved.

KEPT

Chapter 1

Of all the things I had to face that day, the prospect of sticking my hand down someone else's pants as part of my Cognitive Behavioral Therapy, or CBT, just didn't seem right. Mind you, no one was wearing those filthy pants, but even a gal in therapy should have limits. Today anyway.

According to my therapist, I'd somehow give in to my obsessive-compulsive behaviors less often if I occasionally went out of my comfort zone. Still, in my opinion, my current assignment wouldn't help me that much.

Five minutes earlier, standing inside the lobby of the local Jiffy Lube, my best friend, Aggie, had given the hot new mechanic a harrowing speech that left me wondering just how far she'd go to help me out. "My good friend Natalya here is one of those clean freaks. It'd be awesome if you'd help her out by letting her put her hand down your pants.

"Pants pocket, that is." Her eyebrows danced while she grinned devilishly.

So, there I was, ready to do the deed with the mechanic's grimy uniform.

"Oh, just stick your paw in there so we can go home," Aggie begged. "Your mom said she's making her special pot roast."

How would soiling my germ-free hands with a journey into the grimy pocket of the admittedly attractive mechanic help me with my obsessive-compulsive disorder? I suspected that, in the grand scheme of things, it wasn't really about my well-being. Agatha McClure just wanted the mechanic to take his coveralls off.

"Let the healing begin," she purred as he bent over. The lean, yet hard lines of his body were quite evident under his jeans and white T-shirt.

Healing, my ass. She was staring him down like she was a werewolf on a full-moon prowl and he was the next rabbit she planned to snag.

My head swiveled to catch her running her fingers through her red hair. It was a habit she always fell into when she saw a good-looking man. She had such a blissful expression on her face, I felt bad taking the moment away from her. *Eh, let her leer over him for a few minutes more.* I had an emergency pack of baby wipes for days like today.

So I shoved my hand into the pocket and tried to think happy thoughts. Find that Zen place that didn't involve freaking out over how slimy and lint-laden the pocket was. By the time my hand came out, it resembled a chocolate ice-cream bar with nuts sprinkled on it. Those "nuts" were balls of fluff.

"Well, look at that," Aggie said with pride. "You stuck your paw in and you're still alive."

I handed the mechanic his coveralls with a straight face, and then scowled at Aggie. This exercise sucked. Ever since I'd joined my therapy group, Aggie was constantly searching for golden opportunities like this one to "help" me. As a werewolf with an obsessive-compulsive disorder, I began therapy because I tended to stress out over the little things. I still do, mind you, but I've been learning lately to try to focus on the important stuff, like bonding with my family. Over the past few years, I've been estranged from them due to my disorder. I've made some progress, especially with my dad, but like any issue that dredges up painful memories, the healing had taken some patience.

However, that was a subject I didn't want to fixate on right now. It was already hard enough to deal with this little exercise. While I cleaned off my "ice-cream bar" with baby wipes (many of them), I gazed through the window of Jiffy Lube out to the main street of South Toms River. Not many people may know it, but New Jersey in the winter is beautiful. Especially with a light dusting of snow. On the way here, I'd driven past South Toms River Park. There's something about barren trees extending toward the sky. When they're covered with just the right amount of fallen snow, they can be quite calming to the soul.

Even from inside the lobby, I could taste the winter on my tongue. With it came the promise of holiday decorations and Christmas cookies. The most perfect time of the year.

Once the oil change was done, we left. Aggie strolled to the passenger side of my Nissan Altima—a smug smile on her face—along with a coupon for a free oil change in her hand. I would bet good money the guy had snuck his number on there.

I shook my head with a grin. You couldn't keep an outspoken wolf like Aggie down. We'd known each other for a long time. A few months ago, she'd left New York City to travel west, but a pit stop at my place had ended up as a permanent arrangement. I was grateful to have her company, even with her quirks. Really, they weren't that bad. And although my problems constantly haunted me, Aggie's own issue—an overeating disorder—didn't bother her as much. Case in point: Once comfortable in the passenger seat, she whipped out a snack-sized bag of Cheetos and munched away.

* * *

I turned down the street to my parents' house, and Aggie gave me a strange look. "You do realize we need to pick up my cakes at your place, don't you?"

I'd completely forgotten about her baking spree this weekend. How many cakes had she made? Usually, I simply shrugged off her cooking—especially when she cleaned up after herself. But as I drove around the block to head back toward my place, a heavy weight formed in my stomach at the thought of going home.

I'd mentally prepared myself for the trip to my parents' place; returning to my own home would be another unwanted reminder of my problems.

After a few minutes driving through the outskirts of South Toms River, I reached my house. On my good days, seeing the two-level cottage, with its bright red shutters and whitewashed wood, made me feel safe. Its surrounding woods created a haven from the outside. But on my not-so-good ones it was unnerving.

I pulled into the garage but didn't get out of the car. It seemed like a good idea to just let Aggie fetch her food. Of course, my partner-in-crime had other plans.

Her head peered around the door. "A little help, please?"

Instead of getting out, I said, "For what?"

"Nat, get your ass outta the car and help me carry the cakes. What's your problem anyway?"

I tapped the steering wheel three times. Then twice more. I should just get it over with. But after all the time I'd spent preparing myself for a visit to my parents' home . . . I could undo it with one look—one reminder. Thoughts of my house—or should I say, its contents— wasn't something I wanted weighing on my mind while I was at my parents'.

Normal people let things go. Time to pretend to be *normal* and help my friend. I got out of the car.

The hallway between my garage and kitchen was clear. Like it always was. In the kitchen, Aggie stood with her hands on her hips. With a groan, she shoved a cake container in my hands as I approached her, and I caught a decadent whiff of carrot cake with butter cream icing.

I tried to focus on the cake, on turning around and marching back to the car. But beyond the kitchen lay the living room. And, with it, my shame. Renewed and growing again. Stack after stack of white boxes with holiday ornaments mocked me. Christmas ornaments, Hanukkah candles, and even elaborate Kwanzaa displays. All of them taunting me with a reminder that I'd be facing a certain someone at my parents' home. And that someone, a relative, saw me as a *hoarder* and didn't appreciate all the changes I'd made.

On any other day, seeing those boxes and knowing what beautiful things they held would've brought me inner peace. They'd definitely sheltered me during the long days since I'd been ostracized from my pack.

I reminded myself that some things had changed in my life, like Aggie living here. I glanced at the boxes again and bit my lower lip.

While other things haven't changed at all.

I scrambled out of the house with Aggie not far behind. She struggled to balance three cake containers and managed to get them into the car with only one wobble. As her best friend, I should've done a better job helping her, but I just couldn't shake my doubts. I wanted to be well. Be normal. And sometimes coming home didn't help that.

Ten minutes later, we pulled up to my parents' place. Cars filled the street and driveway. Evidence that everyone had arrived already.

I checked myself for the third time in the rearview mirror. Not a single brown hair was out of place. My blouse and skirt were clean (no surprise there), but I couldn't shake the feeling that something about me was screwed up and wasn't fixable.

Aggie opened her car door then noticed I hadn't done the same. "You have plans to come inside?"

"Yeah."

"Nat, what's wrong now? It's not as if you haven't been here before."

"*She's* here," I mumbled.

Aggie rolled her eyes. "Oh, give me a break. Put on your big-girl panties and just brush it off."

Aggie didn't mention the name of the woman I referred to, but I knew we'd see her soon enough. After just one hundred feet, I would reach the house, knock on the door, and then see that particular person opening it. Every step was unnerving. The thought of my dad's cousin greeting me at the door was worse.

As the matriarch of my family in Maine, "Auntie" Yelena Torchinovich led her brood with an iron paw. She'd come here a few weeks ago for my brother Alex's wedding and had decided to stay for an extended visit. She claimed all sorts of reasons—from catching up with my dad to having missed spending quality time with her relatives. Certainly, in the past ten years, she hadn't shown such *eagerness* to be with the family.

Auntie Yelena stood about an inch taller than me, with thin lips and eyes that conveyed her thoughts—and right now, staring at me, they were black and unwelcoming. Her short and sharp black hair added to her dark impression. I stared back at her. From the way her eyes formed slits, I was returning her gaze far longer than she preferred. No lower-ranking wolf stared down a higher-ranking one without repercussions.

"Quite a persistent little thing," she said. "I think you've forgotten your place—"

"Hi, Yelena." Aggie walked around me and entered the house. The move forced Yelena to step back, thus allowing me to step past her. I shifted my eyes to the floor and carried the cake into the house. For once I was grateful that Aggie was a dominant female.

All around me, my parents' home was alive with activity. The dinner had started already, so everyone sat at the tables set up in the dining room and out into the living room. To any stranger, the whole scene would've seemed noisy and crowded. But to us it was normal. I reveled in this chaos—I had missed it.

I could feel Yelena's heated gaze following us as Aggie and I headed to the kitchen.

While I tried to shake off my aunt's oh-so-warm welcome, Aggie appeared to be relishing the loud conversations. Smatterings of English blended with bursts of Russian. Even though Aggie couldn't understand the Russian parts, she felt at home among the Stravinskys. Under most circumstances, I would've enjoyed dinner here, too. As the weather got colder, my mother gave in to her urge to roast anything that could be herded, caught, and quartered. According to my nose, the meal would be extra tasty tonight. No one could resist the siren call of the savory scent of grain-fed Angus beef. To top it off, I knew the meat would be succulent and dressed with thick homemade gravy.

We reached the oversized kitchen to find my mother waiting for us. Thankfully, Overlord Yelena Torchinovich had not followed us this far, instead taking her seat at the dinner table.

Even as her guests ate, my fair-haired mother continued to mind her pots and keep the food coming. She quietly offered us some Russian salami with cheese and then assessed Aggie's cakes.

Aggie said, "Everything smells divine, Mrs. Stravinsky."

I expected my mom to glow with pride, but she only offered a small smile and gestured for us to go back to the dining room and eat. "Don't let the food get too cold," was all she said.

For Aggie and her never-ending appetite, Mom had effectively rung the dinner bell. With glee, she made a beeline for the table. Naturally, only two spaces were left. Both of them were right across from Auntie Yelena. How convenient.

Before sitting down, though, I approached my grandma and greeted her. After I kissed both of her cheeks, she whispered, "I'm glad you came." Grandma Lasovska-ya's face might be wrinkled from centuries of living as a werewolf, but her brown eyes remained young, always shining with the warmth of her love for her family.

My dad sat at the head of the table eating a steaming bowl of soup. When one of my uncles slapped his shoulder after telling a god-awful joke, I expected him to laugh—or at least snort—but he didn't. I guess I wasn't the only one who didn't feel like taking people's crap today.

Not long after I sat, my aunts and uncles nearby passed me bowls of food. A generous spoonful of home-made and creamy *olivie* snuck on my plate first. I emitted a happy sigh. Nobody made potato salad like my mom. She used fresh vegetables and then added bits of chicken. Next up was her famous pot roast. The meat was so tender, the pieces fell apart as they landed on my plate.

Everyone, except Auntie Yelena, chatted and made jokes with me. Even Dad tried to crack a smile once in a while. Just a few years ago my interactions with family had been very different. They'd avoided me back then as if I didn't exist, due to my obsessive-compulsive disorder. Even now, of course, all it would take was just one person to stomp on the precarious relationship I've built with them.

"How long do you plan to continue this charade?" Auntie Yelena asked.

A slice of beef almost got caught in my throat.

The question was directed to me, and I wanted to ignore it. But my grandma had taught me to mind my manners, even with people who apparently had forgotten theirs.

Yelena took a sip from her glass of merlot. "You do realize the trials are coming, don't you?" Her snippy questions wrapped around my throat like a boa constrictor. "I bet you think you can just slide back into the pack like you did with this family."

My auntie Yelena was referring to the trials the South Toms River Pack holds every year. It was a chance for me to not only rejoin my pack but to prove to everyone that I was no longer a weak and vulnerable member of the Stravinsky family.

I guess that even after I had survived the Long Island pack invasion not so long ago, I still hadn't proved myself. I gave everything I had that night. Too bad Yelena still didn't see that I had tried my best.

I sighed and tried not to squirm. The whole time thinking, *The strong within the pack shall prevail, and the weak shall fall.* Wasn't that what the Code—the code of ethics for all werewolves—had taught Auntie Yelena? Being a part of a family that followed the Code for centuries should have given me a measure of pride. I had a history, a heritage. But for me the Code was nothing but a persistent reminder of my shortcomings.

Finally, I found my voice. "Forgetting about getting kicked out of the pack is rather difficult. Especially since I haven't been included in anything for the past five years." Like her daughter's last-minute wedding this past summer to an overweight stripper. I bet she thought we didn't know about her son-in-law's cheesy website and his free *in-home* demonstrations.

From a few seats down, my brother, Alex, spoke up. "Hey Nat, unlike some other folks at the table, my wife is looking forward to seeing you at her baby shower."

I glanced at Yelena, who stared back at me. "I wouldn't exactly call that pack business," she said. "But I guess someone has to take pity on you."

She had some nerve. I should just hand her my butter knife so she could get it over with and stab my damn heart out.

Aggie threw her fork down. "I'm a guest here, but I'm also Nat's good friend. Could you just knock it off?"

Other than my grandma and my father, Auntie Yelena was considered an elder and should be a respected—or should I say *tolerated*—member of the family. No one told her to knock off anything.

Yelena shot to her feet. "Who do you think you are—"

My mom had picked the perfect time to bring in one of Aggie's cakes. "Oh, shut up, all of you," she snapped in Russian.

She slammed the cake on the edge of the table. The poor chocolate masterpiece never had a chance—it plopped on the floor like a gob of mud.

I took in everyone's faces. Aggie's expression was horrified. She screeched, "Man down!" Meanwhile, a few seats from me, my grandma broke out in a fit of giggles. The laughter spread like wildfire, until everyone was laughing.

Except my mom and dad. Mom turned away and began to cry.

Dad sat there silently, then reached out to comfort his sobbing wife. He turned to us. "She had a hard time at work today. I'll take care of her."

"Mom?" I asked.

My dad, ever the hero when needed, tilted his chin

toward the living room, "C'mon, Anna, let's take a walk."

Uncle Boris immediately stepped toward her. "What's the matter, Anna?"

Mom shook her head as Dad led her out of the room. The urge to follow them was strong, but I knew it was best to let Dad take care of her.

Everything settled down once my parents left. While Auntie Yelena continued to give me the evil eye, Alex sat down next to me.

"You've been preparing for the trials, haven't you?" he asked.

The question was a simple one and unfortunately so was the answer. I hadn't done a damn thing. A few months ago, I was completely focused on staying alive while the Long Island pack hunted me down. But even now that the invaders were long gone, I still had yet to find the time, or the energy, to do a push-up.

"I've been planning a thing or two to get ready." *Or none.*

"Good. Then adding a workout routine with me to your schedule won't be so hard." He gave me a wink from his seemingly innocent blue eyes. But I knew they were about as innocent as a carton of milk left in the fridge for too long. You never know what you're gonna get when you finally venture to take a sip.

While Alex and I spoke, Aunt Vera had honed in on Aggie. Out of all my aunts, Aunt Vera's matchmaking tendencies were the most relentless. If she wasn't eating or trying to throw on a dress that was too tight for her pear-shaped body, she was arranging perfect pairings for her relatives' all-important walk down the aisle—or trying to.

"You've been here so long, Agatha. Haven't you found a good man yet?"

This was where I should've rescued my friend. But

from the amused expression on Aggie's face, I thought it seemed best to sit and observe.

"Not yet." She shrugged with a slight grin. "But who knows if Prince Charming isn't waiting for me in a drunken stupor on some street corner?"

My aunt harrumphed. "You don't need just *any* man." She had that mothers-know-best expression down pat. "You're Scottish, right? Well, that means you need a good, strong man. A *Russian* man."

Here we go. For the next ten minutes—or should I say longer, since I got up to do something trivial in the kitchen, my aunt began her spiel. When I came back she was still going—giving Aggie every reason she could think of for marrying a Russian man. That she was willing to say all this while the men in *my* family were sitting at the table struck me as rather bold. Uncle Boris was an overpowering-cologne-ridden lady-killer, my brother used to be a man-whore, and . . . well, the best thing I could say of my three other uncles was at least they had jobs and would be loyal spouse material. That was it. *Unfortunately.*

After picking up a few things here and there in the kitchen, I peered out the back window to see Mom and Dad sitting on the patio in the backyard. Dad's thick arm was stretched across Mom's shoulders, drawing her small frame close to his large one. Even with the contrast in their appearance, they looked like the perfect pair.

Their words were ever-so-faint, but I heard them nonetheless. As a werewolf, my hearing is quite acute, as is that of my family members. To keep a conversation to themselves, my parents often went outside.

"—but it has been too quiet in the house," my dad said.

"It has. I've missed my Natalya."

"I know you have. I never expected things to . . . turn

out how they have lately. But you do believe me when I say that I don't want you to worry," Dad whispered.

Worry about what? I leaned as close to the window as I dared.

"I've waited so long for us to become grandparents," Mom said. "I've looked forward to it."

"And soon you will be one," he replied softly. "You're a good *jena*. The best wife for a man like me. Sasha's baby'll come soon, and Natalya will marry a good man. We're a family again, and there's nothing but smooth sailing ahead of us."

Mom's reply didn't sound as confident. "I hope what you say is true, Fyodor. I really do."

I heard one of them shift to look around, and I immediately backed away from the window. The rest of their conversation belonged to them, but what I'd heard weighed heavily on my mind as I walked back to the dining room. After all the things I'd had to face, what could be coming now?

Chapter 2

I hadn't expected a man—other than my brother—to call me the next day at five a.m. to wake me to begin my training. I recognized the number right away, and it wasn't Alex's. Caller ID really made it hard to be surprised these days.

I let the phone ring three times before I picked it up, then blurted, "Thorn Grantham, unless you're calling to give me a free pass to avoid the trials, there's no reason for you to call me at this hour."

"Meet me at the high school track in thirty minutes." There was a *click* and the phone line went dead.

I hadn't heard his voice in a while, so I wouldn't have minded a "Hey, you" or perhaps a "Sorry to wake you at five in the morning." But all I got was an order to meet him at the track, presumably to start my training.

If my foggy memory served me correctly, wasn't it *Alex* who was supposed to have called me for a training session? And if so, why had my sneaky brother asked this particular person to help me out—the one man I wanted to avoid at all costs? Alex knew my ex-boyfriend was engaged to another woman. His blatant attempt to hook us up was useless.

I heard Aggie snoring in her room as I plodded into the bathroom to get ready. I was tempted to bang on her door and wake her up so she could offer *moral support* at the track.

Ten minutes later, after a cold shower and half a pot of rich Columbian coffee, I hurried out of my house and drove to the track.

While driving, I mentally went over the three individual elements of the trials. Werewolves, like humans, had special initiation ceremonies. In order to be accepted as a productive member of the pack, candidates had to prove they could defend themselves and protect their clan mates—in essence, show themselves to be of sound mind, body, and spirit.

The first challenge I'd have to face was a ten-mile run. If I survived the second part, a grueling obstacle course, I'd then have to show I could dominate my enemies. The ten-mile run and the obstacle course were intended to wear me down before the final hardship—a fight with one of my fellow candidates. I saw this stage as a pissing match in which the combat-ready candidates could shine and achieve a higher rank within the pack. In terms of self-confidence, I didn't have much. I wasn't a fighter and I didn't see myself becoming one. But what I did have was an undying drive to join the pack—no matter how insurmountable the odds.

When I pulled into the lot, the track was empty; it was early morning after all. Just a few lights illuminated the stands, but with my keen night vision, I could see no one was there. It was not until I left my car and entered the stadium that I found a blond-haired man in jeans and a T-shirt waiting for me on the bleachers, gazing at the woods surrounding the high school grounds.

Despite his brusque phone call to order me to come here, I knew that avoiding Thorn was my best course of action. For the sake of my heart anyway. Letting go of the past was a lot easier when it kept out of your way. Yet I'd still come here to meet him.

Thorn was a few feet away when I caught his scent. A chilled breeze brought it to me: a mix of denim, leather, and mild soap. To my nose it was a perfect combination. "How did Alex convince you to do this?"

He stared at me in a way that made me uncomfortable. "Alex said something about you needing help and how he couldn't do it since he's busy preparing for the baby's arrival. So he asked me to train you for the trials and I said yes."

I sighed. "He never planned to help me at all."

"Why would you say something like that?" Thorn indicated I should follow him to the track.

"You don't see what he's trying to do? Get us together here alone?"

He shrugged. "We're both adults. It's not like we don't know what we can and can't do."

Then he glanced briefly at my shoes: a pair of running shoes that hadn't left the shoe box until fifteen minutes ago. "Have you ever run in those things before?" he asked.

I rolled my eyes. "I have to dress up for work every day. That means heels, not sneakers."

"Do you do everything in heels? Never mind, don't answer that. My mind went to the wrong place real fast."

I suppressed a smile and tried not to follow his mind into the gutter. It wasn't easy though, with the way his T-shirt clung to his body. My fingers itched to trace a line along the rock-hard abs under his shirt.

"Are you ready to face the trials?" He took in my appearance, and I wondered if he was thinking that the battle with the Long Island werewolves had damaged me permanently in some way. It had, but not in the way he probably thought. I mean, let's keep it real here: Who could get through a fight to the death in which you watched the man you loved get stabbed in the heart and not walk away just a little bit frazzled? Especially someone in my fragile condition.

"I'm hanging in there. I'll do just fine." I waved my hand as if I wouldn't bat an eye at what he had in mind today.

He studied me. Maybe he didn't believe me. But instead of brushing me off, he began his spiel. "Let's get you started with the endurance stage. You need to show you're capable of a ten-mile run."

"Sounds easy enough. I've run that far many times during the full moon."

His hazel eyes went to slits. "In human form."

My mouth dropped open then snapped shut. *Oh.* I tried to remember the last time I'd run *anywhere* when not in wolf form. As a werewolf I had honed senses and a powerful physique, but I knew that in my human form I wasn't in the best physical shape. I was a size six, but that was mostly due to my skinny Russian-girl genes. (Which my mother loved to remind me would disappear after I had kids.)

"I'll do fine." I left him behind and jogged down the track. Would he follow me? I turned briefly to see him sitting down on the bleachers to watch my progress.

"You're not coming?" I asked.

"You have the pace of a were-sloth participating in the Olympics. You'd slow me down to the point of aggravation."

After a few minutes, and a few laps (I wasn't keeping count), I became winded. As I passed him I asked, "How am I doing?"

"You need another lap to complete one mile. At the rate you're running, I could go pick up a breakfast sandwich and still make it back before you're done with your ten miles."

"A mile?" I glanced at my watch. It had taken me eight minutes to do less than a mile. I had to be in better shape than this if I was going to survive the trials. But my chest burned and my shins ached. As a werewolf, I sucked: Like all werewolves, I had natural agility and speed, but evidently endurance wasn't an automatically included ability.

By the time I completed three miles, I was reduced to walking. I avoided Thorn's eyes each time I passed him. Why stir up his animosity?

Thirty minutes later, I plopped down on the other side of the track and lay between the lanes. All this torture and I still had a long workday ahead of me.

A shadow passed over my head. It was Thorn. "This'll be a long week for you. Expect to be here at four a.m. tomorrow."

"Don't athletes get a day of rest between events?"

He snorted. "A day of rest is for people who exert themselves. See you bright and early tomorrow, Nat." With that he walked off the track and disappeared into the woods.

A part of me warned myself not to watch him walk away. But I couldn't help it. Between training for the trials and wanting Thorn, the trials would be far easier for me to deal with.

My group therapy day was usually Tuesday. A regular schedule made my life, or should I say my stress level, a lot easier to manage. But at this difficult time, with the trials coming, my therapist thought it'd be a great idea to shake things up and have us meet on a Friday. In his phone message last Friday, Dr. Frank explained that he wanted to put me in a new situation to help me learn to accept change. He had sounded cheerful, but his good cheer didn't help me much while I scrambled to rearrange my work schedule.

I told myself that now that I'd had my first "official" day of training, I should spend more time working to improve other aspects of my life. Even though I'd been thrown yet another curveball, with the added Friday session, at least I was on the path to normalcy.

Since I wasn't on the Long Island pack's hit list anymore, it was safe for me to drive to New York City, a somewhat pleasant drive on an early winter day like today. Dr. Frank's Manhattan office was located not far from Central Park. The building appeared to be no different from any other in Midtown. Matter of fact, the regular folks who walked by every day had no idea that inside the ordinary-looking building was a bunch of supernatural physicians and their practices.

I'd been to this building many times before I'd officially restarted therapy with Dr. Frank a few months ago. I'd first come here with my parents back when I was a teen. Mom and Dad had settled into the flow of the city easily, and no wonder, they'd lived here many, many years ago. Perhaps through their eyes, the city hadn't changed much at all from when there had been horse carriages and Model Ts in the streets. But for me, New York City had been a frightening place.

After growing up in a small town like South Toms River, the city that never slept was too bustling and dirty for me. Even Dr. Frank and his office had been intimidating. The only thing I knew at the time was that I had a problem—and my parents felt it was bad enough for me to seek out magical help.

As I drove past a street vendor selling Eastern European food, I couldn't help but think about that first trip. How after I barely survived my session with my therapist, my father had stopped at a cart very similar to the one I now passed and bought me some piping hot piroshki. I remember how the outer breading melted in my mouth while the ground beef within had been spiced to perfection. The whole time, Mom had grumbled about me not needing therapy. But Dad simply bought me the food and told me not to worry about her. He promised me everything would work out. All I had to do was look forward to more *piroshki* when we came back for my next therapy session.

As I walked up to the building now, I couldn't help but think: *If only such memories could make therapy any easier.*

The office, up on the fourteen floor, had the cleanliness of a hospital. It smelled germ-free and had a large waiting room with lots of seats. I went straight past the receptionist to the meeting room, and before I even walked in the door I smelled the welcome scent of coffee and fresh pastries. Dr. Frank liked to keep his patients as happy as he possibly could under the circumstances.

The meeting room had been set up for us, with the chairs forming a circle. Off to the side was a small table with refreshments. For the sake of my sanity, I'd arrived comfortably early this time, and the first thing I did was search for my friends.

I spotted two other members of my therapy group: Raj, the minor Indian deity, and Tyler, a dwarf. Raj nodded my way like he always did. Therapy session wouldn't be the same without Raj clutching his antibacterial wipes. Like humans, I couldn't see his multiple arms, but I bet his hands were covered with gloves to keep the germs away. With the way people kept coughing all over the place this winter, I might feel inclined to wear them, too.

From his seat, Tyler offered a wave and then smiled. It was a rather attractive one; Tyler was a dwarf who could have worked as an underwear model. Although a dwarf, he was actually one of the tallest guys here, except when hunched over like he was right now. My poor friend tried his best to appear smaller, more dwarflike, but it was rather difficult, and I'm sure that gave him even more stress.

Two other friends waved from their seats: Abby the

Muse and Heidi the mermaid. Heidi's wave was far more exuberant than Abby's. The Muse always melted into the background and usually only spoke when spoken to. But when Abby had joined the others in the group to help me fight the Long Island werewolves, I'd seen a side to her that had been a lot more animated.

A warm hand touched my shoulder. Only Thorn could sneak up on me like this without a scent or sound. Dressed in a black trench coat with a black fedora, the white wizard gave me a tantalizing grin. His hat was tilted forward, causing his black hair to cover one of his eyes. His other eye, dark and mysterious, danced with mischief. My heartbeat quickened. It felt good to know someone looked forward to seeing me.

"You look wistful today." Nick Fenton leaned in close enough for me to take in his handsome face, from his strong chin up to his midnight eyes. He was so close his casual greeting felt wonderfully intimate. But after seeing Thorn this morning, I felt awkward: The potential relationship I'd been building with Nick had been pushed a bit off-kilter.

"I'm just a bit tired. With the trials coming and all." I inhaled deeply and waited for the scents to tell me about the man in front of me. Maybe today was different. But, as usual, the only thing I caught was the smell of the others around me. Nick was a blank canvas.

"Do you want to talk about it—"

Our conversation was cut short as Dr. Frank came in and told us to sit down. The old wizard patted Nick on the back in greeting and directed him to a chair. By the time I'd grabbed a coffee and moved to sit, there was only one seat available, and it was right next to the newest member of the therapy group: the wood nymph named Starfire Whimsong. He was as laid-back as ever, dressed in shorts and a T-shirt. On a wintery day. Even worse, his ethereal forest magic couldn't cover up the obvious fact that he stank. It was pretty bad today.

I sat and tried to think happy thoughts. Across the room, Nick glanced at me with concern. He mouthed, "You want to trade places?"

As much as I did want that, I couldn't do it. I was there for therapy. If Starfire brushed up against me, I wouldn't fall over twitching. That was what my antibacterial wipes were for.

On the other side of Starfire sat Lilith. A succubus who, unfortunately, still didn't look as if she'd drained any souls lately. Lilith's skin, which normally looked pearl-white, seemed a bit grayed and unhealthy. Even her eyes didn't appear as bright. Her coat, which was too big, had some kind of furry dead animal wrapped around the collar, and the color of her orange fingernail polish didn't seem like a wise choice with her lavender-and-gray-striped shoes. To each her own, I guess.

"Good afternoon, everyone. The tension in the room is up a bit but not as bad as our last meeting. Great progress." Dr. Frank always had encouraging things to say. "How about we relax for a second to get into the mood?"

Dr. Frank's magic fluttered through me. Oh, the man knew how to soothe a woman! Every worry I had on my shoulders lifted momentarily.

"How was everyone's week? Did anyone have any difficulties dealing with the change in schedule?"

Lilith spoke first. "A change in the schedule is the least of my problems. I thought I'd be happy, now that I'm dating and soon to be married, but things aren't going like I planned with Yuri."

I'd almost forgotten about my distant werewolf cousin in Russia. Yuri had flown in from St. Petersburg not too long ago to live with Lilith. Since he always sucked out the souls of most of my family members, I thought the two of them would be perfect for each other. Evidently not.

"How have you dealt with your relationship problems?" Dr. Frank asked.

Lilith played with her fingernails. "I've wanted to run away."

Now, that was a change. Most of the time you'd find Lilith eagerly feeling up the male members of the group.

"Keep going," Dr. Frank encouraged.

"He calls me all the time. While I'm at work, while I'm on my way home. He's like this leech I can't get off my back."

I rolled my eyes. This story wasn't anything new. Yuri had clearly just switched targets.

"I simply want to be happy with someone," the succubus said bitterly. "I wanted to attract someone, but not like this."

"Maybe you've finally realized you don't always get what you want," Heidi mumbled.

"Good to hear you speak, Heidi," Dr. Frank said. "What would you do in this situation to reduce anxiety?"

"You're making things a lot harder than they have to be." Heidi leaned forward and continued, "Stop being a doormat and take control of the situation. You're a damn succubus, for goodness' sake. Tell him to stop calling you so much."

"And what happens after I do that? Should I still marry him?" Lilith whined.

Heidi covered her face with her hands. Maybe to keep herself from saying something crass. I knew *I* wanted to. Our group therapy sessions often spun into relationship counseling.

"Maybe you should be happy someone wants to marry you. My new dwarf girlfriend dumped me." Tyler crossed his arms and gave Lilith a dark look.

Heidi rolled her eyes. "I'm saying you need to stop crying about it and make a decision on your own, as your own woman. Whether you like the consequences or not."

"Good advice. We can't cling to our typical behavioral patterns if we want to make progress in our recovery." Dr. Frank turned to me. "How have you been since we last spoke, Natalya?"

Everyone's heads swiveled my way. I'd expected him to talk to Tyler next, maybe even Starfire since he rarely contributed to the conversations.

"Good," I squeaked. "Nothing new to report." Sadly, the only positive thing I had to look forward to was Nick and Alex's new baby. Otherwise, I had plenty of stress-inducers in my life: the impending trials, Thorn's marriage to Erica, and now I was wondering what bad news my parents were hiding from me.

But I smiled and nodded with emphasis. *Yep, I'm all good here.*

"Well, hopefully you'll open up at our private session." That white wizard had a raised eyebrow that told me he'd read through me like a cheap tabloid magazine.

"Anyone else want to talk?" Dr. Frank asked.

"Right now I'm pretty upset about the construction on the Brooklyn Bridge," Starfire began. "They are polluting the East River with all those chemicals and the machinery—just to repair the overpass. It's ridiculous. And the new bill in Congress that didn't get passed to keep the chemical D-128 out of pesticides. It's environmental suicide to allow farmers to spray that on our food."

Raj and Lilith rolled their eyes. I had the same feeling, but I tried to be a good girl. Unless someone interrupted Starfire, he'd argue for hours about every little thing he couldn't control. All of the things that worried him were beyond even a white wizard's power to manipulate.

Dr. Frank glanced at everyone to make sure we behaved ourselves. For once, Lilith kept her mouth shut and gave Starfire five minutes to get it all out. I had to admit that maybe she'd changed a bit since Yuri had come her way.

While Starfire spoke, Dr. Frank nodded at the appropriate times. But when he had a chance to jump in, he did. "Those problems do sound unfortunate, Starfire. But how about you tell us *briefly* some of the activities you've planned to reduce your stress?"

That question appeared to push the nymph a bit. "I've had trouble—acting on solutions to my problems."

"Have you found a coping mechanism?" I suggested.

"Something that usually gets your mind off polluting factories—" Abby said.

I jumped in again. "How about volunteering whenever you feel overwhelmed? There's plenty of opportunities to be found."

"Good idea, Natalya," Dr. Frank said. "That's a great suggestion."

The others made suggestions, too. Heidi suggested that Starfire help out at the youth center where she volunteered once in a while. For a second I wondered if that was a wise move since he'd potentially knock out anyone with a sense of smell, but who was I to keep a guy from helping the community?

Raj mumbled his offer, but it was a constructive one nonetheless. "If you'd like to join me tomorrow for racquetball, you're more than welcome."

Starfire nodded with enthusiasm. "That'd be wonderful. No one's ever invited me to anything before."

A quip lingered at the back of my mind—but his final words tugged at my senses. The smile on my face disappeared and for a brief moment I wondered how lonely his life was. Did Starfire have a family? Did he have any-

one in his life, like my grandma, who loved him uncon-
ditionally?

By the time we'd worked through Starfire's extensive
list of problems and offered him some solutions, our
time was up. Everyone stood, and I expected Nick to
accept my offer to go out for dinner, but he immediately
shot my hopes down.

"I've got a Friday evening shift at the pawnshop.
Sorry." The disappointment on his face was clear.

A sigh escaped my mouth before I could hold it back.
A small knot formed in my stomach and a familiar feeling hit: loneliness.

Maybe when I got home Aggie would be there to hang
out with me. But I doubted it. Lately she'd been spending more and more time socializing out of the house.
And Aggie was my best friend and all, but I refused to be
the tagalong friend while she was getting some action.
So that meant I'd be spending my evening like I always
used to: alone at home with what few ornaments I had
left, making s'mores, and commiserating with my only
company—my memories of the past.

The ride home was quiet. Even the vast array of jazz
stations that usually mellowed out my mood didn't help
much. I tried to brighten up and think about my ornaments. They'd be waiting—and if the holiday sales kept
coming, I'd have something to look forward to.

Thankfully, Aggie was home. But a cozy evening with
my friend came to a quick halt.

Aunt Vera had left a long message for me on the an-
swering machine.

Aggie sat quietly—for once not eating anything. From
the expression on her face, what she'd heard probably
made her lose her appetite. The impending doom gave
me the same feeling. How did I always end up in this
position?

When I played the message, I was glad I was sitting down. It left me with the same sinking feeling I'd felt when I learned my brother had been kidnapped by the Long Island pack.

But now it was my father who was missing.

Chapter 3

The drive to my parents' house was a somber one. Even though Aggie came home from her part-time job before I'd arrived, like a good friend, she still rode with me. Still, during the drive, I couldn't shake the guilt from holding back yesterday. Why hadn't I asked my parents what was going on between them? Surely I could've asked what was wrong?

"Don't worry, Nat. I bet your aunt's worried about nothing." Unfortunately, Aggie's words of reassurance didn't make me feel better.

When we arrived at the house, I noticed that no one else was here. If my father was missing, where were my uncles and cousins?

My brother answered the door. His expression only deepened my anguish.

"Where is everyone?" I asked. My ears told me Grandma was asleep upstairs while Mom cooked in the kitchen. From all the banging noises she was making, she wasn't very focused on her task.

"We're not sure what's going on yet. Aunt Vera called me since Mom's acting weird about Dad."

Aunt Vera emerged from the kitchen and took us to the side to explain she'd managed to get Mom to tell her Dad was missing, but that was it. Instead of gathering the whole family, as we always did in an emergency, and sending them out to search for Dad, Vera thought it best to call us to help get her sister to open up first.

We entered the kitchen to find Mom leaning against the counter. Stains covered the front of her blouse, and strands of her blond hair escaping her ponytail made her look harried.

My brother approached her first, but I was the one who spoke up.

"Mom, what's going on with Dad?" I searched her blue eyes. When she avoided my gaze I knew that something was very wrong. She took a cup of coffee from the counter and gripped it tightly. Squeezed her eyes shut and swallowed deeply.

"This morning he said he'd return home before dinner. I told him not to go," she whispered. "That I'd find some way to help him with his debt."

"What debt, Mom?" I knew it: I *should've* pressed further when I saw how reserved Dad and Mom were being. If I'd told Alex, and he and I had pushed the matter, they wouldn't have been able to hide this secret from us.

Mom's voice was practically a whisper. But the heavy silence in the room helped us hear her. "His moon debt with a werewolf in Atlantic City."

She didn't need to say more. From behind me, I heard Alex curse.

To me, Atlantic City meant only one thing. Trouble. And it was all because of my dad's past. When most kids' parents needed an odd job here or there to help out with the bills, they worked at Walmart or hauled materials over at the old mill in town. But as a powerful werewolf with a menacing build, Dad was able to make a buck or two doing something very different: He was once a bodyguard for the supernatural crime groups. He'd made good money and kept a roof over our heads.

But at what price?

My belly ached with dread over the moon debt. To most people, "debt" meant monetary debt. But for werewolves, debt can only be paid in sweat or blood. According to the Code, debt had to be repaid sooner or later—with servitude or death. I didn't know when my dad had incurred the debt, or what he owed. All I knew was that the look on my mom's face was of deep sorrow. And that when she feared something enough to cry, it was never good.

An hour later, Alex and Aunt Vera managed to convince Mom to talk. Aunt Vera got Mom to gab after she convinced Mom to spend some quality time in her haven—the kitchen.

Mom baked a cake to keep her nervous hands busy. After the cake was safely in the oven, she stood quietly staring at the stove, her right hand locked around a glass of whiskey. My mom didn't drink often, but a visit from good ol' Uncle Jack Daniel's would settle her nerves when necessary.

I must've been staring at nothing too long, because Alex tried to cheer me up. "For all we know, Dad might show up any minute now."

Did my brother really believe that? Mom was crying, for goodness' sake. "I called his cell," she said, "but he didn't answer."

"Has he *ever* answered his cell when expected?"

Alex had a point there. Dad and the newest technology didn't exactly go hand in hand. Dad was from the old country; dealing with newfangled gadgets always drove him to scratch off what little hair he still had on his head. Most of the time, either Alex or I had to upgrade the cell phone he rarely used.

"So what do we do now?" I asked.

"Nothing," Alex murmured. "He'll likely turn up in the morning."

"What about the moon debt?"

The side of Alex's jaw twitched. When he worried about things, I could see hints of Dad in his face. My younger brother took after my mom, with the same blond hair and blue eyes, but bits of Dad lingered under the surface.

"Don't worry about it. Dad's probably drunk and settling the debt with a few card games." Alex smiled at me, but I could see through his false reassurances.

"How's Karey?" Changing the subject to his wife should ease the climbing tension in the room.

Alex's face brightened. "She's great. A bit grumpy, but if I were carrying around a kid in my body, I think I'd be cranky, too."

"Have you finished the baby's room?"

"Not yet. Karey has all these plans to create an environment suitable for a nymph baby. I have to remind her once in a while that I should have a say."

I snorted. "Good luck with that."

"At least I can help with the furniture and things. Dad was supposed to help me with the crib." His voice trailed off.

"Have you seen the instructions for most cribs?" I managed a laugh. "We have a few antique ones at The Bends. Bill said they would bring in the lazy customers who don't feel like putting a new crib together themselves."

When I wasn't fending off relatives who couldn't wait to ostracize me again, I worked at the Bend of River Flea Market—known locally as The Bends—in town. Its owner, Bill, wasn't the best boss, but he ran a profitable business.

"Are you sure The Bends should be selling cribs?" Alex asked. "Don't antique cribs have safety issues?"

I cackled loud enough to make my brother laugh. He sometimes forgot my last name should've been "anal-retentive." I always thoroughly cataloged and verified *everything* that went through the store. If my stock were a person, I'd have known their credit rating as well as the last time they picked their nose in public. "Don't worry, they're safe. Most of our cribs would've been used a century ago. A few of them are haunted, if you're interested in that kind of thing."

"A haunted crib? Who'd buy something like that?"

A hand touched my shoulder. It was Aggie joining us in the back of the kitchen. She held a plate with a warm slice of cake. Under most circumstances, the chocolatey dessert would've begged for my company, but right now I was too distracted to eat.

"Rich people buy eccentric shit like that all the time," Aggie said. "They see it as the easiest way to show how big their wallet is compared to the size of their pecker."

"Our most profitable supernatural sales come from auctions for the wealthy," I said.

Aunt Vera joined us. "Does anyone else *besides* Aggie want a piece of cake?"

As usual, Aggie didn't look the least bit insulted by my aunt's remark. From the pleased look on her face, I could tell the generous piece Vera gave her made up for the loss of her chocolate cake to the floor yesterday. But I shook my head.

"Your mother was hiding this in her pocket while she was cooking." Aunt Vera tilted her head to make sure Mom wasn't looking as she took something out of her own pocket. "She kept pulling it out, trying to read it secretively, but I saw her."

Alex took the note and read it slowly. For some reason he turned it sideways, as if a different angle would reveal some important clue.

"What does it say?" I asked.

"I don't know. Whoever wrote it probably did so with their eyes closed."

I extended my hand. "We're lucky you're able to read and write at all, Alex. Just give it to me."

After reading the note, I had to concede my brother had a point. It was in Russian, but whoever wrote it barely knew how to scribble using Cyrillic letters. No wonder Alex had tried to read it sideways. I stared at the note a few times, and it eventually became clear:

Fyodor, any time you want to score a big hit, you come see me. Just look for Old Leslie Leatherback to take good care of you. I could always use a helpful hand when the next opportunity comes up.

"There's some other stuff in there—a bad joke or two—but nothing else useful. It's also signed, Roscoe Skins." My nose turned up. "What kind of name is that?"

"Sounds like a bad hair band from the eighties or a brand of potato skins," Aggie said through a mouthful of cake.

"It says nothing about the debt, though," I said.

"You three should go home," Aunt Vera said. "I don't think the note's of any use."

Alex rose, but I didn't follow.

"Natalya, I'll make sure your mother gets to bed all right." Aunt Vera's face was reassuring.

Now that I was an accepted member of the family again, no one could prevent me from doing what I wanted. Especially since my father was missing. "I'm staying here with Mom until Dad comes home," I said.

Dad didn't show up that night, or the next morning.

The day began like any other Saturday, with my mother rising early to make breakfast for Grandma and Aunt

Olga, who was Grandma's caretaker during the day. By noon, the sun had risen, and my father was still missing.

For some reason I felt drawn to the porch, where I stared out at the busy morning street. Cars went by, their passengers taking care of weekend business. None of them turned into my parents' driveway or waved in my direction.

Alex had work today, but he pulled up to the house around lunchtime. He sat down on the chair next to me. "No sign of Dad, huh?"

Out of nowhere, my stomach growled. How long had it been since I'd eaten? "Nope. I guess it's time to call the cavalry. I'll do it."

"No." He grabbed my arm, preventing me from standing. "We have our honor," he whispered. "This is our burden to bear, not the others'."

I rolled my eyes and stifled a groan. "Don't give me that BS. If the family bands together, we stand a better chance of helping Dad."

"So we help Dad by going to his debtor with twenty people, to help him further lose face? Not happening."

I looked at the road again and pondered the man sitting next to me. For the longest time, Alex was known among us as the womanizer who took life as seriously as he took the next lay who fell/jumped/skydived into his lap, but now he was a different person.

He continued. "One debt. One wolf. That's the way it's always been. He's our sire, so we should be able to speak to him, see him at least."

"When did you start caring about the Code?"

"I started to care when I realized pretty soon I'm gonna have to be responsible for teaching someone else our way of life."

I crossed my arms and bit my lower lip. Of all the times for Alex to grow up. If I weren't so afraid for Dad,

I would've been proud. Maybe he had a point—*if* he had a solid plan.

"Our friends and family won't like this," I said. But, then again, they weren't here to offer their opinion. "So what should we do?"

He had a conspiratorial gleam in his blue eyes. Seeing his determination made me smile. "Pack a quick bag and hightail it out of here before Mom notices. We'll drive down to Atlantic City and find Old Leslie Leatherback."

After I acknowledged his plan with a nod, I made it home in record time. Since it was around lunchtime, I didn't expect anyone to be home. Aggie worked the lunch shift at Barney's Pickles.

But instead of finding a quiet house, I heard whispers from the living room. A tiny moan and then the frantic rustling of clothes, with the associated snaps and zips. I strolled into the kitchen with a wide grin. *Should I give Aggie and her guest a bit more time?* I asked myself. I was in a hurry, but I grabbed a glass for orange juice and checked the rest of the glasses to make sure they were lined up correctly. All the while, I made plenty of noise to show I was in the kitchen, before I entered the living room.

"Hey, Nat," Aggie yelled. "What are you doing home? I thought you were scheduled at The Bends till late today?"

Under normal circumstances, I did work the Saturday shift, as well as the Sunday and Monday ones. But a quick call to my boss while I'd driven here had gotten me a few days off. Speaking of taking things off, apparently Aggie was spending the afternoon taking off someone else's clothes.

Not more than ten feet away stood a blond-haired, hazel-eyed man with a deep flush in his cheeks. Will

Grantham continued to button up his shirt, his eyes avoiding mine.

"I did."

I could've excused myself to give her some more time, but after every little trick she'd played on me over the past few months, seeing Aggie flushed with embarrassment for a minute or two was *so* worth it.

I took a step toward the stairwell. "I need to change out of these clothes. You two can hang out for a while."

While I marched upstairs, I couldn't help yelling back down, "There's no sex allowed on my couch, you two!"

My shower didn't take too long. I even managed to only second-guess myself four times about my outfit before I settled on a pair of blue jeans. This wasn't a business trip. My standard wardrobe of blouses, heels, and pencil skirts wouldn't cut it. Especially if I had to defend myself. I actually owned only one pair of jeans, but I rarely wore them. They'd been used so infrequently, I had to take the brand-new tags off them.

Once I was uncomfortably dressed, I prepared an overnight bag.

"Hey, Nat!" A knock on the door drew my attention.

"Yeah?" I moved faster.

"You hungry for lunch? Will is heading out for burgers."

"I'm good. I just need to go out for some air. I'm really concerned about Dad and need to sort things out." I shook my head after I said it. Heading out for a casual stroll in the forest would never happen. Especially with all the mud and gunk out there.

A loud snort came from outside the door. "Go out for some air?" She tried the doorknob and found it locked. "What are you doing in there? You're not planning anything stupid with Alex, are you?"

I groaned silently and cursed Aggie for having a midday tryst instead of going to her job as manager at Barney's Pickles. Why didn't she have her weekend sex-fest with Will over at his place? But when I thought about it, I remembered that Will lived with his dad and Thorn, which meant that if my place wasn't available, it didn't exactly leave many hookup spots other than the local Holiday Inn.

I almost grabbed a shirt for my bag, but Aggie knocked again. "Nat, I can smell a mistake coming. If you think I'll let you march out of here and . . ."

I stopped listening. In two strides, I made it to my bedroom window. The latch clicked silently and, with a few smooth movements, I leaped out the second-story window. I landed on the ground with no problems—but the urge to climb up and close the window hit hard. (What if it rained? *Sleeted?*)

It didn't matter. There was no time to take care of it. As I made it to my car, I heard Aggie thundering down the steps. I gunned it down my driveway and made a beeline for my brother's place.

While I drove, I took stock of what had just happened: I'd packed a bag containing a *single* shirt and barely any toiletries. And I was on my way to save my father, without enough time to plan out a damn thing. Pulling together a search party had to be easier in the olden days, when you strapped on a gun and rode to the rescue with a tin star.

One thing I did know was I had to pick up Alex—really fast, before Aggie's cunning little mind found a way to stop us. I could practically hear her now: "Have you sorted one too many antiques, Nat? Because I'm questioning your sanity here. These are dangerous people you're trying to meet."

I was one block away from my brother's home when I pulled off to the side of the road. The ticking clock nipped at my mind, but what I'd imagined her saying made me stop and think.

Other than the obvious question of what the hell was I doing, thoughts of my brother also came to mind. He was married, with a child due any day now. As his older sister, I was responsible for him, and I shouldn't allow him to put his life in danger. Instead, I should go by myself. It felt like the right thing to do, but the result was a painful one. I'd have no one to help me.

But on the other hand, if the worst happened, how could I ever face Karey and my future nephew or niece to tell them that I was there when my brother died and I didn't even try to put my own life in his place?

My fingers tapped the dashboard. I had the note and a general idea of which casinos to search. On the way I could stop for cash. I could do this. It wouldn't be hard at all.

I hoped.

After driving a half hour, I had to stop for gas. Since I hadn't planned to escape, I hadn't filled the tank.

It was still early afternoon so I had plenty of time to reach Atlantic City before rush hour. While an attendant filled my car with gas, I went inside to grab some food. If they had any that passed my stringent standards. There wasn't much to choose from. In the end, I decided I could always trust a bag of chips. Not the healthiest choice, but at least it was sealed shut. Armed with a bottle of water and my chips, I headed back to the car.

I hadn't gotten more than ten feet when I spotted Thorn leaning against my car, his arms crossed, an even expression on his face. Damn it. He always managed to sneak up on me. Even from downwind. No sounds. No scent. If he'd been an enemy, he could've brought me down without a struggle.

"So how long did you think you could run from us before I found you?" he asked.

I strolled past him and dumped my purchases into the backseat. I shouldn't have been surprised by this. Will had been at my house with Aggie, so he'd called his older brother as soon as he knew what was going on. And now that Will had poked his paws into my business, I had no choice but to face Thorn.

Alex, frowning, headed over from his truck. "Did you plan to call anyone to say you were leaving without me?"

I stared at the pavement. What could I say to them? They knew very well what I was doing.

"I was worried something might happen to you if I let you go to Atlantic City," I said quietly.

Thorn snorted and then scratched the back of his head. I guess he thought my sacrifice was foolhardy.

"I'm my own man. There's nothing you need to worry about," Alex grumbled.

"Alex told me a thing or two on the way here. I'd ask why you decided to go it alone, but we both know, based on your past history, the answer to that one."

I wanted to say, "What do you care?" Or more specifically, why should he care about what goes on in my life, since we couldn't be together anymore? But what I actually said was, "Alex and I can handle this on our own. You don't need to worry about our father."

I stole a glance at Alex. Hadn't we agreed to keep our father's secret to ourselves? Wouldn't telling people our business just bring gossip out into the open? Especially with the way my aunts loved to gab?

"Fyodor is pack," Thorn said. "I'm concerned about his whereabouts as much as you are. If I were in the same position, I know he'd do the same for me."

It was so easy for him to flip things around. But he did tell the truth. When the Long Island werewolves had kidnapped my brother, Thorn was there to search with me. He'd fought bravely and helped save Alex. If I recalled correctly, he'd snuck up on me then, too, when I'd tried to join the rescue team.

"Since you're so eager to find your father, tell me, what's your plan?" Thorn's smug look made me want to kick him in the shin. Hard.

"I have a note from my mom—with a lead."

"So you plan to track him that way? With a note? Does it have an X on it maybe?" My frustration rose with every word Thorn said.

"Can you two stop fighting and get in Nat's car? I thought you guys were done with arguing like this. Good God, it's like you're married or something."

I gave Alex a look that could've melted the flesh off his face. Thorn only chuckled.

They both could go to hell.

"What about your truck?" I asked Alex.

"I'll send Uncle Boris a message to pick it up after he gets off work. He'll take any excuse to go to the bars around here."

Those poor women. They weren't ready for Lady-Killer Uncle Boris. Until he'd knocked up a wood nymph and married her, my brother used to be just like him. Now it was just my uncle who roamed the bar scene. One woman had jokingly told me that his cologne was so disgusting, it smelled like the Black Death. If Boris ever told us over family dinner that he'd knocked someone up, the first thing I'd wonder was if she had a sense of smell.

I paid the attendant in cash. By the time I approached the car, only one seat remained empty: the back one. The two coconspirators sat in the front seat chatting away, most likely about where they planned to go first and what steps they'd take.

This was gonna be a long day. And I'd already completely lost control of the situation.

Chapter 4

When Atlantic City came into view, the neon lights made me wary. For anyone else, the sight would have promised a good time. Lights. Gambling. Fast music, faster women, and enough liquor to guarantee a drunken stupor. But we weren't here for fun. And we most certainly weren't here to see if we could make enough money playing the crap tables to build a college fund for Alex's unborn child.

All we had was a couple of names. Not the best of leads in a city as large as this one. We entered town via the Expressway, and I wondered if this road would lead us in the right direction.

Alex must have had some plan I didn't know about. He made a few turns and headed farther into the city.

Meanwhile, Thorn stared out the window. For once, I was glad I was sitting in the back, so I could steal a glance or two at him. Waves of soft blond hair peeked over the headrest, beckoning my hand to run my fingers through them. Then his own hand snaked up to touch the curls, and I'll admit it—I envied the damn thing.

Thorn's head tilted to the side, and I caught his profile. My gaze roamed from his eyes down to his lips. Guilt poured over me as the familiar hunger hit, and I immediately turned away. He had to have noticed. My quickened breath. My racing heartbeat. But this shouldn't matter to him. Or me. After all, an invisible line existed between us—one that couldn't be crossed at any cost. No matter how I felt.

I directed my attention elsewhere. "Are we close to the main strip of casinos, Alex?"

"I think so." But he didn't sound *that* confident.

My brother was just as stubborn as I could be. I'd offered to use the GPS I stored in the backseat, but he refused. That didn't stop me from pulling it out and turning it on now, though. Why, yes, *there* was the strip of hotels next to the coast. And why, yes, here we are going in the *wrong* direction.

I turned up the volume on the GPS so Alex could hear the woman's voice. *"Turn left now."*

"Could you shut that thing off?" Alex grated.

As the late-afternoon traffic increased, I knew we'd be here forever, so I left it on.

My brother tried to pretend he was ignoring it, but he made the turns as directed, and soon we were back on track.

"That thing's pretty nifty," he finally admitted. "Although the voice is kinda boring. It'd be hotter if they used Pamela Anderson or something."

With a grin, I clicked a few buttons. The GPS unit said, *"Take the second left, you must, or you will fall to the dark side."*

Both Alex's and Thorn's heads snapped in my direction.

"Yoda?" Thorn asked.

"I got quite the deal from the manufacturer," I said. "I can even have Han Solo or Darth Vader berate him, if you like."

Thorn chuckled, low and soft. "I don't think even Stormtroopers could convince Alex to go in the right direction."

I wanted to tease my brother further, but he didn't give in to the dark side. He followed Yoda's directions, and we reached one of the nicer hotels and parked in a nearby garage. As we walked inside, I pondered the question neither of them had brought up. Where would we stay? What were the *sleeping* arrangements?

And most importantly, how the heck was I going to survive with no meds, one shirt, and nothing else clean to wear?

No one said anything about the two beds in the room or who'd be sleeping in them. Of course I had other things on my mind, such as the fact that the room could be harboring countless germs. In recent years, hotels in the northeast have had some bedbug problems. The very idea that I could settle into one of these beds without a careful inspection was impossible. This trip was stressful enough as it was.

"Lay low for a bit," Thorn said to me. "I'm taking Alex out to talk to the people in the note. Once we get a solid lead, you can check it out with us."

Here we go. I should've known this was going to happen. "You're not serious, are you?"

"Nat, you don't know these kinds of people. You'll have more problems than your missing father if you show your face to them."

Anger welled up inside me, furious and flowing. "What's that supposed to mean? I've held my own before."

His face remained even. "Your bravery—and stubbornness—isn't the problem. It's how other werewolves perceive you."

No matter how much I strived to keep my universe sparkling clean and free from germs, there was something I still couldn't control: the fact that other werewolves thought my scent was inferior. My inferior scent was the one thing I couldn't scrub off. Worry, doubt, and fear clung to me and alienated me from others.

I stood and marched to the door. Thorn meant well and all, but reminders weren't necessary. "If we're leaving, we should do it now."

Alex got up from the other bed and tried to hide his smile. "I don't know why you try, man."

As we walked out the door, Thorn groaned. "I don't know either."

My first visit to a casino should have been on a vacation with my girlfriends. A night out to enjoy drinks and perhaps snag a good Russian man to bring home. Or at least a clean one anyway. Instead, I stood in the middle of the Golden Saddle Casino trying to find my missing father. As of this moment, my only option was staring at the multitude of blinking machines within a fog of never-ending smoke and other people's body odors. A few of the valued customers hadn't bothered to get up from gambling their mortgages away to freshen up for the day.

As we browsed the aisles looking for leads on Old Leslie Leatherback, every part of me wanted to hose this place down with bleach. Who in their right mind would touch these slot machines after everyone else had put their grimy hands on them? Some of the patrons were even stranger. Humans weren't the only gambling addicts. In between the regular customers, hidden with glamours, sat supernaturals. A zealous brownie, dressed in a tweed jacket and dirty brown pants, stared at another customer playing the slots, perhaps hoping to feel the excitement of a win. Personally, I would've been creeped out to have someone gaping at me like that.

A werewolf, thin and hungry, clung to a machine,

pressing the buttons continually. He looked to be around my age, twenty-five or so. A cigarette precariously hung between his lips and dipped every time he pressed the button. Press. Dip. Press. Dip.

"Nat?" Thorn touched my shoulder.

We pressed on and I tried to ignore the persistently skeevy feeling while I passed a group of human men who were taking a succubus to the nearby bar. The female sex demon's glamour was strong and brightened her white skin. But even under all her glamours, she couldn't disguise her scent from my well-trained nose. She stunk of magic. Not your average clean white magic, but the kind that could give you more than a mystery venereal disease. Those poor guys had no idea she planned to drain both their wallets and their souls. With a smile, she took them to one end of the bar while Thorn directed us toward the other.

From there, I spotted two werewolves enjoying a drink. The men smelled old—quite old by werewolf standards. They were even a bit older than my father. However, to humans they looked to be in their late forties. One wore dressy clothes while the other sported a worn brown leather jacket with jeans. The dressed-down one had a shaggy haircut that gave him the air of a hardened ranch hand.

When Thorn stood before them, the dark-haired man in the nicer clothes spoke. "Can I help you?"

He eyed me next, slower than I'd prefer. Long enough for Thorn to push me behind him. The wolf's gaze switched over to Alex.

"I'm looking for Old Leslie Leatherback. You heard of him?" Alex asked.

The man who'd addressed us rolled his shot glass between his fingers. "Who's asking?"

"I'm—" Alex began.

"We'll introduce ourselves once we find Old Leslie," Thorn said. "Our business is with him."

The dark-haired man offered a small smile before he stood. Thorn had a good few inches on him, but the other man had a cockier stance.

"That's enough, Jack," the dressed-down man warned. "Quit acting like everything's a pissing contest." Not long after, he laughed. "I'm Old Leslie. What's your business, son?"

Jack stepped away from Thorn and sat, but he kept his eyes on Thorn.

Old Leslie continued. "You're definitely not a pup," he said to Thorn. "You're much too powerful to be one."

From behind Thorn, I could see Alex stand straighter, but I doubted he'd made much of an impression.

Thorn said, "I was told to come see Old Leslie Leatherback if I was looking for work."

My mouth threatened to drop open, but I kept it in check. What the hell was he doing?

"Do I look like an employment office?" Old Leslie chuckled.

"You look like a man who has connections." Thorn shrugged. "I've heard a thing or two."

"From whom?"

I bit the inside of my mouth.

Thorn didn't hesitate, though. "Fyodor Stravinsky's from my area. I haven't seen him for a while, but he told me if I needed quick cash you'd be the man to see."

"I haven't seen Fyodor in a while either, but he's good enough folk."

He stared at Thorn for a few seconds. From my angle, I couldn't see Thorn's face. But I had an idea what was happening. I'd seen my father do it with other wolves. Their eyes would examine each other in an elaborate dance that spoke words I didn't understand. I suspected it was some kind of male thing where they measured each other's machismo.

"Good enough, then." Old Leslie flicked his fingers in Jack's direction. "Meet up with them right here at ten tonight and take them to Roscoe." Then he said, "You better be as good as you look."

Jack's frown filled his whole face when he met up with us later that night. Maybe his life as a thug and working for Roscoe was the reason he was so talkative and cheerful.

None of us said a single word as we followed him from the bar and then out of the casino. The streets of Atlantic City around the Golden Nugget Casino buzzed with life. People walked along the street holding drinks in their hands, holding conversations with their friends. The stench of cigarettes and cheap beer clung to their clothes. Ugh. To make matters worse, we passed a man who staggered toward us after he'd upchucked on the sidewalk. A part of me was grateful I'd mostly missed out on that particular tourist attraction. The only thing I did enjoy was the succulent scent of fine dining. We'd eaten a light meal while waiting to meet up with Jack, but we hadn't made any plans for a *real* dinner. Alex and I had been far too worried about Dad to think about that.

Jack led us three blocks down the street before we reached the entrance to the Jersey Juniper Resort. This place wasn't as large as the Golden Saddle, but it had just as many customers. Supernaturals swarmed as both customers and staff. The entryway beckoned to us with obnoxious maroon and dark pink lights. Two unfortunate souls, both of them dressed in costumes from the latest hit Broadway show, passed out flyers and tried to generate excitement for their show with an elaborate singing routine.

Alex took the lead into the hotel while Thorn brought up the rear. I followed my brother with my arms crossed, hoping I wouldn't come into contact with anyone. Jack led us down several corridors in the hotel before we finally came to a door labeled FACILITIES. The scent of wolves lingered here from one corner to another. Their musk filled my nostrils and made me wonder which pack controlled this area. The last I'd heard, the Atlantic City pack had severed into several factions after its leaders had quarreled. I wasn't sure if one of the rival packs held Dad's debt or if it was held by a single person. The name Roscoe didn't ring a bell, so I had no idea what we were about to face.

From the locked door we walked down several flights of stairs until we reached the facilities floor. We didn't run into any maintenance employees, so no one stopped us before we reached the final set of doors. Two burly guards stood in front of them. I froze. It wasn't as if I hadn't seen guns that big before, but seeing two men as large as my father holding them made me twitch in fear. Like my dad, the guards were thickset—muscle built on muscle. The guns they held were most likely to ward off any curious humans, but from the way they softly growled at us, they saw us as a threat, too, even with Jack as a tagalong.

Jack's hand rose. "They're with me. Old Leslie cleared them to see Roscoe."

The guards parted and reluctantly allowed us to pass. The room we entered looked like I could fit my whole cottage inside it. From one end to the other, it was a palace for men who liked to play: pinball machines, luxurious black lounge chairs, a full bar. Not far from the pinball machines sat a large desk with a massive screen. The whole setup screamed gamer.

The only thing that seemed off about the room was the stacks of crates behind the pinball machines. Their strong metallic scent led me to suspect Roscoe's boxes stored weapons, not holiday cheer like mine.

But the room wasn't relatively empty of people. Only a few sets of eyes flicked in our direction. Jack led us all the way down to the end of the room, where a man sat at the desk playing on a computer. When you thought about crime rings and gangsters, you didn't picture a guy around my dad's age playing a computer game. At least I didn't. I tilted my head slightly to the side to get a better view of the computer screen. A dark-haired man with a beak-like nose was playing World of Warcraft, but he wasn't playing as just any old regular WoW character. He was playing as an elf—a well-endowed blood elf death knight who could also have been a real dark elf hooker snagging a john on a corner. Why he preferred to play as a woman wasn't any of my business, I figured.

"Old Leslie told me to bring these people to come see you, Roscoe," Jack said.

Roscoe flipped off his headset, giving us at least a part of his attention, though his right hand still flew across the keyboard, as if he planned to continue to fight orcs while he spoke to us. "What do you want?"

His black-eyed gaze swept from Alex to Thorn, and then finally his eyes rested on me—on my boobs anyway. His grin wasn't attractive. Not with those over-sized chompers. "Perhaps I need to make an addition to my stable."

Most werewolf men who approached me didn't say such things. When I walked around town, strangers would leer at me in my pencil skirt, but once they actually met me, my behavior told another tale—I wasn't like all the other werewolf girls.

"What kind of place is this?" I asked Thorn.

"One that your father hadn't meant for you to ever see," he murmured. He kept his face forward, his eyes focused on the guards.

Even though Thorn wasn't as large as them, the guards assessed him with wary, alert eyes.

"We're here on business," Thorn said.

"You men don't look like the type who usually come looking for people like me." He switched his gaze to Alex. "You're rather scrawny."

Looking at the guards standing around us, I had to concede that he had a point. Alex matched my height of five foot seven. He had a muscular build and all, but he took after my mom, and she definitely didn't have my father's girth.

Roscoe's gaze went to Thorn, and I wondered what the older man thought of him. But instead of lingering on Thorn, he assessed me. "I have plenty of men—but I could always use a pretty girl."

"No, thanks," I whispered. "You don't want me in stock at your little store. I have cooties."

At the same time, Thorn said, "She's with me."

Roscoe laughed. "Interesting. So, what does an alpha want in a place like this? No need to deny it. You practically have most of my men hungry to fight you."

Three of the guards faced Thorn head-on, but no one else looked directly at him. They didn't need eyes to see his stance. The way he filled space with his powerful presence.

"What is it? You lose a few thousand at the tables?" Roscoe's bushy eyebrows danced. "You need to buy back the *farm* you came from?"

"Not exactly. I'm actually here looking for someone." Thorn motioned for Alex to speak.

Alex seemed hesitant but stepped forward. "We're

looking for Fyodor Stravinsky. He had business here recently."

Roscoe made a sarcastic snort. Then he rolled his tongue over his teeth. "What do you care for that *ublyudok*?"

I tried to take a step forward, but Thorn grabbed me. How *dare* Roscoe call my father a bastard? I tensed as the urge to attack him strengthened. Thorn's hand on my hip tightened painfully.

Alex was far less reserved. In Russian, he spat back, "Watch your words if you value your tongue. Are you the man who owns his debt?"

"What if I am? Take your piss-poor honor back home, pup." He sneered, revealing a single canine. In English, Roscoe said, "Grown men take care of their own moon debts."

"I want to see my father," I said.

Roscoe leaned forward, abandoning his computer game. "Do you know what it means to fulfill a moon debt, *devushka*?"

"I have an idea." I also knew what a blood debt was, having recently had one on my own head for the death of another, but that had nothing to do with the problem at hand.

Thorn moved in front of me, but he couldn't prevent Roscoe's gaze from boring into me.

"A long time ago, when the Code was first being forged, men always paid their debts one week after the full moon, when they were fresh from the hunt and ready to fight. Since I saved your father's life, he owes me such a debt." Roscoe waited for me to speak, but when I didn't he continued. "Have you ever been to Russia?"

He'd addressed the question to me, so I shook my head. He laughed at my frown, but I wasn't ashamed.

Traveling overseas to visit my distant relatives wasn't a cheap affair. The Code was also strictly enforced over there. That made it low on my places to visit.

"When I first encountered your father in Russia, he was a businessman who supported the White Army. I, on the other hand, supported the Bolsheviks and their noble revolution."

Since Thorn was a bit of a history buff, I didn't need to play the role of an encyclopedia and fill him in on the Russian Civil War of the late 1910s. When my dad drank a few too many beers with my uncles, he'd tell us stories of his work with the White Army. None of them included Roscoe. He evidently had never gotten *that* drunk.

"As we always did, the party went from house to house to rally support among the citizens of St. Petersburg. When my comrades and I arrived at the Stravinsky home, we found quite a surprise." Roscoe grinned. "It was a shame we uncovered White Army propaganda there. A few guns as well. At first my comrades wanted to search the house peacefully, but Fyodor's father, Gregor, didn't have the sense to *give* us entry."

"So you just waltzed inside, huh?"

Thorn's chin twitched. I really should behave, but an asshole like Roscoe brought out the worst in me.

"Gregor was a proud man, *devushka*. Since he was a White Army sympathizer, we had to search the house. But your grandfather Gregor had to open his big mouth and get Fyodor in trouble." Roscoe chuckled. "When the other men held your grandfather down and threatened to kill him, your father made a foolhardy move against my men. He attacked them. Very successfully, I may add.

"Somehow, perhaps due to the fact that Fyodor's a survivor, he managed to escape and elude my men—until I caught him not far from the house. He begged for the lives of his family, and I felt inclined to offer it since he promised to fulfill his moon debt when I was ready to call on it."

"And what does he have to do?" Alex asked.

"That's between Fyodor and me. But if you really want to know . . ." He smiled at me suggestively.

I rolled my eyes. The man had to be around my father's age. Over a hundred and still horny for younger wolves. Good God. He took "dirty old man" to a new level.

"Stop checking out my goodies and tell us."

Thorn's head snapped in my direction. His expression warned me to shut up.

"Moon debts aren't simple things, *devushka*. They require a sacrifice equivalent to the one made by the other person. I saved not only his life but his father's and his ancestral home. Therefore, your father must do work for me before the end of this moon's cycle."

"Could you be more specific, please," I mumbled. Why did some people feel the need to do this kind of stuff, drag things out all the time?

Roscoe continued. "Fyodor must first retrieve something that was stolen from me a long time ago. A family heirloom that was my great-grandmother's. He needs to hurry before that piece-of-shit goblin dealer sells it off again. He'd trade my compact for one of those tires he loves so much."

" 'First part'? You mean there's more?" Alex asked. A faint buzz filled the air. The noise came from Alex's leg. His phone. He ignored it and remained focused on Roscoe.

My first thought was that Dad wasn't done. How could fetching an heirloom fulfill such a large debt?

"It should've been an easy in-and-out job. All he had to do was get me an antique compact case. He left around dawn yesterday and hasn't returned." Roscoe grinned. "It's too bad he won't fulfill his debt to me in time. Especially since I have more for him to do."

I rested my hands on my hips when Thorn shook his head. "A compact case? Even if it's a Romanov dynasty heirloom, I doubt such a simple task could take care of his debt."

Roscoe continued. "The case has a few trinkets hidden inside that I'm interested in. A few stones."

Stones as in *precious* stones, I'm sure. "Is that it? It still doesn't seem enough. What else does he have to do?" I asked.

Thorn gave me an exasperated look and then said to Roscoe, "When Fyodor returns, could you kindly tell him to call his son or daughter? They're concerned for his safety."

Roscoe was all smiles. "Of course! I wouldn't want Fyodor's family to be in the dark over the whole thing. Right now his life belongs to me, but he'll be safe and sound with them when the debt's all cleared."

"Why are you hiding things from us?" I couldn't resist advancing forward.

One of the guards closed in fast, grabbing my shoulder. Thorn growled, ready to fight, but Roscoe's hand shot up.

"*No member of the debtor's family may be harmed in my presence!*" he thundered.

The tension in the room was thick enough to make it hard for me to breathe. The guard released me, keeping his eyes on Thorn.

Thorn took a step backward, pulling me with him—but Roscoe stopped him by offering a card. "There's no need for us to part on such poor terms. My *associates* are rather protective of me.

"You might not be interested in a little spare cash right now, but you never know when a strong man like yourself might want some. Or maybe in the future you'll need an extra hand or two to keep your pack safe and sound?"

Thorn's face was even. "I'll be sure to think long and hard on it."

Roscoe laughed. "I'm sure you will."

Chapter 5

G_{oblins}, like my boss, Bill, tended to keep to themselves. They even preferred not to work with other goblins—especially when it came to money. Bill always had his fist around a wad of cash, and he was paranoid about holding on to it.

The way he was always looking around outside and grumbling about how the older goblins made him pay a lot of money to keep The Bends open made it seem as though he was constantly under attack.

These little nuggets of information about goblins led me to where we needed to go to find out if Dad had met up with that black market dealer. Most goblins liked to sell their wares outside of the cities and along major roads, because the city was far too busy and cluttered with other supernaturals. The goblin black marketer we were looking for would most likely not operate in the city. If we wanted to find him, we'd have to follow our noses. For example, if he sold or collected rubber tires, I could find him easily enough. Rubber had a distinct scent. A bit overpowering, in fact. Of course, Google would provide enough information for me to locate all the tire distributors along the Expressway, but our noses would reveal the exact location of his place just as effectively, if not more so.

Before we could set out, though, we had to wait for Alex to finish talking on the phone.

"Are you sure, Heather?" he asked. "Does my mom know that my wife is in labor?" Heather was his wife's former roommate—a fellow wood nymph.

While I did a little search on the Internet, I couldn't help but overhear most of the conversation. As I listened, joy filled my heart . . . and dread soured my stomach. It was time for my brother to go home—he was going to be a father soon.

My gaze went to the window and the world beyond it. I could go back with him. A part of me didn't want to be here to face this without my brother. Or be alone with Thorn. And for all we knew, my dad could already have obtained the compact and be heading back to Roscoe.

I sensed Thorn's gaze on my back. He really hadn't looked at me this way since we'd begun our trip. It was like a caress at the nape of my neck that swirled down my back.

I swallowed a bout of nervousness.

"It's an hour drive," Alex said, "but I'll get there as soon as I can. I'll rent a car."

"No you won't!" I piped in. "You're borrowing my car. This is Atlantic City. If I can't find a rental to use, then this tourist trap isn't doing its job properly."

So, it was settled. And hopefully in a few hours I'd be an aunt.

We all left the hotel at the same time. Not that I couldn't tolerate being in a room alone with Thorn, but due to everything that'd happened with my father, I was as jittery as a newborn pup. It wasn't as if I hadn't seen Thorn lately. I'd seen him the other morning at the track, certainly. But today something was different. As we walked to pick up my car from valet parking, I sensed a change inside me. I was looking forward to being alone with Thorn. I had so many things to ask him since the battle with the Long Island werewolves. Most were about that night, when he'd saved me from the pack leader. What had happened to him?

"You got plans to get in the car, Nat?" Alex's tone was persistent.

I'd drifted off again. It was all too easy with Thorn, my father, and my brother's new baby weighing on my mind. This whole situation was an information overload.

Not more than thirty minutes later, even in the middle of night, Alex had driven off in my car and we had a rental. An SUV. Not my first choice, but Thorn had haggled me out of a nice little four-door vehicle.

"Do you seriously want to do a getaway in that?"

"What's wrong with a Honda?"

He sighed. "If something goes wrong, I'm not making a run for it in a Honda Fit."

I laughed. "Have you seen the gas prices around here? In the city?"

He got into the driver's side of the SUV and sighed. "It's the principle of the matter. You wouldn't get it."

Thankfully, I did get my way in one regard. I got my leather seats. Cloth seats weren't the easiest to clean, so if I had to ride in a rental, I made sure it had leather seats. Easy to wipe off with an antibacterial wipe. Still, the leather seats in the SUV had a strange smell, as if the rental company hadn't cleaned them very well, or often enough.

"You need help?" he asked.

As I cleaned the head support I mumbled, "No, I'm good."

He didn't hurry me, simply checked the stations on the radio until he found a mellow jazz one. Quite nice.

"You still like to listen to Miles Davis before bed?" he asked.

The question came out of nowhere, making me halt my cleaning. "I'm more into John Coltrane now. The local station turned me on to him. He's really good with the tenor saxophone."

I finished my work and settled into my seat. We had a few possibilities in mind for the location of the goblin's market, so I sat back and kept my eyes on the well-lit road.

Questions bubbled in my mind while the music played. Why *did* Thorn come here with us? Why not let us find Dad and settle this debt on our own? Since he belonged to Erica now, he had no business helping my family—yet here he was—with me, all alone. Was it friendship or did he still care for me?

The soft lilt of the sax and drum set pulled me in and pushed my mind away from my troubles. I think that's why I've always preferred jazz music. Especially when I was a kid. My aunt Vera loves jazz music and used to play it whenever we ate dinner at her house. Since my mom's food is far better, and she loves cooking and serving it, I could pretty much count on one hand how many dinners I'd had at Vera's house. But the exposure was enough to teach me the greats of jazz and harness their soothing effects on my anxiety.

"You never answered my question," Thorn said. "Do you still listen to Miles Davis before bed?"

My mouth went as dry as my lips. The question brought about memories I'd buried deep and only retrieved on my loneliest of days. Us naked, with limbs intertwined. His fingertips lazily drawing figure eights along my clavicle bone. My soft sighs as his hands drifted over the tips of my breasts. All the while, in the background, a haunting trumpet would play, its horn lulling me to sleep with the promise of a sweet dream next to Thorn.

My voice was jittery when I spoke. "Once in a while I do."

"I still do, too."

I was glad I was facing the window and he couldn't see my face flush with heat. My body was most likely betraying my feelings. It was something wolves couldn't hide from each other: the quickened breath, the heated skin. But I refused to look at him and acknowledge what he'd severed when he left me five years ago. It was plain and simple. We were simply friends now—maybe even something less than that if I ever managed to stomp my raging hormones into the dirt.

To violently stab and bury my libido as quickly as possible, I asked, "Does Erica like jazz music?"

Thorn laughed. "She's educated and all, but her idea of music, whether classical or modern, is a pop video with dancers gyrating."

I rolled my eyes. "Isn't that what guys like? Buckets of breasts and thighs shaking like they're fresh out of the oven from Kentucky Fried Chicken?"

We'd finally left the city and were now driving westward along Highway 30. We'd hit the first place pretty soon.

Thorn continued. "Not every man needs to see that kind of thing to be entertained."

"Oh, c'mon. You can't tell me you don't like watching scantily clad women doing a stripper-pole dance in what *someone* would call a music video."

"If you want to put it like that, then yes. On occasion I've enjoyed a video or two enough to press *rewind* on the DVR a few times."

I cringed for a moment, thinking about the conditions of the Grantham cabin. Back before the battle with the Long Island werewolves, I'd gone to Thorn's father to seek protection by rejoining the pack. During my (blessedly short) visit, I'd come to find so much disgustingness around old Farley's La-Z-Boy—crumpled-up chips, a greasy remote, and much more—that I found myself wondering how I'd survive another visit if it came to that. "You actually *touch* the remote in that house?"

Thorn didn't answer my quip. My gaze went to the window again. I'd seen as much of the city as I'd ever want to take in, but it distracted me nonetheless.

A few minutes later, we pulled off the highway and into the parking lot of a newer building right off the road. A sign with the words "Flat Iron Tires and Servicing" hung in a precarious manner. The building was obviously far newer than the sign, with its bright red brick and three closed garage doors. Through the windows, I spotted cars waiting for repair inside. We'd sold garage equipment at The Bends before, so I could tell the equipment didn't appear to be in the best shape. But it was otherwise just your normal mechanics garage.

Not far from the side of the building stood a set of tire racks. A few tires were stacked carelessly—perhaps waiting to topple over a hapless human. After a few steps toward them, I caught the goblin's scent. A rich and earthy one, yet slightly metallic, similar to what I often noticed on Bill.

Our target obviously had a budding black market enterprise that had garnered him enough money to buy a newer business front. I smiled, thinking about all the humans at The Bends who never knew they were handing their credit cards to a scheming goblin.

Bill always said, "Back in the Dark Ages, I could squeeze cash out of a rock if I tried hard enough. You need to have that mind-set, Nat. Stay focused on the prize and just hand the customer some lube so it doesn't hurt as much when you screw them over."

Right. I'll be sure to keep that lube handy.

So far, no sign of Dad. No scents. Nothing to indicate he'd been here, from what I could tell.

Thorn strolled around the front, but I motioned for him to join me in a walk around the back. Everything was quiet until Thorn's cell phone rang. Didn't he put it on vibrate like most werewolves? Otherwise, stealth with all that potential noise wasn't possible.

"The goblin won't show up at the front door," I said. "One thing I do know about them, they prefer people to think they run a regular business with normal business hours."

A breeze blew against my cheek and tried to sneak into the warmth of my coat. It whistled softly through an outcropping of trees next to the building.

The back of the garage looked like any other. A few older tow trucks and cars were parked in the spaces, while one truck blocked the back garage doors.

The shrill ring of Thorn's phone continued.

"Don't you have voicemail?" I hissed.

He cursed under his breath and ignored the phone.

The phone rang incessantly until Thorn grabbed it and made a beeline for the street. Not glancing my way, he spat out, "What is it now?"

I kept my distance. Enough that I could tell nothing more than that the caller was a woman.

"Yes, I'm with *her*." His face remained stiff, yet anger pooled under the surface. All I could do was wait.

"Don't start with me," Thorn grumbled. "I haven't touched her. Nor do I plan to, so you can stop calling. You'll see me when I return."

I winced with every stinging syllable. I could barely hear her voice, but Erica didn't even have to be here to drive the wedge of their pending marriage between us.

"This isn't the time or the place for us to get into this," Thorn said.

Erica practically screamed into the phone. Thorn had definitely offended her, probably making her feel embarrassed about her obvious possessiveness. Not that I blamed her. I wouldn't want to share Thorn either.

"You'll be my mate in less than a month. Why can't you just—"

And with that, I left with my back stiffened, determined to focus on the mission at hand. I already tortured myself on a daily basis by passing up most Christmas sales. I didn't need to do it by hearing him try to pacify his wife-to-be.

I made it no more than five steps before a hand caught my arm. The grip was warm, yet firm.

"You're angry." His voice was soft.

I shook my head and refused to face him. "Only indifferent."

He was silent for a moment but didn't let go of me. "I'm sorry you had to hear that."

I shrugged as my throat tightened. To speak would expose me. What could he say? What could I say?

With a sigh, I said, "If you need to go, you should do it now."

"Don't be that way."

"If your girlfriend needs you to stay away from me, what are you doing? Why are you here? Are you a glutton for punishment?"

"I said those things to protect you from her. She doesn't understand our friendship."

It took everything I had to keep my mouth sealed shut. We couldn't be friends. We couldn't even be acquaintances. There was no way in hell we could be anything at all if I continued to want him like this.

A yearning as deep as I felt meant we could never *just* be friends.

"Damn it, Natalya."

I tugged away again, and he finally let me go. Maybe if I walked fast enough I'd reach the back of the building and he'd think seriously about returning home. Maybe after I checked things out, he could take us back to Atlantic City. I could get my own car and we'd part ways amicably. It'd make things easier for both of us.

I briskly went to the back door and then froze. A sound, very faint, came from the trees to my left. I tilted my head to scan them for movement. It was just the trees, most likely camouflaging small animals. My nose told me I was alone. So why had the hairs on the back of my neck stood up? I turned to look at Thorn, but he'd vanished.

Damn it, Thorn! Couldn't you have waited a few more minutes before you listened to me?

Alone and unsure of where to go, I slowly backed toward the garage as the sound echoed through the trees again. Goblins had spells, but they only went so far. I'd never seen Bill defend himself—but he told me most goblins' magic was defensive in nature.

Forms shifted in my direction. A low growl rumbled in my throat from the wolf straining under my skin. When I came into contact with the building, I crouched low. They had to have seen me by now. Where was Thorn? Now I was sure he'd gone off hunting the goblin alone, leaving me behind. This wasn't the first time he'd done this to me—he'd briefly left my side to rescue my brother.

The strong scent of goblin magic suddenly filled my nostrils from all sides. It scratched at my throat every time I swallowed. No matter how deeply I crouched, I sensed danger everywhere.

Something grabbed my arm, and I lunged toward it. Whatever I fell into had a solid form, but I couldn't see it. I sure felt it, though. My weight crashed us onto the concrete. As soon as we hit, I jumped off my attacker to strike again. But nothing was there. Almost as if a breeze had swept through and wiped the slate clean of magic.

No scent. No sounds. The only thing I could hear was my heartbeat, beating loud enough to burst my eardrums. For once I wished I had a friend or two around. Nick, perhaps.

Out of nowhere, a knife appeared at my pulse point. Its silver glinted brightly. "Don't move, bitch!" The voice was gravelly, almost as if they'd smoked way too many cheap cigarettes.

It cackled. "Little wolves shouldn't come playing in Scabbard's backyard. Unless you're here for an oil change?"

The olive-skinned hand that held the blade hovered close under the guise of glamour, an invisibility spell that most goblins employed.

From the corner of my eye I peeked, but I couldn't see its—Scabbard's—body, only smell the overwhelming stench of its magic as it flared strongly. This goblin was more powerful than most.

"Only cowards who offer shitty oil changes hide behind a blade," I managed to bite out. My words stumbled a bit. "Face me if you plan to kill me."

He jabbed a few times with the blade again, this time eliciting a cry. I'd been stabbed before—a lot deeper, if I recalled correctly—but the new nicks on my neck and body burned like hell.

My attacker giggled. A strange sound from such a hoarse voice. "My little intruder's bold." The presence shifted around me and now came from the front. "Where's your friend? Scabbard can't sense him anywhere."

His presence quivered slightly in front of me, shimmering in the dim moonlight. Then it crept closer. Close enough for me to feel the inhale and exhale of his garlic-laden breath on my face. "Perhaps if Scabbard pricks you a little bit more," he whispered, "your friend will show up. A nick or two to wet his blade again?"

My breath locked in my chest, and I couldn't help remembering the feeling of another blade piercing my side. A much deeper cut. I'd had little fear on that other night, but now, tonight, was a different story. Everywhere he'd cut me pulsed like a bitter bee sting, and I was afraid.

Before the hand could jab at me again, a form rushed at us and slammed into where my attacker stood. Sounds—a grunt, a painful croak—filled the air. The knife clattered against the concrete several feet away.

I turned to see Thorn in wolf form hovering over the moaning goblin. He snapped and growled at his prey.

"Don't kill Scabbard," the goblin begged.

Thorn continued to tower over him, his claws digging into the goblin's shoulders. I gasped at the sight of the creature. I'd never seen a goblin up close before without its glamour. This close anyway. Bill had never revealed his true form to me. And now I knew why.

Goblins were ugly as hell. Either Thorn had beaten the shit out of this one until his face resembled somebody's wart-covered ass, or his face just looked like someone's ass.

I touched my neck and winced at the bleeding wound. He'd done far more damage with a few pricks than a regular silver blade could do. What the hell had he used on me?

"Do you do this to all of your potential customers?" I grated.

"No-no." His voice quivered from under Thorn's glare. "Scabbard was warned to look out for werewolves tonight."

I paused. "Did another werewolf come tonight before us? A larger man?"

"You're the first. That's why Scabbard was prepared for you."

My fists clenched and unclenched. *Damn it, Dad, where are you?*

Then another thought came to mind. "Who warned you?"

"Who do you think?" the goblin sneered.

Thorn growled and then snapped at Scabbard.

The goblin cried out like a startled cat. "Scabbard was just stating the obvious—Roscoe told him."

"We're not Roscoe's hired thugs," I said. "We're looking for someone. Thorn, get off him."

Thorn didn't move. Matter of fact, he tilted his head enough for me to see how much he disagreed with my idea.

"He'll play nice," I said to Thorn. "Because if he doesn't we might have to use his own knife on him."

I retrieved it. The knife had to be no bigger than an envelope opener. A simple butter knife. While I examined it, Thorn jumped off the goblin.

"What the hell is this thing?" I asked.

The goblin laughed in his hoarse voice. "You like it, Wolf? It's one of Scabbard's expensive toys he has for sale. Its magic's built to alter its form to the prey. Rather useful, regardless of the enemy."

"It's vile." I turned to Thorn, who circled a few feet away. "Any sign of my father while you were out partying in the woods?"

Thorn shook his large head and continued to pace.

"We should go back to Roscoe to see if my father's there." My fingertips brushed against my neck again. Not only did it hurt, but it itched as well.

"So you're just gonna leave Scabbard here bleeding, without giving him anything for his pain and suffering?" the goblin asked.

And I thought my goblin boss took things too far at

times. But I'd only met Scabbard a few minutes ago, and I was already sick and tired of him referring to himself in third person. "I'm not the one who attacks people without provocation. Between the two of us, the one on the ground bleeding could've answered the door when I planned to knock on it."

"Scabbard's protecting his territory. This place is rampant with you *werewolves*. The leprechauns aren't any better either."

I rolled my eyes. "As much as I'd like to argue this little matter with you, we need to get going. We're heading back to Roscoe. If my dad shows up—and he's a lot bigger than Thorn, by the way—I suggest you answer the door when he knocks. *If* he knocks."

The goblin swallowed visibly. "Bigger, you say?"

I flipped open my phone and showed a picture of my dad with my uncles. "He's the one in the back who looks like he could crush you with his bare hands."

"Fair enough," the goblin whispered.

Thorn took a step toward the front of the building. I followed.

"W-wait," the goblin stammered. "If Scabbard gave you the compact, could you keep that bigger fellow from coming here? The rest of your family, too?"

I shrugged and feigned a sour face. "When someone attacks a member of my family, we usually have no choice but to retaliate—in great numbers. And you attacked me." I matched Thorn's pace and gestured wildly with my hands. "I have several uncles, a few mean aunts," I called to the goblin. "And good God, I've got cousins all over the place. Big, burly men, like my dad."

"Now, you don't need to keep threatening Scabbard. All he did was protect what's his from people like you." Even after grumbling a few times, the goblin got up and hobbled over to the building. His hand shook when he reached for the doorknob. It served him right for stabbing me with his magical butter knife.

After changing back into human form, Thorn followed us.

The inside of the garage was nothing I hadn't seen before. The office was against the far wall, inside a glass-walled area. We walked around in darkness before the goblin clapped two times. A sharp light filled the room.

The Clapper, huh? Who needs magic when you've got human innovation at your fingertips—or smacking hands, as the case may be?

The goblin's office wasn't too shabby. From the endless packets of sugar and empty coffee cups, it was evident that he had the sweet tooth of a sugarcane farmer. Not a single scrap of paper—other than from the sugar packets—sprinkled the desk.

"Now, Scabbard expects you to keep your promise," the goblin said. "He'll give you the compact and jewels and you'll leave him alone."

He reached into a drawer and pulled out a black bag. As he reached inside, I noticed the bag was velvet-lined. Fine quality, my eyes told me. But then, what he pulled out would make any girl sigh. A square compact case, about the size of my palm, filled his spindly hand. The outside shined from the bright light above and made me notice the swirls etched into the surface. My first thought was, *Timeless and expensive*.

The goblin clicked on the tab to open it. Nestled inside the compact lay seven gems. Four of them were cut, while the other three were raw. I most certainly wasn't a jeweler, but I knew the raw gems would be valuable to a dealer, who'd want to further divide them into certain cuts for his customers.

One of the gems, a raw-cut diamond, beckoned to me like a discount rack Christmas ornament. It wanted me to pick it up. To clean and protect it with the rest of the goodies at home. I usually didn't like shiny things other than ornaments, but this one was different. It was imperfect, but with a little love, it would become pristine.

My distraction almost kept me from looking closely at the inside of the compact. The goblin was in the process of closing it when I saw the flaw. The mirror caught my eye. It was far too clear. Why would an antique give off such a bright reflection? That too-perfect perfection screamed the compact had been manufactured in the past century. But Roscoe had said it belong to his great-grandmother.

"You like it?" the goblin asked.

He mistook my expression for interest. At first it had been, but now I was more than suspicious.

"It's a very pretty piece," I said. "From what century?"

Let's see what he pulls out of his ass this time.

"It's very old. Illya's been waiting decades to try to take this from Scabbard."

"Illya?" Thorn's eyebrow rose.

"That must be Roscoe's *real* Russian name," I whispered.

I turned to the goblin. "How old again?"

The goblin shrugged. "Scabbard doesn't know."

I took the compact and examined it. After another glance inside, my suspicions were further confirmed. The interior had chipped-off paint on it. Barely perceptible but a sign of a fake nonetheless. No one in their right mind would use paint on an antique compact. Of course, anyone who wasn't in the biz, which I was, would've mistaken the flaw for a discoloration in the metal. What the hell was going on here?

The goblin rubbed his hands. "Don't forget our terms."

I offered him the compact. "I won't. Especially after you give me the real one."

"You think Scabbard would just hand off something this valuable so easily, huh? Well, Scabbard values his business and his life."

I placed the compact on the desk when he didn't take it. "That part of the job is really shitty. I'm guessing Antique Metallic Brass spray paint. Maybe the Hammered Metal Finish? What do you think, Thorn?"

"It all looks red to me. Like someone's splattered corpse on a wall." His lips formed a thin line.

The goblin's hands went up. "Now, now, there's no need for violence again."

This place looked like an office, but something in the garage was giving me the creeps. "How about you produce the real compact, so we can leave."

After mumbling under his breath a few times, the goblin led us out of the office and into the area where he stored tools. While he sorted through one of the larger storage compartments, I noticed something gleaming along the opposite wall. Underneath the shelves with parts in boxes, another metallic object glinted. It was blurry, as if my vision had been smudged with grease, but eventually it cleared more and more, since I was familiar with this type of magic.

What I finally saw was a set of cages. Two of them, stinking of burnt cinnamon from binding magic, were a few inches shorter than my height and were barely wide enough to lie down inside. The beginnings of fury stirred in my blood. That piece-of-shit goblin had planned to keep and sell whatever he'd caught. Namely, us. The dark magic in the cages was the sort spellcasters used to entrap werewolves.

Based on what I'd learned from Nick, warlocks used black magic for nefarious spells. Wizards like Nick were restricted to white magic—which meant we might need to watch for a warlock in this area.

Scabbard turned to us, holding an object that appeared far older than the fake compact. This piece had all the signs of fine workmanship: It was a nearly flawless silver case with embellishments like seashells along the surface. I was almost afraid to pick it up, it appeared that delicate, but I had to fulfill the debt. We hadn't been captured—nor would we be tonight.

"Is everything okay?" Thorn asked. He gave me that look that said he knew something was troubling me.

"We're good," I managed to say. "Let's take the compact and get the hell out of here."

We left the garage, Thorn taking up the rear. The goblin limped ahead of us and remained silent. As soon as we reached the car, Scabbard stood to the side with a frown.

Before I got in the SUV, he asked, "Can Scabbard have his knife back?"

Why not just give him the knife back so he can stab and cage others? Against my better judgment I replied, "Check your mail in a couple days."

I might've wanted to tear the goblin apart, but I refused to lower myself to his level.

Chapter 6

W_e reached the Atlantic City limits before I fell apart. The nagging pain from the wounds Scabbard had given me didn't help either. I tried to focus on what I had to do next, but my mind clung to the web of deceit I'd fallen into. If Thorn hadn't saved us, I would have been caged right now. And all the blame fell to Roscoe. He'd set a trap for *us*.

It was all there in front of me. Why would Dad be given such an *easy* task for the first part of his debt? And if fetching the heirloom was the only task, we shouldn't have been able to get it from Scabbard as easily as we did. The facts swirled through my mind: the cages, the warning beforehand from Roscoe to Scabbard. All of this stank of trickery to get us either captured or shoved out of the way. *But for what reason?*

Another question suddenly came to me, but the very thought of it stole my breath. If this was all a wild-goose chase, then what was the real task my father had been asked to do? One that would be suited to a man like Dad—a skilled killer? My frown deepened. Whatever it was, it had to be something *so wrong* that perhaps my father didn't want any part of it. Which meant Roscoe was hiding something very important from my brother and me about our dad.

"I want to kill, Roscoe," I breathed.

Thank goodness Thorn was driving. Rage stirred inside of me and I wanted to lash out. To lash out at anyone who tried to contain the wolf.

How long had it been since I'd vented properly? The battle with the Long Island werewolves? I'd waited far too long to give in to my desire to tear something apart.

With a man like Roscoe, should I be surprised that something bad like this happened? After seeing his place and meeting Scabbard, this whole situation would only get worse.

I swept my fingers over the heirloom—a fancy piece of shit meant to bait us into going to see that goblin. My boss at The Bends—even with his crotchety attitude—had more honor than the people I'd encountered tonight.

A curse in Russian escaped my lips, and I tried to suppress a wave of anger with clenched fists. Darkness suffocated me and made me wheeze with each breath.

"Calm down," Thorn said softly.

I didn't want to.

I'd always been like this. Calming the wolf. Restraining it under my desire for order and organization. My hands clenched the seat, ready to form claws. My back hunched slightly. The change was close to the surface.

"Pull over," I demanded.

The car rolled to a stop, and I stumbled out. Like a tightly pulled rubber band I ached for release. Maybe screaming would help. Before I could turn to run for the nearest set of woods, Thorn's arms slid around me and clutched me tightly. When I tried to fight him, he tightened his grip.

"Let me go," I growled.

"When you calm down I will." His deep voice held hints of the change. He must've sensed the wolf straining to be free within me and was reacting to it.

Time passed. I wasn't sure how long. One of Thorn's

warm hands slowly slid upward along my arms until it cupped my face. A thumb brushed a single tear away.

Instead of feeling comfort, all I felt was shame. A deep ache that made me want to hide my face in my hands and never expose the inner me to Thorn. I'd seen angry wolves before. When they succumbed to the bloodlust, they attacked and slaughtered without thought to their actions. If I knew anything, it was that the Code taught us those kinds of wolves weakened a pack.

No wonder old Farley Grantham had kicked me out.

"You're telling me he just *gave* it to you?" Roscoe hid his disbelief with a laugh.

Under most circumstances, I would have wondered if we were fools for coming back, but what choice did we have? I wanted answers, and Roscoe was the only one who could give them.

I tossed the compact to one of the guards. The man gingerly tried to catch it. I snorted. Why were they bothering to pretend they cared about it? "Here's your compact. Isn't that what you expected my father to fetch?"

The guard handed it to him. Roscoe rubbed his fingers along the ridges before he lobbed it on his desk. Just as I thought—he didn't care about it. He'd abandoned another video game to chitchat with us. This time, he'd taken the form of a death knight with an elaborate set of armor.

"Are you sure you didn't barter your firstborn child?" He appeared smug. "Most goblins don't take too kindly to folks messing with their profits."

"We found a way to persuade him," I said. "You could say I have a way of seeing through people's lies."

The side of Roscoe's mouth lifted to show the hints of a smile. "Do you, now?"

"Cut the bullshit," I said. "I know very well you warned Scabbard about us. Which pretty much screamed to me that your little bullshit run was to get me captured by another party while you continue to *persuade* my father to fulfill the job you set for him. What was it you said last time? 'No one is allowed to harm the family of a debtor in my presence'?

"The only way you could get my dad to do whatever shitty thing you wanted him to do was to have me captured and then force him into doing it by saying Scabbard would kill me. Do I have that about right?"

I hate to admit it, but I felt really smug—until I saw the lack of enthusiasm on Roscoe's face.

Slowly, he walked over to me. "Fyodor is a strong one. One of the strongest werewolves I've hired." His voice lowered, and his black eyes focused on mine. "I've seen him crack a human's back with his bare hands."

"Where's my father?" I whispered.

"He lacks something most of my men will always have: fear. I've never seen him afraid—only angry." Roscoe continued while I stared at him, my own fear creeping up my back.

"Over the years, I've come to have many enemies. A few of them needed to learn a final lesson only Fyodor can teach. Since your father's moon debt was high, I told him he'd have to take care of a few of his former associates and then make a delivery for me." Roscoe leaned forward, switched his gaze to Thorn's. "Do you know what he said to me? He told me he wasn't the kind of man to kill his friends—even if he didn't work with them anymore. He wasn't a killer like me. Ha!"

When Thorn didn't react, Roscoe looked at me. "But you know what? A killer will always be a killer. A wolf's always a predator waiting to strike its prey. Of course, none of those truly matter to a man—especially when he has a weak point: a *family*."

My heart sank.

"Your father left me with no options—so I offered

him none in return." Roscoe gestured to a guard and jerked his head to one of the doors to the left. Thorn and I watched the guard as he entered and closed the door behind him.

Time passed, and all the anger I'd pooled earlier turned into an icy ocean of fear. What was behind the door? If my father didn't want to fulfill the debt, what had they done to him? Had they killed him?

My mouth dried painfully, and every breath took effort to inhale. No matter how angry I got, no matter how much rage boiled inside me, I would never be a match for the guards around us. I prepared for the worst, but I was still hit hard. The door opened and the guard returned, dragging something on a chain. A large form rolled along the floor.

I heard a soft cry and then realized it came from me. No one stopped me when I rushed to Dad's side. He was wide awake and blinked at me. Something about his gaze almost made me want to turn away—as if he was ashamed to have me see him like this.

My hands reached for the chain—over an inch thick—which circled him, from over his shoulder to around his neck. I tried to pull it off him, but failed.

Those filthy bastards. I stood, but a hand locked over my shoulder. He hadn't meant to—but Thorn's hand brushed against the wound near my neck. Just another reminder it still hadn't healed yet.

"Not now." Thorn's voice was low, primal.

"I'm definitely not the person you want to *fuck* with, *devushka*." Roscoe watched me with a grin I wish I could claw off his face. "Unless you're finally interested in showing me what you're made of."

"Release him," I hissed.

"He's perfectly free to leave, when the debt on his head is clear. Of course, he hasn't fulfilled any of it yet, so the answer to your demand would definitely be no."

If I'd had a gun, I would've fired that puppy until my trigger finger fell off. But Thorn was right. My anger wouldn't save my family. Roscoe had boxed my father in, and now he knew he had the Stravinskys by the balls.

My shaking hands clenched into fists. This whole mess made me want to bury my head in my hands and escape to a quiet place where stress and pain couldn't find me.

The sound of my teeth grinding together pushed me back into reality. I had to do something. Alex wasn't here. Mom wasn't here. The debt was my father's, yet the weight of the debt affected the whole Stravinsky family. And now this burden was on my shoulders. I knew very well that I wasn't a mercenary trained to kill.

I approached Roscoe. Every footstep made me feel weaker. A tingling sensation coursed down my arms. He'd resumed his computer game, as if we had left the room. Why bother to worry about us when he had enough firepower and guards to knock us into next week?

Slowly, I managed to find my voice and bury the heat of my anger. "I've come to take responsibility for Fyodor Stravinsky's moon debt," I said.

"Hmmm?" Roscoe swiveled his chair and regarded me in amusement. "You'll take on your father's debt?"

Thorn was at my side and twisted my arm to make me face him. "What the hell are you doing?"

"The right thing." From the way his features tightened, I'd prevented him from doing what he'd planned. I guessed I earned two points for beating him to the punch, but I was sure I wouldn't hear the end of it when I faced him alone.

Thorn turned to Roscoe. "I will help her repay this moon debt."

"You don't have to do this," I said. He wasn't my mate or even my boyfriend. He shouldn't play the hero.

Thorn ignored me and continued to stare Roscoe down.

"No," was all Roscoe said.

"No?" Thorn took a step toward Roscoe.

The guards shifted to intercede, in case Thorn got too close.

"The terms of the moon debt are quite clear. A Stravin-sky must make the hit. The pack in Jackson's expecting *one* werewolf. No more, no less," Roscoe sneered. "She can joyride with fifty humans, for all I care, but no were-wolf assistance."

He added another word for good measure when I didn't speak. "None."

The thought of doing the hit nauseated me. "Unlike my father, I'm not trained to kill. But I'm more than willing to fulfill the second part."

"What makes you think that's good enough for me?"

"You said the final task was a delivery. To where and how soon must it be done?"

"A week to make the hit and then afterward he had to deliver my goods to Jackson, Maine. What? You inter-ested in picking up a gun?" he purred.

"I-I can't do the hit, but I'm willing to sweeten the deal by making the delivery in twenty-four hours." I hated it when I stammered.

"That's not good enough for me."

I sucked in a deep breath, searching through my mind for solutions.

"Other than performing the hit, what other options are *acceptable*?" Thorn asked. This whole time, Thorn's gaze had never left Roscoe. From the way he stared him down, I feared Thorn was contemplating doing some-thing really heroic and stupid.

"Let me think." Roscoe paced a bit. When a smile ap-peared on his face and then grew, the nausea in my stomach reached painful levels.

"Under the Code, I have the right to kill your father. But since you're willing to take care of the delivery—in under twenty-four hours—I'll make a nice profit from the sale of my goods to the Jackson pack. But, then again, I should be compensated for the lack of a hit man."

His gaze flicked to the guards. A silent signal. Three of the larger ones advanced on my father.

My stomach lurched, and I tried to step forward. "No! You can't do this!"

Everything happened too fast. Thorn grabbed me around my waist to hold me back. The first guard swung his boot and kicked it into my dad's belly. The second leaned down to punch him in the face, while the other stomped on him repeatedly.

For the first time in my life, I fought Thorn. I tried to claw at his arms—twist my body to free myself. Anything to reach my father's side and help him.

"Natalya, stop!" My father barked out his command between a grunt of pain.

I stopped but not without utter disbelief. So Dad meant for me to watch? To stand by and do *nothing*?

A sob escaped my mouth, and I tried to turn my head away.

"You shouldn't turn away, Natalya." It wasn't Roscoe who whispered this, but Thorn. He gripped my shoulders, but his hands offered me no comfort. "He's doing what a man must do for his family. Accept it."

The urge to squeeze my eyes shut was so tempting. What kind of sane daughter could watch her father get beaten down like this?

As if that bastard couldn't show any more of his indifference to us, Roscoe went to his computer and resumed playing his damn game. The computer's noise did nothing to drown out the sounds of suffering. Time passed too slowly, as my dad's blood flowed. When the guards finally removed his chains and then backed away, I ran to his side. He was barely breathing.

"Why?" I asked him softly in Russian. But Dad didn't answer me. When I touched the only spot on his head that wasn't bleeding, he didn't move either. His bruises weren't visible yet, but they'd come soon enough.

I wanted to comfort him. To tell him that everything would be okay—that I'd do what needed to be done. But it was time to leave. Thorn slowly hauled Dad's unconscious bulk over his shoulder.

"Do you need help?" I asked.

"No."

Somehow, I stood in front of Roscoe without spitting on him. "I'll be back at dawn."

Roscoe continued to play his game, his fingers twirling to send us on our way.

"Can't wait to have you come back to play."

Chapter 7

Since I didn't trust anyone else in Atlantic City, I asked Thorn to take my dad home in the rental.

"You're asking a lot of me," he said.

We stood in the parking garage of the Golden Saddle, facing the vehicle where my father rested. He hadn't stirred when Thorn offered him food and water.

After Thorn's soft words, it seemed best to avoid looking at his face. "All you have to do is drive him home to a healer."

"You know that's not what I mean."

I blinked, unsure of what to say.

"You know I'll find you. Wherever you are."

"You can't help. You mustn't." I emphasized each word to make my warning clear.

"That may be true. But you know me—you may not see me, but I'll always be around."

His words dug into me and made my stomach clench. I'd heard them before. Back when the Long Island werewolves hunted me at every turn. Just like now, he'd been my protector. My white knight, even though he'd been promised to Erica. Right now I wanted something eloquent to say. Something witty to convey how much he still meant to me and how grateful I was that he gave a damn about me and my family.

What came out instead wasn't as profound.

"You say that, but you don't seem to be around when I really need it," I joked.

I sensed his warm smile. "Most people define needing help as having their car battery jumped when it's dead or fixing their stopped-up toilet. Your needs turn out to be much more elaborate."

A quick peek beyond the parking garage showed a still-dark sky. I'd have some waiting to do. The night wasn't over yet. It would be a night I'd spend alone.

"I think I'll go get some sleep."

He took a step toward me. "Are you sure about this?"

"I am." I couldn't say more without sounding weak.

Thorn sighed. "Can you promise me you'll try to stay out of trouble? Just make the delivery?"

"I don't go looking for it. But that shit seems to always be looking for me."

He chuckled and took another step. I couldn't help but steal a glance at him. He was close enough for me to make out a trace of blond stubble along his chin. I kept my gaze away from his eyes, and somehow it settled on his lips. How long had it been since I'd run my fingertips over them? He licked them and forced me out of my reverie.

Time to take a step back.

I started to take it, but he stopped me. His hand snaked out, and he pulled me into his arms. My face was buried in a warm spot right under his chin. I didn't wrap my arms around him—I refused to do such a thing. But damn, he fit me just right. My body curved into his, at the perfect angle for our bodies to rub against each other. Even through my clothes I sensed the hints of his arousal. Smelled it. He still wanted me—and it convinced me all the more to increase the space between us.

Once we separated, I managed to find my voice. "You should go. The healer's waiting for you two."

He only nodded before getting in the SUV. A part of

me wanted to turn away when he drove off, but I watched the vehicle leave the garage and disappear into the night.

All alone, I made the most of my time. I took a shower and switched into some clean clothes I'd bought at the gift shop. I tried to get a few hours of sleep, but my racing mind kept me wide awake. My hotel room wasn't much of a comfort either. I checked the alignment of the coffee glasses next to the coffeemaker. I washed my hands five times. Then I arranged the towels. Whenever I tried to go back to bed, I'd rise again to seek out the comfort of a repeated activity.

When I finally settled enough to lay down again, I realized I still hadn't taken any of my meds. Nor would I be able to for the next twenty-four hours. I still had some anxiety medication running through my system, but given my current highly anxious state, I'd surely be an obsessive freak by tomorrow. Not a good thing at all.

Sadly, I got only about forty-five minutes of sleep before I reported in to Roscoe. He wasn't there when I arrived, but one of the guards had a set of keys for me and a note with my instructions.

"It looks like you're getting a DT 466," the guard said as he led me out of the building.

"A what?" He'd spouted some other language most likely. The language of vehicles and their associated models wasn't something I was familiar with. In a past life, my time in New York, I'd been a fervent researcher of knowledge to verify facts for a publishing company, but trucks were not in my repertoire.

According to the note, I had to deliver the truck by dawn tomorrow at a park near Frye Mountain in Jackson, Maine. It shouldn't be too hard to do this.

The guard gave me a quick ride in a Jeep to a large vacant lot not far from the marina. The whole area smelled of fish, construction, and sewage. A lovely combination on a Sunday morning. From what I could see, the lot had a bunch of cars, trucks, and such in various stages of disrepair. Dread hit me when I realized that none of these vehicles looked new—or clean.

"When you get to the Atlantic City Expressway, use the second lane at the toll. Roscoe's got a wolf stationed there, so you shouldn't have any problems getting through."

"How kind of him to check on me."

The guard shrugged. "One more person to keep you out of trouble."

"Or in line," I mumbled.

We continued to drive through the lot before another important question came to mind.

"Did Roscoe tell you what I was transporting?"

"Naw. It's none of my business." He paused for a moment to turn down one of the lanes in the lot. "You shouldn't concern yourself with it either."

I snorted. "I should probably know if I'm carrying enough narcotics to get the entire New England coastline high. You know, just in case I need to gun it if the police are on my tail."

If Roscoe was having me carry drugs, what would I do? I'd have no trouble smelling them and would definitely know if they were in the truck. But could I transport drugs, even to help my family? Under most circumstances, I knew I'd do bodily harm to anyone who hurt my loved ones, but transporting drugs or harming kids was on the list labeled HELL NO.

The guard said nothing, so I remained silent. Fine. I'd find out soon enough.

We pulled to a stop next to what couldn't exactly be called a truck. My body steeled up, and I mumbled, "Is that it?"

It was a damn dump truck. Not a new truck or even

one that had been recently cleaned. It was one of those rectangular trucks people used to haul crap around. There was no way this was a regular delivery truck. It had gigantic stains, peeled-off paint, and endless rust spots. I could smell it from over fifteen feet away. It *sure* as hell didn't smell like cocaine, pot, or some other rave-based happy pills.

As I got out of the Jeep, for a second I wished I *were* transporting drugs, so long as they were in a brand-new dump truck.

"This is the transport," the guard said. "You got until tomorrow morning." He used a set of keys to unlock the door, he opened it, and then he threw them to me.

When I didn't move, he chuckled. "Sunup these days comes between six and seven a.m. so I suggest you be on time. The client's a stickler about time."

"Trucks this size require a D class license to drive them." The words came out of me like a robot. I hadn't expected to say that out loud, but I did. I didn't know much, but at least I knew that little fact.

"Good luck with that. Don't forget to fill it with diesel." He jumped into the Jeep and sped off.

I continued to stand in the spot where I'd gotten out.

The first thought that came to my mind was, *I'm so screwed.* The second, *I'm in deep shit,* fit even better.

I took a step toward the truck and then immediately took one back. After ten deep breaths (didn't work), I opened my shoulder bag and pulled out my antibacterial wipes.

One look at my sorry little package, and I groaned, "I need a Costco-sized box of these."

Finally, I approached the truck. All the while, I repeated to myself, "For my family. For my family. I can do this. I've been through worse."

The door was open so I stood on the step-up. The inside wasn't any better than the outside. The truck had two blue seats, which appeared to have been mauled by small rabid animals. For some reason, the floor mats were missing and in their place was a layer of petrified food bits and mud thick as a shag carpet. The steering wheel even had a slimy sheen—oh, gross—as well as a broken-off turning handle. (Maybe if I jabbed something in there it would work?)

I cringed. It was absolutely, positively disgusting.

My chest constricted, so I took a short walk for some air. The cold breeze from the Atlantic brought me some comfort, but it wasn't enough to keep me from thinking about what I had to do. It was time to focus on the truck. Take stock of it or something. I circled the vehicle and checked the tires. The treads were a bit worn, but they'd hold for the trip. I didn't know what other things to look for, since my dad and Alex were the ones who took care of this kind of stuff. But there was nothing broken or hanging off to give me any concerns.

Something about the back of the truck caught my eye, though. A thick padlock sealed the door shut. At first I was scared about the contents behind it, but somehow I let it go. I told myself, *If it's dirty, I don't need to see what's inside.* And I damn well didn't want to *handle* what could be inside either. Let it stew in the funk, for all I cared. I didn't smell narcotics. Matter of fact, I didn't smell anything at all. What the hell was I carrying? The curious wolf in me urged me to reach out to touch the door, but I stopped myself. Eww. No thanks.

A quick glance at my wristwatch convinced me I'd wasted too much time. I had less than twenty-four hours to make a twelve-hour trip. In a vehicle I wasn't legally qualified to drive, and without GPS.

The perfect Sunday drive.

When I got back into the truck cabin and shut the door, I faced my next problem.

I didn't know how to drive a truck.

Well, at least I could start the damn thing. I turned the key in the ignition, and the truck roared to life. Good, one more thing to check off the list.

While the cabin warmed up, I took out my wipes and did what I could with the steering wheel and whatever else I could reach. No one had bothered to clean out the candy wrappers or the empty fast-food bags on the seats. I always carried a plastic bag in my purse for waste, so I just threw everything away.

Soon enough, the cabin was nice and toasty, so it was time for me to grab something, or push something, and make this thing move. It was just like a car, right? I'd driven a stick shift before. But, come to think of it, that was over seven years ago. Still, wasn't driving like riding a bike? A few minutes and I'll be good.

It took me a half hour to leave the lot.

The dump truck was cumbersome, and steering it was like driving . . . a humongous truck. I'd driven my father's truck before, but that was another story. I had no idea how to make wide turns or avoid the mountain bike I ran over. (I left a note and some money—next to the pieces anyway.)

I had a few blocks to the Expressway and prayed the cops wouldn't pull me over. I sure as hell would have pulled me over if I saw the driver of a huge dump truck was some chick gripping the wheel like she was attached to the damn thing. By the time I spotted the exit, I breathed a sigh of relief. Once I was on the highway, things would go a lot more smoothly.

Or so I thought. The window to view the sides didn't help at all. How the heck did truck drivers see out those things? I craned my neck to see beyond the lane to make sure I didn't run someone off the road. The first hints of traffic loomed on the highway, and I needed to make progress before I got caught in it.

I didn't even have to cuss out any drivers to get on the

highway. Everyone kindly got out of the way. I could've gotten into one of the left lanes, but why bother tempting fate?

The drive to the toll road went well. Of course, every time someone honked near me I wanted to bare my teeth at them. Not only was I a first-time dump truck driver, but I was an anxious one.

I made it to the toll booth in the second lane just like the guard told me to do. I whipped out a few dollar bills, but when I reached the booth, the werewolf, a man who appeared to be in his late forties, just smacked his lips and gestured for me to roll through.

"Good luck," was all he said.

"Uh-huh." I had a feeling I'd need it.

The Atlantic City Expressway eventually got me to my turnoff to the Garden State Parkway. This route was familiar to me, since I'd taken it numerous times to get home from my various little shopping trips. From here, I'd ride past smaller towns and patches of forest. My speed was a steady fifty-five, since I had trouble shifting up to the next gear. Why hurry anyway? I had all day to make the trip, and a faster speed wouldn't keep me from driving through the day into the night. According to the directions, I had about 550 miles. If my math was right, driving at the speed limit would get me to my destination by the end of the day. Easy peasy.

My confidence faltered when I noticed a car following close behind me. The black SUV looked a bit beat-up, with a scratched front fender. My first thought was, *Thorn?* But he'd been in the dark red rental SUV when he'd left to take my father home. His SUV at home was black, but the outside was in immaculate condition. *Don't get me started on the inside.*

At first I expected the SUV to pass me, like everyone else, but it simply matched my speed.

Suspicious, I slowed down a bit. Why not go Cindy-Speed-Limit to see if they passed me with a frown?

But they just slowed down even more.

Shit.

I reached for my phone but stopped. Who could I call? My brother? He might be busy helping his wife give birth. If I called Thorn for help, I was opening a can of worms.

Of course, I could approach this a different way. I picked up the phone and dialed Thorn's cell.

"Hello." It was a woman's soft voice.

Crap. "Is Thorn there, please?"

A slight pause. Out of all the voices in South Toms River, I knew Erica Holden's right away. If all stuck-up bitches had a particular type of voice, then Erica would be their poster child.

"What do you want? He's busy." Her normally chipper voice now had an edge to it. If I was in front of her I would've cowered at her dominance.

"I need to check on my father. Thorn delivered him to a healer."

"I see."

She didn't speak for some time. I knew she wasn't moving or checking with Thorn. It was just her way of being spiteful and making me wait.

Finally, I found my voice. "Can I speak with him, please? Unless you know if my father's okay?" I tried to be nice. I really did. My grandmother would be proud I didn't tell Erica what I really thought of her.

"Thorn." Erica yelled the word and then dropped the phone on a hard surface. Most likely a table. The jarring noise reverberated against my eardrum and almost made me jerk the steering wheel to the left.

"Damn it all the hell," I hissed.

Of course, that was when Thorn picked up the phone. "Nat?"

"Hey, Thorn. Is my father okay?"

"We're at the healers right now. She's still taking care of him." He sighed. "He's in really bad shape."

I flexed my fingers on the wheel. "What exactly did the healer say?"

"Don't worry about that right now. How are you holding up?"

My thoughts went to Erica, who was most likely standing close to his side and listening in on the conversation. I bet she wondered if I'd beg for him to come help me. I almost laughed and thought bitterly, *I'm all alone, and now you've got him all to yourself. Enjoy your sloppy seconds.*

"I'm great."

The vehicle behind me slowly ate away the distance between us. I checked the speedometer. I wasn't slowing down.

"How long have you got to get there?" he asked.

A few feet separated me from the SUV now. I sped up. The SUV matched my speed.

"I-I just started out not too long ago," I stammered. "I'll be there tonight and should return home tomorrow."

"You don't sound as confident as you did last night."

I heard Erica say, "Thorn, I'm hungry, let's go get some breakfast."

"Just a minute," Thorn said. "It won't take long." I could sense his exasperation.

"Go ahead and take Erica to get something to eat," I told him. "You don't need to stay with my dad. I bet Mom's there already."

"Yeah, she's here." Then he was silent. Words hung between us, like always. Maybe the conversation could've gone like this:

"Are you sure you don't want me to come help you?"

"*Actually, I do want you here. I'm kinda scared and grossed out.*"

"*After I check on your dad, I'll be there.*"

But that wasn't what happened.

"Stay out of trouble, Natalya."

"I will," I said softly.

Then he hung up.

Thorn wasn't behind me. A flash of disappointment hit my gut. I guess I'd gotten used to him protecting me. But he'd done a great deal for my family by delivering Dad to the healer. It was a damn shame Erica played tagalong to watch him while he waited for news.

Which brought another question to mind. Who the hell was driving behind me?

A second later, whoever it was rammed into the dump truck.

Chapter 8

When the dump truck swerved, my head swung to the left hard enough for my neck to jerk painfully. The dull screech of metal against metal made me cringe. I glanced ahead and behind me. No cops, thank goodness. But there was also no one around to react to the SUV hitting me. When I sped up, they matched my speed again. And then I could go no faster—I'd need to shift again to do that. My trembling hands attempted to switch the gears. Every time I fumbled with them, the truck grumbled and groaned at my half-assed attempt to head into fifth gear. For once I wished I'd spent more time with my brother when Dad was teaching him the basics of mechanics and cars. Instead, I'd been more than happy to hang out inside the house and watch soap operas with my grandmother.

The truck jostled as it was hit again.

"Damn it!"

My exasperated breath fogged up the front window. With one hand, I managed to grip the wheel and roll down the window to let in the chill. Which, when my attackers came around the truck, I realized wasn't the best choice. A cold gust entered the cab, but the chill didn't affect me as I watched the SUV gun it down the opposite lane to approach me.

It came at me fast, since no cars were coming the other

way. I pushed on the gas even more. "Faster, you piece of shit!"

I could pull over at the next exit, or I could slow down enough for them to either pass me—or shoot me.

The SUV's darkened windows didn't reveal the occupants. And now I watched with horror as their windows rolled down. My mouth slowly dropped, expecting a gun to appear. But nothing came out.

Another car approached from the opposite lane, so the SUV pulled ahead of me.

For a moment, I sighed with relief. Maybe it was nothing.

But then a faint scent hit my nose. One I'd never smelled before. It was like a washed-out meadow after rain. Muddy and rich. Nymphs? Fairies?

Then I heard scratching noises along the side of the truck. A peek out the side window revealed nothing amiss. But my ears and nose never lied when I was on alert. Something was on the truck. The SUV remained ahead of me, an even length away.

Oh, shit. Had they left me a little present on the truck? Should I make a stop at the closest car wash?

I swerved a bit to avoid a pothole and heard rustling along the top of the truck. Tiny scrapes like claws moving along the metal. I looked up and wished I'd brought a weapon with me. The scraping got louder as whatever it was crawled along the roof, then descended down the side.

My mind drifted away for a second—racing to figure out how to defend myself.

A tiny voice in my head screamed, *Hey, genius, roll up the window!*

I scrambled into action, using the rusty handle to raise the window. Along the driver's side, the noises increased until my ears told me they were right above the windshield on the passenger side. And they were heading for the driver's-side window.

Said window groaned with each pull upward. I cursed every turn with all the bad words I could think of in Russian. I even said a few I'd heard Uncle Boris use when he thought the kids weren't listening.

The taps and scrapes grew louder as my pursuers approached faster—the scent of magic increased to the point where I knew it was a hairbreadth from attacking me.

And then, just when the window was halfway closed, the freaking handle broke off.

With one hand on the wheel, I used the other to crank what was left of the handle to roll the window the rest of the way up. I didn't make it.

Something black and slimy stretched into the truck and swiped at my head. I tried to move to the right, but it snatched a nice handful of my hair. I growled and tugged to the right again, only for my head to be pulled back toward the window. When I released the wheel to protect myself, the truck rolled off the road before I could manage to grab it again. The car behind me honked again and again.

Another rough yank on my hair and my claws emerged to scratch at the hand. Black blood, warm and stinking of bitter copper, filled the cabin. Whatever fought to pull out my hair now tried to crawl farther into the cabin. No matter how much I hissed and clawed at my intruder, it stubbornly held on to my hair.

The arm extended farther inside and was followed by a tiny bald and black head. Skin as shiny as wet rocks felt slimy to the touch. With white, pupil-less eyes, it glared at me and hissed, "Pull oooo-ver!"

I reached down and clutched the broken door handle. When a vicious jab, I stabbed my attacker in the face. It screeched and then rolled off the truck. Through the

rearview mirror I watched the creature fall on the highway and then get run over—by an ice-cream van. Should
I call it magical roadkill now?

A tired breath escaped my lungs. The SUV was out of
sight. But I felt wary and on edge. I'd been attacked, but
not by werewolves. Werewolves didn't employ these
kinds of creatures.

The side of my head ached. I'd been stabbed in the
neck with Scabbard's magical knife, and now I was driving
with shaking hands. What little control I still had over
the truck was precarious.

After driving in fear for twenty minutes, I decided to
stop and get my shit together. Time to pull over. I spied
the first exit advertising diesel fuel, in New Gretna. With
some gas for the truck and a nice cup of coffee for me,
perhaps I could piece things together.

Scratches covered the front part of the truck. Not just
your average scratches you see on an old truck. But the
kind that made you wonder if a badger had mauled it.
While an attendant pumped the gas, I tried to think of a
million excuses to call Thorn. Didn't I need to check on
my sister-in-law? Didn't I need an update on how my
father was doing?

I wasn't even halfway to my destination and I'd been
attacked already. By a magical creature.

Once the tank was full, I pulled out my cell phone.
With a sigh, I scrolled through the names on my contacts
list. It would only take a second to dial Thorn's number.
But one name came before Thorn's, so I dialed it.

The phone rang twice before someone picked up.

"This is unexpected. Hello, Nat." The voice was mas-
culine, soft-spoken. It promised the possibility of
much-needed help. I was instantly glad I'd called Nick.

For a second I almost felt shy, but words soon came
out. "Hi, Nick. How's it going?"

"Good," he said. "What's up?"

I groaned. Where the hell could I begin? "I've got a few problems."

"Wanna talk about it?"

I spilled the beans. My dad's moon debt. The trip to Atlantic City. My choice to take my father's place after Roscoe tricked us. Nick listened quietly the whole time, and I didn't feel the need to hold back any details. Talking to Nick was different than with Thorn. I felt like I could speak freely to Nick—minus the baggage I had with Thorn.

"So, what do you think it was that attacked me?" I asked.

"Trouble. Where are you?"

"A truck stop in Jersey." I closed my eyes and hoped he couldn't sense where I was. White wizards had many tricks I didn't know about, and I wouldn't be surprised if cell phone geo-location spells existed.

"*Nat.*" His voice rose, scolding me.

"I'm thinking it was something magical. What about you?"

He sighed. "You can't do this alone. From the description you just gave me, I'm pretty sure it was an imp."

My eyebrows rose. I'd heard of them before, but I'd never seen one. "Well, getting run over by an ice-cream truck killed it."

"Getting run over by a truck pretty much squashes almost anything." He chuckled, and then his voice grew serious again. "Imps are creatures that do the bidding of other magical creatures. Dark ones." I heard movement on the other end of the phone. The click of keys on a keyboard.

"What are you doing?" I asked.

"Looking up a few facts. And e-mailing my boss at the pawnshop to tell him I'm not coming in today."

I rolled my eyes and stared at a happy, noisy family

while they piled into an RV across from me. At least they'd be able to enjoy their trip today. "I'll know what I'm up against so I'll be careful the rest of the way."

"Uh-huh. You're about ten miles from Tuckerton, right?"

So my tricky little wizard figured out my location. "What spell did you cast this time, Mr. Wizard?"

Nick laughed again. "I'm a good listener, Nat. It's not hard to figure things out when you listen to the conversations around you."

The happy, loudmouthed family in the RV had apparently revealed a few clues . . . but only another werewolf would've been able to hear them. This wizard had a few new tricks hidden in that black trench coat of his.

I wanted to question him further, but Nick spoke first. "Don't move. Stay in the truck, in an area where humans are moving around, until I show up."

"Nick, I don't need—"

Then that damn wizard hung up on me. Evidently, no one could say good-bye to me properly today.

A hand tapped on the window and I turned to see I had a visitor.

I'd expected to have to wait over an hour for Nick to show up from NYC, but he made an appearance in less than a half hour. *Not too shabby at all.*

A giggle escaped my mouth, and I breathed a sigh of relief. Nick was definitely a welcome sight. His best feature—his smile—was brief, but he did offer it when mine appeared.

I unlocked the truck door and he opened it to the cold. "How did you get here so fast?" I asked him.

He leaned inside, blocking most of the chill. I took in his lips up to his eyes. After a brief moment passed, I realized I'd stared at him too long when our eyes met.

That was embarrassing. He chuckled softly before he turned to scan the parking lot.

His laugh became an easy grin. "You know me. I've got enough jump points in my pocket to travel from here to Death Valley if I wanted to."

My face soured. "You still trust those things after what happened to us?"

I avoided jump points like the plague since the time Nick and I had been attacked heading from group therapy back to my house. We'd been ambushed in an old nasty basement and Nick barely made it through alive. After that, for the first—and hopefully last—time in my life, I carried an unconscious wizard home on my back.

"One can't be afraid of the dark forever."

I caught a whiff of something and took a step out of the truck. It wasn't Nick. He never left a magical scent unless he cast a spell or two. This one was faint, like when the breeze from the ocean hit my nose. Not more than five feet away stood two women with wide grins on their faces.

"Surprise!" one squealed. It was Heidi. The mermaid might fear the ocean, but she sure didn't have a problem standing close to a dump truck like this one. In a pair of army boots and an old bomber jacket, she looked comfortable. In contrast, my other new arrival wore only a sweater, blue jeans, and a small smile. Most of her chestnut-colored hair hid her face, but I immediately recognized the Muse named Abby.

Both of them were a welcome sight.

"Where did you get this hunk of junk?" Heidi laughed while I frowned.

I snorted. "I'm moving my collection up north. A nasty truck seemed like the best option."

"Maybe in the ninth circle of Hell it would be," Nick said. He eyed the truck with distaste.

"What are you two doing here?" I glanced at Abby

and Heidi before looking at Nick. "How much do they know?"

"We got a little phone call from Nick here. He told us enough for us to figure out you're in deep shit and need help." Heidi placed her hands on her hips.

"As much as I'd like to accept your help, I can't. Something attacked me not too long ago and I don't want you in the middle of my mess," I said.

Now the Muse appeared—well, amused. "I think you've seen we can handle ourselves just fine."

My thoughts drifted back to the battle with the Long Island werewolves. Both the Muse and the mermaid had worked a blade with a finesse I hadn't expected. But even if the mermaid could gut a whale with her trident, I still didn't want them to sacrifice themselves to help me.

"No. You don't need to do this for me."

"Whatever. I need to take Abby up to Maine anyway, so the least you can do is give us a ride for saving your ass awhile ago." She winked as she checked out the truck cab.

I frowned. "Why can't she drive herself?"

The mermaid sighed. "Maybe I should simply let Abby drive herself so the cops can notice her car doesn't have a driver?"

Whoops. With Abby standing there quiet all the time, I sometimes forgot she was invisible to all humans—except for the authors she inspired.

"Sorry, Abby," I mumbled.

"It's okay." Her soft voice drifted to me on the wind, her smile soft and sweet.

Heidi then examined the truck. "Looks like you got a DT 466."

"That's what the guy who gave it to me said. What is that anyway?" I asked.

"It's a truck, that's all you need to know." She appeared thoughtful and then whistled. The noise was shrill and hurt my ears. "Hey, Nick, come take a look at this."

Nick followed Heidi. He peered at something and nodded at her. "Yeah, I saw it when we walked up."

They'd spotted what had put me on edge while I'd filled up the truck. A bunch of scratch marks from my attacker.

I joined them. "You still thinking it was an imp?"

"Yeah, but what I'm worried about was what or who dropped an imp-care-package on your truck."

"And if they're coming back," Heidi added.

"Oh, they'll be back." Nick circled to the back of the truck. We all followed.

His hand hovered near the dirty handle to open the back compartment, but he never gripped it. I couldn't gauge his feelings, other than seeing his face, but I was sure he was as grossed out as I was.

He examined the lock but didn't touch it either. "Nat, did they show you what's back here?"

I shook my head. "The guy just handed me the keys and sent me off on my merry way. They told me not to take a peek at my Christmas presents."

"Have you tried to open it?" he asked. "I'm getting weird vibes from this thing."

I tossed the keys in his direction. He caught them with one hand.

When he gave me an exasperated look, I replied with one that said, *You asked, you open it, pal.*

Nick tried the lock; it didn't budge.

"Is it jammed?" Heidi asked.

"It's sealed." Nick tried again, but no dice. "With magic."

I scratched my head. I'd been attacked by an imp, and now I'd learned the back of the truck had been sealed by magic, presumably to keep people out. Should I add to the list that werewolves *rarely* use or even know any spells, so the fact that magic was involved made it even worse?

Nick approached me with a frown and leaned in to look at me closely. His oh-so-faint scent of magic tickled my nose and made me think of fresh cinnamon rolls from the oven. "You have any plans to remove that curse from your neck?"

I touched the burning area where the goblin had poked me. "I have a curse?"

"A minor one. I don't sense a deep wound." His warm fingertips rubbed the spot for a bit, and the pain vanished. I avoided staring at him again as he checked me over, gently touching the places where Scabbard had cut me.

Once finished he said, "I call shotgun."

But I wasn't done with him yet and grabbed his sleeve. "So what would've happened if that goblin had really stabbed me?"

"You wouldn't be alive, that's all." He said it way too calmly. "Thankfully, he only nicked you. The curse would've killed you in a month or two, though."

That didn't sound too good.

"What about the lock?" I asked.

"There's nothing we can do about it now. I'll dig at it while we ride." Nick made a beeline for the passenger seat. Abby climbed in after him while Heidi and I used the driver's side.

"You might not want shotgun after you take a look inside." Perhaps my face said it all, but when Nick entered from the other side, his already pale face appeared even paler.

"The inside definitely looks a lot worse than the outside." Nick opened his coat and pulled out two long blankets. With a whisper and a tap from his fingertips, the blankets spread along the seat to cover it, stretching until the two seats melded into one long one for all of us.

I couldn't help but spout, "Don't you have a spell in there to clean this place?"

Nick frowned and then climbed in. "It would take more than a spell to clean the filth off this thing."

Like me, Nick wasn't too fond of germs. I'd have to thank him profusely later for being willing to get inside.

When I attempted to get in the driver's seat, Heidi pushed me aside. "Do you even know how to drive this thing?"

"Sort of," I replied.

She took one long look at me and then shook her head. "Not only are you lined up all crooked next to the pump, you hit the fucking thing."

With an innocent voice, I said, "I merely brushed against it."

Heidi started up the truck. It roared to life and the heater turned back on. "Uh-huh."

She focused on the truck. "I sometimes drive semis when I need to get away from the coast. I usually prefer a bike between my legs, but a truck is just as nice."

"Was that a bike or a biker you tried to get between your legs last week?" the Muse asked with a wry grin.

Heidi kindly offered the Muse her middle finger.

I think I vote for the biker.

Not long after, we set off northward up the Garden State Parkway. During the ride, I was snuggled between Heidi at the wheel and the Muse on my right. Poor Nick took up the leftover space against the passenger door.

I warily watched the pine trees along the Parkway, trying to keep my mind focused on anything except an obsessive activity. Over the past few hours, I had been fighting an incessant itch to wash my hands. Ten years ago, I used to wash my hands all the time. Hour upon hour of running my hands through the lukewarm water.

To shake away the revitalized compulsion, I spoke. "So. Where are you and Abby headed to in Maine?"

Abby answered. "A small town. Not too far from Bangor."

"Sounds quaint. Do you go up there every couple of months? As needed?" For a second, I almost pictured Abby as a call girl. Heading up to an author's place to provide her *services*.

"She doesn't do it often enough." Heidi snorted. "I'm forcing her to make this trip."

I could tell the Muse wanted to cross her arms, but she had little space to move. "I didn't need to go. He'd be just fine without me."

"Yeah, right. He's not the problem, and you know it." As I watched their exchange, I wondered how Heidi managed to drive and gesture at the Muse. It was rather fascinating—and slightly unnerving.

Heidi continued. "If you don't do your job, you go all Patrick Swayze *Ghost* on me, and then I have to drag your butt to your next gig."

I couldn't help but say, "Aww. That's one of my favorite movies."

"Me, too," Abby gushed.

Next to me, I detected Heidi making a gagging face.

Nick leaned forward. "So if you don't inspire your authors, you start to disappear?"

"Just a little," Abby said.

"She doesn't just disappear," Heidi said tersely. "She goes transparent. To supernaturals, too."

Abby turned to me. "So, what's your favorite scene?"

Her attempt to change the subject wasn't bad. Better than my usual attempts. "The part where he has to go to Heaven is mine."

Almost as if on cue, we both said Sam's loving words to his wife before he went to Heaven.

Heidi groaned. Nick followed not long after.

"You really do know that movie," Abby said.

"I've had a lot of movie nights." Sadly, I'd had many more than even most married couples. "So, why do you disappear?" I asked. "What do Muses *do* during the day?" For the longest time, I'd assumed her kind simply hung around with their authors and inspired them to write books. After working in nonfiction publishing for a few years, I wished I could've employed one or two of them to make the company's authors produce better books.

"Muses influence mortals through our physical presence." She smiled a little. "All I need is to be within one hundred feet to inspire them. They don't need to see me or talk to me. When the connection's right, the author—whether they're a poet, screenwriter, or even a child scribbling on paper—will feel compelled to work on their craft."

I nodded while she spoke. It seemed logical.

She continued. "We get our assignments from the gods. They prefer to give us mortals who will create literature or art of great importance." She sighed. "I don't think they choose very well when it comes to *mine,* though."

"That last guy in Queens you hung around wasn't too bad. Well, when he wasn't drunk or hooking up with those cheap prostitutes," Heidi said with her gaze focused on the road.

Between clenched teeth, Abby said, "He wrote about this crazy small-town physician who sewed his tools inside of people. In-side of peo-ple." She emphasized every syllable with a look of distaste on her face.

"Hasn't he been on the bestseller list for the past nine weeks?" Heidi asked.

"I don't care what list he's on," Abby said. "He made my skin crawl every time I had to look into his head. What kind of human thinks this kind of stuff up?"

Even though Abby was upset, I couldn't help but snicker. "A man who wants a paycheck?"

The Muse lightly swatted me, apparently unoffended. "Oh, shut up."

Nick, who'd been quiet for a bit, spoke up. "Just out of curiosity, how did you get the name Abby?"

She quickly said, "Oh, that's not my real name. But I've had it since the Black Death in 1349."

I couldn't help but shudder. Abby had to be germ-free after all these centuries, but a small part of my mind couldn't help imagining the superflu lingering under her fingernails.

"And your real name?" he asked.

Now this I wanted to know. Abby didn't seem like it fit her as a Muse.

Our quiet friend grinned slyly. A rare one for her. "Only my authors know my real name. And they never kiss and tell."

Chapter 9

Not far outside of Bloomsfield, we stopped for lunch. We were still in New Jersey, but we'd made great progress. After riding in close quarters, the chilled air was welcome. Heidi's choice of where to eat . . . not so much.

"Has this place passed any state legal codes to serve food?" I asked.

"Oh, c'mon, you two." Heidi eyed Nick and me as if my personal tastes were a running joke. If only I could find the ketchup and mustard smear along the sidewalk equally hilarious. Or the greasy feel of the metal handle on the door.

"Nick, you don't want to touch that," I advised.

"Already ahead of you." He pulled out a napkin and used it to hold open the door for the rest of us. "If I didn't want to look like a weirdo, I'd have on plastic gloves right now."

I reached into my purse and yanked out two gloves from a brand-new bag. "I bring them in case of emergency. Now you're not alone."

Thanks to being a clean freak, I was used to being stared at by the other werewolves back at home. In comparison, a few humans I'd never see again didn't seem like a problem. The cheap plastic gloves brought me a strange comfort just looking at them.

Nick offered to put one of them on me. "Here you go." His hands were warm and smelled of fresh mint. I rather liked the smell of both mint and antiseptic. Most folks wouldn't get off on such things, but the scents made me feel safe.

"You good?"

I'd been staring at my hands. When I glanced up at Nick, he flashed that warm smile he always had on his face when he looked at me.

I couldn't resist the smile that tickled my lips. "I'm good." Then I held up my hands. "I've got my protection on."

His eyebrows danced as we strolled up to the counter. "You shouldn't do *it* without protection."

I snorted, but my face warmed nonetheless.

Heidi was at the front of the line and obviously couldn't resist joining in. "I've always wondered if safe sex was possible in the ocean."

"I don't," Abby said with a laugh.

While Heidi ordered, I checked out the eatery. The inside of the restaurant wasn't the cleanest. Matter of fact, I suspected the mermaid just picked the first place she could find that had gas. To her, this place was clean, but after I picked up my tray of food, I noticed it felt slippery underneath.

"It's just water from the washer." Nick must've noticed my expression. "I should've offered to carry your tray."

Heidi laughed and then whispered, "Why not just levitate them to our table?"

"And frighten the humans?" the Muse asked.

Nick chose a spot in the corner, a booth where Heidi and Abby sat on one side. I took a seat on the other side with Nick.

Heidi said, "We could do anything in here. Half of these truckers look like they're barely running plays on the field right now." She'd hardly sat down and she had her burger unwrapped. Somehow, on the way to the table, she'd inhaled half of her bottle of water.

I expected things to quiet down while I performed surgery to extract my food from the wrappers, but Heidi continued to gab. Nick, my ever-present sidekick in cleanliness, took my wipes and went over the table and condiment containers.

"I find that most of these places have really interesting people," Heidi said. "I once met a trucker who was a dark elf hiding out from the leprechaun gangs."

I laughed. "Did he steal their pot of gold?"

"I hope not. They cut off people's hands for stuff like that."

Once Nick finished helping me, he excused himself. "I need the keys to move the truck."

Heidi frowned. "Is something wrong?"

"Other than the fact you parked it right out in the open?" he replied.

"We can see it from here." Heidi gestured to the window next to us, through which we could see the truck.

Nick extended his hand. "Keys."

"Whatever. Don't hit anybody." She tossed the keys at him. "Or ruin your nice plastic gloves."

The Muse picked up the conversation, taking her food from Heidi's tray. When Nick returned, I couldn't find a single sign of the truck.

"Where did you put it?" I asked.

"In a warded place," he replied. "We're not safe here anymore."

He gestured with his head to two patrons along the far wall. They were seated closest to the door. My nose told me they smelled like humans.

"What's up with them? They look like tourists to me," I said.

"You don't see them like I do." He'd taken off the

plastic gloves to drive the truck, so he offered his hand to me. "It will only take a sec, and you can wash your hands after I'm done."

"Okay. But the humans better be naked or something cool like that."

The mermaid's hand shot out real fast. "I sure as hell wanna see them if they are."

Nick mumbled a few words under his breath. As to what tongue he spoke, I didn't know. His palm wasn't warm like before. It blazed hot and made me grimace from the touch. His black eyes, usually shiny, reflected a fire that made me want to look away.

I slowly turned, in a manner that wouldn't alert the couple, and saw through Nick's eyes. The whole place changed. I should have focused on the couple first, but everything around me writhed with life. Strange little creatures that looked like caterpillars shuffled along the checkout counter. On the wall above the spot where customers could get straws or packets of condiments, something that resembled a speck of light pulsed along the wall. Another one from the other side of the room joined it.

Like a curious kid, my hand almost went up to point at what I saw, but then I noticed my hand—or should I say I noticed how my hand looked. It glowed. Almost as if coals burned under my skin. Fire churned there, surging up and down my fingers. My skin barely contained what swam underneath.

I thought, *Holy shit,* and turned to Nick in amazement—and saw the unthinkable. Nick was pure light. An absolute white without a speckle of dirt or darkness. The urge to reach out and bathe myself in his warmth pulled at me. Was this what all white wizards looked like when they truly checked out each other? Without glamours or walls of magical protection?

I only knew for sure it was him when the lights that

were once his eyes blinked a few times. Something that had to be his lips smiled.

"Behave yourself, Natalya." The white wizard's grip on my hand tightened, and he chuckled under his breath.

My head turned to the couple. I wanted to look at the mermaid or the Muse, but I'd fulfilled my curiosity enough for today. Whatever signal Nick projected was feeling slightly weaker by the second. The couple in the corner had skin the color of coal. Not a natural color either. Their skin appeared shiny, as if dipped in oil. I wanted to focus on them, but something inside warned me not to stare. A tracker takes in information quickly to stay on the trail. I let my mind snap a photograph, and I processed what it took in: One of them was tall and thin, while the other had a medium build. The tall one focused on the door, the other one maintained their disguise by eating. Their heads had a fine sheen of black hair. As shiny as their skin.

"Who are they?" Heidi's smile had disappeared. She was all business now.

"Assassins. Most likely dark elves employed by whoever—or whatever—used the imps. Maybe fairies," Nick said.

"Not good," the Muse responded. "They usually leave people alone."

"Unless their target has something they want." Heidi eyed me.

I should've been afraid. But naturally the first words out of my mouth weren't productive. "What kind of fairy assassin scopes out their target in a fast-food joint?"

Heidi shrugged. "One that not only wants to kill you but also wants fries along with a double cheeseburger?"

"What do we do now?" The Muse took a sip from her drink, then swallowed a final bite of her burger. She had resigned herself to the fact that it was time to go.

"They're heavily glamoured," Nick said. "Since I had

to use a nice dose of magic to see them, they should know by now that I'm not human."

He'd released my hand not too long ago, but my palm still tingled.

"If we go out the door, they'll just follow us to the truck."

"How do you know there aren't more of them waiting for us by the truck?" I asked.

"Well, instead of leaving it out in the open, I parked it in a safe place." He stood. When we moved to follow, he gestured for us to stay.

"A no-fairy parking zone?" the Muse joked.

"You could say that. Stay here and wait for my signal. They'll follow me; after you get my signal, make a run for it outside. I'll meet you there."

He didn't say what his signal would be. Naturally, him being a wizard, it would be something we couldn't miss. At least I hoped so.

Nick walked toward the door, but instead of leaving, he strolled to the bathroom.

Every part of me cringed, and I mumbled, "He's definitely taking one for the team if he heads in there."

Heidi said, "Not all bathrooms are disgusting, Nat."

"It's not what your eyes can see that's the problem."

The dark elves rose, and then put their food away in a waste container. They casually talked between themselves before one followed Nick into the bathroom. Bingo. The other one stayed put.

"So," Abby whispered, "what's the signal?"

Faintly, I heard a *thump,* and then smelled the scent of something burning. Like someone searing cinnamon in a pan.

I resisted the urge to stand. Nick had gone in there alone. Was he all right? I clutched my hands together and waited. The other elf glanced at his watch then rushed into the bathroom. I guessed even though people saw the elf as a woman, it wouldn't stop his cohort from helping his friend out.

"So?" Abby leaned forward. "The signal?"

"We need to go in there and help Nick." I stood, but the mermaid grabbed my arm.

"Look." She glanced at the table. On one of the napkins in the center, bright red ink flowed into words: *What the hell are you doing? Run!*

Heidi didn't need to pull me away from the booth. We ran for the exit. The door to the bathroom slammed open. As I burst outside, I caught the faint clicks of claws against the tile floor of the restaurant. The scampering of little feet raced after us. The snapping of jaws.

"Where did he put the fucking truck?" Heidi yelled.

I followed my nose—searching for the horrible scent of the truck. All of our scents lingered on it, but its foul odor drew me to it like a nauseous beacon.

"This way!" I ran past the restaurant parking lot toward the area where the main truck stop was located. Trucks continued to drive around us—oblivious to the hoard of imps racing in our wake. I could smell them, and my stomach rolled from eating burgers and then making a run for it.

We ran across the parking lot. Not far beyond I spied where the scent originated: the truck stop's car wash. I looked for the dump truck, but my eyes couldn't see it. When we ran around the car wash, I noticed a tall black fence. A fence made of thick iron. And just beyond it, the truck.

"How did he get it in there?" the Muse panted, nearly out of breath.

With a running start, I easily leaped over the fence.

"Hey, slow down!" The mermaid reached the fence right behind me and formed her hands into a boost for the Muse. Abby stepped up on them and vaulted over the fence.

On the other side, I jumped on the railing and offered Heidi my hand. Not far behind her the imps were coming. At least twenty of them. Their mouths moved hungrily, just like the first one I'd seen.

I grabbed Heidi's outstretched hand, but it was too late. One of the closest imps jumped on her back. I growled at it, my claws out and ready to swipe.

Heidi was no wallflower ready to die. She belted out, "Son of bitch!" and grabbed at the imp. But the creature scampered all over the place, reaching and scratching. Not far behind, the others prepared to join it.

In my back pocket, something burned and vibrated: the knife from the goblin.

I pulled it out of my pocket and jumped off the railing. The knife glowed and drew me toward the imp on Heidi's back. When I touched the blade to the imp, its skin sizzled like bacon in a hot pan. The creature screeched and jumped away—trailing a line of black blood. The others closed in but kept a healthy distance.

The two dark elves appeared. A disturbing sight, one holding a sword and the other a knife. A tourist couple ready to gut the locals—how nice.

"Climb over." I knelt down and offered Heidi my cupped hands. She wouldn't like the ride I was about to offer, but things didn't look too good. When she got into position, I jettisoned her over the fence—she landed with a painful *umph* on the concrete. I heard it but kept my eyes on the dark elves and imps. They glared at the blade in my shaking hand.

"C'mon!" I said hoarsely. "Who wants to play with my little knife next?"

One little knife against twenty or so imps and two dark elves carrying much bigger knives. I had a great chance—when Hell froze over and the devil opened a Popsicle stand.

An obviously bold imp jumped forward, only to have

a limb fried off by yours truly. They had numbers on their side, though, and I only had one blade. They swarmed toward me, some leaping toward my arm while others jumped on my leg. The wolf within whined, urging me to change. To give in and let it fight.

I had almost decided to do so when the roar of a horn and the blast of a cranky engine belted toward us. The imps that didn't move were crushed. As the truck came up beside me, the passenger door flew open. A hand snaked out and grabbed my arm, two imps still clinging to me.

The rush of the truck propelled me forward, but Nick's hand around my arm held firm.

A yelp snuck out of my mouth from the biting pain on my arm. My two passengers clung to me for dear life. Perhaps they'd hoped I'd fall off and develop a road rash like their other comrades.

The truck veered wildly out of the parking lot, then settled into a hard pace on a side road. I expected Heidi to drive toward the highway, but she kept roaring down the side street.

Using the goblin's magical blade, I swatted madly at the two remaining imps, now clinging to my leg. Damn, those little bastards were persistent. Their claws dug into my jeans until they pierced the thick material.

"Hold on!" Nick held on to me with one hand, the other gripping the truck. The open door swung into him.

A rough bump kept me from slicing into one of the imps. One of them crept up my leg again, while the other tried to maintain a foothold on my backside. That one bravely took a leap toward Nick. Boy, did it get the surprise of its life. A light brighter than a set of stadium lights filled my vision and burned my eyeballs. It was painful enough for me to curse madly in Russian.

"Shit! Shit! Shit!" My grip on Nick faltered. The wizard had picked a great time to use his little flashlight to protect us.

The blinded critter fell to the road. The other imp scrambled off me to find a safe spot on the side of the truck. Over the wind, I heard it hiss at us.

With a rough yank, Nick tugged me inside. I landed on his lap with a grunt. By the time he slammed the door shut, the second imp had climbed to the window. It glared at us, perhaps throwing curses in whatever grunt-like language it used.

The Muse was as close to the mermaid as she could get without impeding the driver. Heidi had the intricate focus of a neurosurgeon—until the imp scrambled over the top of the truck and landed square in her line of sight.

"Fuck me!" The mermaid swerved hard to the right. Everyone inside flew to the right.

Abby whimpered, while I screamed, "Wipers! Damn it, wipers!"

The imp had its face plastered against the windshield—its large eye swiveling side to side, pretty much mocking us as well as any middle finger.

The wipers moved, banging into the imp's body. The little shithead didn't budge.

To add to the fun, a set of honks and a growing police siren ahead alerted us to big trouble.

"Could you stay in your lane, please?" Nick yelled.

The truck jumped again to the left.

Abby slapped Heidi's arm. "Don't regular people drive on the right side of the road?"

"How about you grab the wheel and take it for a fucking spin if you know what to do?" Heidi checked her seat belt. Umm, that wasn't a good sign. "I suggest you hang on."

"To what?" I mumbled. I was still on Nick's lap—with

no seat belt on. "What are you doing, Heidi?" I said with a growing frown.

The honks increased as the truck sped up.

"We need to stop," the Muse begged.

The honks grew closer.

The Muse squeaked, "We're going be a roadside pancake."

Heidi stomped on the brake.

The imp, with its beady eyeball trained on us, flew forward. Everything that came next almost happened faster than my eye could catch. Nick's grip on me tightened.

Since he didn't have a seat belt on either (future lesson here), we both crashed forward.

Hello, windshield, my name's Natalya.

I'd never had such an up-close introduction with a windshield before. My forehead *thunked* soundly into the windshield before it bounced back and then hit the dashboard. I guess I should be grateful that they saved me. Poor Nick, trying to keep me from getting hurt, ended up smashing me farther into the truck.

Sounds around me didn't make much sense after that. Heidi cursed a few times in a language I didn't recognize before the truck jerked forward. We hit a squishy bump, and she snorted.

By the time we rolled to a stop a few feet later, I could only hear one thing: the sound of a single police siren in front of the truck.

Chapter 10

Even though I was at my wit's end, I knew we were in trouble. Reckless driving. Evading a police officer. Murdering, or should I say running over, a supernatural creature.

"Does everyone have their license on them?" Heidi asked.

"It's in my other trench coat," Nick mumbled. He didn't sound too good.

"Will he see mine if I pull it out?" The Muse laughed lightly.

"Not funny." Heidi rolled her eyes. For once, I had to agree with her.

A speaker from the cop car blared, "Everyone out of the truck with your hands up. Nice and slow."

Nick managed to unravel his hands from around my waist. I slowly pushed myself upright and rubbed the monstrous goose egg that was forming on my brow. Underneath my skin, I sensed my body already at work to mend anything that might be broken. But I'd still hit my noggin pretty hard. My upper lip felt a bit swollen, too.

Heidi opened her door and held her hands out. Should I be alarmed that she looked as if she knew *exactly* what to do? I'd seen enough cop reality shows to know most folks would be wetting their pants and professing their innocence. Heidi, however, just marched out with her hands on top of her head, as if she'd been arrested every Sunday.

The Muse slowly followed her and tried to mimic her movements. She didn't need to bother, of course.

On the other side of the truck, Nick opened the door with a groan. "My neck's killing me."

"I'll trade your whiplash for my concussion," I said.

He slumped out of the truck. "I'll pass."

"You ever been arrested before?" I whispered as we moved over to Heidi's side of the truck.

"I distinctly remember asking you that question not too long ago."

"And I remember you telling me you've never been." It hurt like hell to rest my hands on my head. "I guess I get to say yes if you ask me again."

The officer approached us and belted out, "Shut up!" Through his shoulder mike, he spoke briefly to dispatch. "I got 'em, off Shaw Road."

The mike responded immediately. "ETA on backup is ten minutes, Stan. We got a 246 in Burnsville."

"Roger that." The cop marched up to us with his gun extended.

The pain in my head increased to the point where my vision doubled a few times. I wobbled a bit but still managed to stand.

"Okay," the cop said. "Which one of you was drunk enough to take up two lanes for the past two miles?"

We exchanged glances. I tried to say a few things, but it came out as globbledygook. Then Heidi spoke up. She began the harrowing tale with a hitchhiker, along with his pet monkey, trying to get a ride with us. She lied through her teeth pretty well, didn't even hesitate or stammer. The hitcher had tried to take over the truck, apparently. We'd managed to get rid of him, but his vicious monkey somehow ended up on the hood. Through Heidi's quick thinking (and this was where I thought she began to sound like she was full of shit), she'd managed to slam on the brakes and get rid of the monkey before we crashed into other innocent drivers.

No one said anything after that. What the hell could I say to back up a story about an evil hitcher and his trained killer monkey?

The officer's face suddenly reddened. "Do you think I'm gonna believe some cockamamie story like that?"

Well, at least Heidi'd tried.

Nick groaned and then shrugged at the cop, unsure of what to say.

"Stanley?" the Muse addressed the cop and took a step forward.

The cop's gaze flicked in her direction. "Ma'am, you need to stand with the rest of them and keep your mouth shut."

Abby whispered, "You shouldn't listen to your wife about your book."

All of our heads turned to her. First of all, the cop *saw* her. Second, what the *hell* was she talking about?

"Ma'am, this isn't funny."

"Go home and tell Rebecca that you've got a great story. The plot just needs a little work." While she talked, something about her was different. It was as if only the two of them existed. It was like one of those scenes you saw in soap operas where the edges of the TV got all fuzzy. Abby's features softened. And was I mistaken, or did she just lick her lips in a come-hither manner?

The Muse continued. "You will finish that book. You will get it published. You simply need to make sure she supports your decision."

"I love Terry and Velma so much." The hardened exterior of the cop faltered.

My hands plopped down to my sides. This whole scene had to be one of the effects of my concussion.

"I know you do," Abby said softly. "The gods favor your efforts as well, but they won't bestow their hand upon your words until you focus on those pages."

"I will. I'll do it today." He nodded vigorously and stared at her adoringly. "Is this a dream?"

"A wet one?" the mermaid mumbled. I elbowed her to keep quiet.

"Only if you're on the right path," the Muse whispered. "Go home now. Your wife took a half day today." She waved as the cop headed to his vehicle. "I expect you to finish chapter five tonight."

"I will." He waved fondly in her direction.

We watched the cop car speed away, its lights off. For a few minutes, Heidi, Nick, and I stared at the gravel road, none of us finding words to talk about what had transpired.

Heidi broke the ice. "That was fucking awesome."

"That was nauseating," I said. My stomach quivered at the thought of the cop coming back. I turned to Abby. "How come he saw you? I thought only the authors you inspired could do that."

Abby shrugged. "I'm not paired with my new author yet. Anyone who needs inspiration is fair game."

We climbed back into the truck. The passenger-side door was in pretty bad shape as well as the window. A quick glance at my watch told me the obvious: two hours of travel time were gone.

While I brooded, Heidi teased Abby. "I've known you for years, and all this time I've never seen you in *action*."

"In action? You make it seem like I'm a *porn* star or something."

Heidi laughed so hard I wondered how she continued to drive. "I wasn't the one licking my lips or pushing my boobs up for the cop to see."

Abby appeared shocked. "Heidi! He's a married man and an officer of the law."

"How did you get so prudish all of a sudden?" Heidi's hands left the wheel for a second and I about grabbed it. "When was the last time you had someone subscribe to your lady softness newsletter?"

Abby groaned. "Oh, don't give me that again. I talk to guys on the phone sometimes."

Since the wheel was safely back in Heidi's hands, I felt it was safe enough to speak. "According to my best friend, Aggie, gentlemen callers are for virgins who aren't giving it up."

"Precisely," Heidi said. "I go straight to the meat-packing plant. No need to wait for the spinsterhood delivery service."

"What kind of term is 'lady softness'?" Abby asked.

Heidi snorted. "You're a Muse and you don't know every term for a gal's wooha?"

"I do. A man's as well. But I don't inspire people to use something as vulgar as the terms you use. I rather prefer the ones used in romance novels."

"Oh, here we go." The mermaid shook her head. "I'd like to apologize in advance for what's about to happen."

The Muse took a deep breath before she spoke. "There's the quintessential classic phrase, 'manhood.' Then there's 'purple-headed warrior,' 'sword of ecstasy,' 'pulse-pounding hammer,' and 'velvet steel shaft.' One of my personal favorites, from a science-fiction romance I helped an author write, was 'staff of felicity and fervor.' The alliteration is utterly delightful."

"*Felicity and fervor?*" I mumbled.

"Why did I agree to help you again?" Poor Nick sounded horrified.

Abby continued to list crazy names for a man's love package, while my mind drifted back to calculating the time we had remaining to reach Maine. Only fourteen hours, and we still needed eight for driving. Heidi drove the speed limit—at my request—so we could avoid little visits from the police.

We settled into the drive. After Abby thankfully stopped with her list, no one really talked. We all seemed to be on edge, as if we were waiting for someone else to attack us. I glanced at my phone repeatedly, to see if anyone had texted me about my dad or Alex's baby, but there weren't any messages. I actually had to keep myself in check from messaging anyone to vent about how I've been feeling: anxious, scared, out of control.

The pounding headache from my forehead meeting the windshield and dashboard didn't help either.

Every time I managed to focus on the important things—like what I might face in Maine—my mind fought to drift away. It was like I had some strange person living in my head alongside the wolf. She caged it, keeping the place tidy and well kept—all the while the wolf circled and waited for the house of cards to fall. And right now those cards were teetering like crazy. Who in their right mind would drive a dump truck with who-knows-what inside?

Strange music penetrated my thoughts. Heidi had turned on the radio and evidently thought the classic rock station could pleasantly fill the silence. I wouldn't have minded—except that one of the first songs that played was Jimi Hendrix's "Purple Haze." My mind was separating at the seams while Jimi droned on about how he didn't know if it was day or night (daytime?) or why he was actin' funny (he was crazy?). My hands began to shake. The headache increased tenfold.

A hand took mine. "You doing okay?" Nick asked.

On any other day, I might've snatched my hand away, but something deep inside me whispered that at least his hand was clean. Of course, even though my nose could smell the antiseptic on his hands, the compulsion was still there.

Was a part of it related to Thorn? Was he the real reason I hesitated? To shove thoughts of Thorn away, I
gripped Nick's hand tighter. A wave of magical warmth
hit, and I couldn't help but sigh.

This was the feeling I needed. No worries.

"You're tense." His voice was a mere whisper. Low
enough for the wolf to barely register it. Even with the
others in the truck, I wondered what Nick was thinking
as his white wizard calming energy bathed me. I dared
not look at his face.

Unexpectedly, my heart started to race. Here I was,
snuggled next to Nick, his hand holding mine, and all
my anxieties caught on the brisk breeze outside and
floated away. Bits of snow along with rain hit the truck,
leaving the roads potentially precarious. But I didn't
give a damn.

The warmth flowed up my arm and settled into my
chest. My breathing slowed—then quickened. The sensation raced down my legs—fast enough for my toes to
curl. What the hell was he doing? From the corner of my
eye, I saw the wizard looking out the window, taking in
the view—while I was getting off on his happy magic.

Another surge pulsed through me, and my nipples
tightened. My tongue snaked out to lick my dry lips. I
wanted to let go of his hand. To let go of this strange
pleasure flowing through me. I didn't want it to go *there*.
To get me excited enough to snatch that damn wizard
from his seat and make out with him on the side of the
road. The wolf within me writhed and rolled over on its
back. How long had it been since I'd been this breathless? This fluid feeling from my belly to my center? My
fingers twitched—and then my body completely melted.

I barely managed to swallow the whimper that tried
to escape my mouth.

Embarrassment, both hot and warm, touched my
face. I immediately let go of Nick's hand and tried to sit

straighter in the seat. I'd just gotten a subscriber to *my* lady softness newsletter. At my side, the Muse had dozed off, while the mermaid appeared to be unaware of the mystical make-out session not far from her. She belted out the lyrics to "Afternoon Delight"—how appropriate— while I tried to pull myself together.

Off-key, she sang the chorus, which pretty much talked about two people rubbing each other's happy places before they did the horizontal mambo.

Yeah, Nick wasn't rubbing anything on me, but he had sure set off some fireworks. And he had the hugest grin on his face. Damn him.

I elbowed him with my right arm, but the movement bounced off his hard stomach. Damn his rock-hard abs as well.

Here I was, aroused as hell, and I barely heard his heartbeat on most days. I was so glad there weren't any werewolves in this truck. They would've smelled my arousal immediately.

But then I caught it, the flare of his nostrils. The slow inhale and exhale when our gazes caught. For a second, only the two of us existed, sitting next to each other in a dump truck. I took in the contours of his face. Lips that I wondered what it would be like to kiss.

I opened my mouth to speak, but what the heck could I say? "Stop healing people and turning them on"? But then, he'd told me a few months ago that with the right person, the spellcaster felt as much pleasure as the one who received it. That made my face redden even more.

"You need to behave," was all I managed to whisper.

He winked at me—a sly smile on his face.

Instead of more embarrassment, *Why?* was my first thought. *When can he do it again?*

Chapter 11

We had plans to drive straight through Connecticut as the night went on, but the warning light for gas told me we'd have to stop at the next gas station. We'd filled up the truck before the imps had attacked us, but I noticed with despair that the gas didn't last anywhere near as long as it did in my car. Either something was wrong with the truck, or Roscoe had given me one with the worst fuel efficiency ever.

The flashing red light bothered the hell out of me. "Does anyone remember the number of miles until the next town with a gas station?"

Abby shook her head, while Heidi looked grim.

Nick said, "Maybe ten miles?"

I groaned softly. I asked Nick, "Is there any chance your staff squirts gas?"

"As in farts?"

I gave him a lethal look.

"You opened the door for that one," he said with a laugh. "I simply walked through it."

The engine sputtered, and everyone fell silent, barely breathing. It didn't take long to sour the mood.

"Is that a bad sign?" the Muse asked quietly.

"Of course not." But Heidi didn't sound as confident as her words.

With each breathless minute that passed, we watched

the mile markers go by. The red light continued to flash, mocking me with the threat of an ended trip.

When it seemed as if I'd start babbling about pushing the truck down the road, we spotted lights from buildings off the exit.

I grunted, "If they don't have diesel, we're going door-to-door until someone gives us some."

"I know how to siphon gas out, if necessary," Abby said.

My head whipped her way as we pulled into the only station off the exit. From the way she spoke and acted—until the cop pulled us over—Abby came off like the poster child for the Girl Scouts.

She rolled her eyes at my look of disbelief. "I learn these things from my authors."

"Uh-huh," Heidi said.

There weren't any other cars when we pulled up to the gas station. The lights from inside were far too bright after we'd been traveling on the dark road for so long.

We waited a bit for the attendant to come out, but no one did. The whole place seemed—too quiet. I leaned over Nick and peered inside. No one waited behind the counter.

"Maybe we have to pump our own gas in Connecticut," I said. "Which would be nice, since I'd like to get back on the road sometime today."

I tapped Nick so I could get out. We strolled over to the pump, and I whipped out my purse. Time to get some gas and get the hell out of here. With my luck, the pump wouldn't take credit cards—and it didn't.

"Nick, I gotta go inside—"

"Nat, you need to see this." Nick's voice was quiet.

"Just a sec, I need to run inside real quick to pay for the gas."

"That can wait." He took my hand and tugged me

toward the place where he'd stood before. At first I grumbled, but then my noise turned into one of horror.

Our gas tank had a few extra tiny holes in it. And this was a problem, since it shouldn't have *any at all*.

"How did that happen?" I asked.

"Do you need me to explain?"

I frowned. "Can you seal the holes?"

"I'll see what I can do, but right now I'm running low on juice."

After rubbing the sour spot on my forehead, I nodded. I knew from past experience that Nick's powers had a limit.

I strolled over to the building. On the way, I heard someone yell out behind me, "Make sure you get a few bottles of water, would ya?"

I didn't need to look behind me to know where that request had come from. The mermaid should own stock in bottled water companies.

My hand reached for the glass door before I noticed it didn't have any glass. What was left of the door swung outward, and I stepped inside . . . to a war zone. Bodies of imps—long dead—lay on the shiny tile floor. All around them were the remains of food from the shelves: smashed and ripped candy bars, broken bottles of beer, crushed boxes of cigarettes.

Something told me to leave this place, to flee and not investigate what was wrong, what had caused this. Why stick around to see what had killed those hateful things?

But still, I crept toward the counter to look for the register. Maybe if I left a few bucks, we could get some gas? The idea came and left quickly, as I knew I'd have to call the police. I couldn't just leave the place like this.

"When did you plan to call me?"

I jumped and just about knocked out Nick for scaring me. "With all this around me, I didn't exactly have time to plan the memo I meant to send you," I hissed.

Nick assessed the damage, stepping over the bodies around us. He leaned over to examine where something had punctured the soda machine and the hot dog machine—as well as the coffee machine. Whoever had attacked all these imps, and there were many of them, had used a staff or spearlike weapon on everything in the place. Judging from all the black blood, whoever had done this hadn't bled any of his. Unless it was black, too.

We checked the office and noticed the station's back door was open. A trail through the snow showed the imprint of a small shoe. Most likely a pair of sneakers. Hopefully the gas station attendant had beat a hasty retreat, escaping down the highway.

"What were they doing here?" I asked. "Shouldn't they be out there, planning their next attack on us?"

"Yeah. But maybe the fairies left a group of imps here to attack us, since they knew we'd be low on gas."

My dread deepened. "So how come they were dead before we got here?"

He shrugged his shoulders. "Somebody killed them. Do you smell anything?"

I'd scanned the store when I came in. Other than the bloody footprints of the imps, any of the tracks of their attacker were nowhere to be found. The imp assassin also hadn't left much of a scent. What kind of creature had stealth like that?

My mind went to Thorn. He could do this kind of damage—but he never used a weapon like a staff, and he'd definitely leave a scent behind.

Nick shook his head at the carnage. "I need to call the Supernatural Municipal Group to bring in a cleanup team."

I rarely heard them mentioned by other supernaturals, but the Supernatural Municipal Group was apparently some kind of governing body that provided services to keep us in line.

"Are you sure we shouldn't just get a mop and bucket? I saw them in the corner."

He offered a dry snort.

Nick flipped open his phone to make the call while I sidestepped around a heap of bodies. One of the imps had its hand locked around a Klondike bar. I guessed if it thought it was gonna die, it at least wanted to die with a smile on its face.

From my angle, I noticed something lying on the floor in the corner. Someone had scrawled something on the paper roll used for receipts. Gingerly, I picked it up and squinted at the strange symbols.

"Nick, do you know what this is?" I sniffed at the paper but didn't detect a scent.

He'd finished his call, so he took the note from me.

"Holy shit!"

Nick and I turned to see Heidi take in the scene. Abby followed.

"What the fuck did this?" Heidi said as she carefully stepped over broken glass.

"We don't know, but they left a calling card of some kind." Nick's face wrinkled as he checked the note more closely.

"I hope you're about to say it's written in some ancient wizard language that only you have studied for the past ten years," I said.

"Nope." He handed it back. "It's gibberish to me."

"Let me see," Heidi asked.

We all stood there waiting for her to say something, since she studied it a lot longer than Nick had. Long enough to make me wonder if she'd read it out loud. But she didn't. Matter of fact, she crumpled it up and tossed it over by the pile of bodies.

"I can't tell what it says," she said quietly.

"What the hell?" The Muse beat me this time. She

headed over to the pile to pick up the crumpled note, but now it was smudged with blood. "I can read over twenty languages. Why did you throw it away?"

"I'm sure it wasn't important." Heidi shrugged it off and then looked at her watch. The whole time I stared her down with suspicion. What was she trying to hide?

She jumped over the counter and pushed a few buttons on the register. "Did you call a cleanup team, Nick?"

He nodded.

"Then we need to use our time efficiently. When they get here, we need to have the tank filled and be ready to go."

"Do we have to wait for them?" I asked. We *were* a bit pressed for time.

"I need to give them a statement about what we saw," Nick said.

It was rather childish when I did it, but I still kicked at a fallen candy bar in frustration. It flew across the room and landed with a disgusting *plop*. More delays, more problems.

I whipped around to face Heidi to question her about the note, but she'd already left to go fill up the truck. I moved to follow her, but Abby grabbed my arm.

"Leave her be."

"Why? She knew what that note said."

Abby nodded. "It really upset her. I can tell. Just give her some time on the road and I might be able to get it out of her."

"Some time? Did you see the holes in the soda machine? You can practically see the brick wall on the other side. If she knows what attacked these imps, why withhold the information?"

"I don't know," Abby said with a shrug. "But what I do know is, she wouldn't keep anything from us that would hurt us."

I made the move to go outside, but her grip tightened—and then disappeared. Her hand passed right through me. My mouth gaped at the sight, but she kept her gaze focused on me. We both knew what her disappearing act meant, but Abby's mind was on Heidi.

She asked, "Can you trust me, please?"

"As long as you don't disappear on us, I won't bug her about it."

"Agreed."

A half hour stretched painfully along. I hated to admit it, but I pondered how it would look to my friends if I took the truck and left them behind.

Apparently it wouldn't turn out well, since Heidi had a death grip on the keys.

"Do you have any patience at all?" Nick asked me.

I ignored him and continued to pace.

Finally, the Supernatural Municipal Group's cleanup team arrived. Just as when the Supernatural Drunk Bus had picked up the drunken shape-shifter I'd encountered a few months ago, this van had the same Linda Leeks Bread Company logo on the side. I expected several people to show up, but only one man did—Mike, the very same warlock who had picked up the drunken shape-shifter.

He frowned when he spotted us. "I didn't expect to see you two again so soon."

"We didn't plan on being here."

"I suggest you watch yourself, Ms. Stravinsky. I hope not to see you a third time. Especially since there's been rumors of trouble brewing in this area with the fairies. They've been getting mischievous and restless." He took in the room again. "And if this is an indicator of what's to come, hopefully you'll remember my warning."

I kept a straight face, but naturally my first thought

was: *Does any of this trouble have to do with what's in the truck?*

Somehow, I found a civil response. "Thanks for the tip, but I think that spiel should be saved for the drunken shape-shifter who always gives you trouble."

I didn't say just *how* civil I'd be.

Chapter 12

N_{ight} deepened as we left Connecticut. Thanks to Heidi's faster driving, we'd made good time. After the incident at the gas station, no one asked to stop, and we refrained from eating. Nick had offered a few snacks from his coat, but no one seemed interested in wizard candy. (Although it did smell rather good.)

I'd never had a chance to travel through this area before. The shadows along the roads looked no different from those along the Garden State Parkway at night, but something about this place made me uncomfortable. The fairies hadn't attacked us yet, and with so many hours on the road, it seemed logical that they would've come for us by now. Not too many cars passed us either. It was late at night and most travelers were safe at home. A place I'd prefer to be.

"I don't like it here," Abby said.

"You and me both," I replied.

Heidi's voice sounded wary when she said, "We're deep in fairy country now."

I muttered, "Perfect." Why not just show up at their back door with some freshly baked cookies?

"We'll be in Maine before dawn. Not long at all. You should make your appointment on time." Heidi turned off the radio.

The silence wasn't welcome. "I liked it better with the radio on," the Muse said quietly.

"I'd prefer to hear some warning if we're about to get run off the road by imps—"

The truck jolted to the side as if something dragged us. Our bodies slammed to the right. We crushed poor Nick, but he only grunted. The truck twisted and then came to a rest on the grass, slightly off the road.

From my position with the Muse's arm under my head, I continued to gaze outside. Maybe an attack would come soon. But nothing stirred outside.

"What the hell was that?" I asked quietly.

Nick peered at our surroundings. "We need to get out of here. Right now."

I shifted my gaze to look in the same direction. In the darkness, I spotted lights. The lights of many eyes staring at us. Some of them bright red.

Heidi twisted the steering wheel and pressed against the gas, but after a few feet, the truck rammed against an invisible barrier.

"This is not good," she groaned.

Nick slowly opened his door—his eyes on the forest, where the red eyes continued to stare us down. From his coat, he pulled out a worn black staff. He pointed toward the barrier. When he approached the front of the vehicle, the staff encountered something, and a brilliant white light bounced off it.

"Nick?" I asked.

"A fairy roadblock," he said. "You can come out now."

"Are you crazy?" I hissed from the truck. "With them out there?"

"They could come for us anytime they want. But they won't, because of the wards I put on the truck."

Slowly I got out and joined him. "When did you do that?"

"When I took that little joyride to hide the truck behind the iron gate, I infused some of the iron in the truck—to be safe."

I nodded. "Good thing you did."

The others joined us.

Abby said, "I see so many of them."

A faint sound—but grating, like fingernails against metal—came from the back of the truck. Curious, and slightly alarmed, I left the others to check. I sensed Nick not far behind me.

"What is it?" he asked.

"Something's going on back here."

Nick aimed his staff at the door. We were both silenced when we noticed the lock was beginning to corrode. Bits of metal flaked off and fell on the ground. Also, the seam between the door and truck bed had begun to warp. Whatever was in there wanted to get out.

"Oh, shit," I mumbled.

Nick approached the door, but I grabbed his arm. "Are you nuts?"

"I'm pretty sure I can tell what's inside now."

"And you want to investigate?" I gestured to the crumbling lock. "When whatever it is can do *that*?"

"Trust me."

I trusted him, but not what was inside the truck.

"When we hit the barrier, the magic sealing whatever it is inside the truck broke a bit," Nick said. "Enough for it to start busting out."

Heidi joined me. "I agree with Nat. We should care about this because . . . ? We need to find a way past the fairy barrier and get the hell away from this potential bloodbath. If what is in there is some kind of monster, we shouldn't hang around to have a couple of beers with it."

Nick took another step forward. "I know what it is."

He tapped his staff against the door. Light bounced

against the lock and sizzled when it encountered the spell. The smell of burnt cinnamon made me back up a few feet as the door folded inward. Smoke filled the air while Nick worked on the lock again, and whatever was inside also tried to open it.

A part of me wondered if we'd squished Nick too hard when we'd crashed and he had lost his mind. Then the door crumpled outward. I waited for a hand to come forth, for something dark to emerge and attack us.

Thanks to Nick, the padlock finally fell with a *thump* to a snow-covered patch on the ground.

What was left of the door opened with a soft groan.

The light from Nick's staff shined inside, and Heidi said what I thought: *We are so fucked.*

Chapter 13

Inside the cargo area stood a child. She had to be no more than eight or nine. She looked no different than one of my cousins. All she wore was a simple blue pair of slacks and a dirty shirt with a cartoon character on the front. Her skin was so white, I could discern the blue vessels running under her skin. Hair as black as the darkness surrounding us was cropped short and stood straight out from her scalp.

The skin around her wrist was blackened from an iron bracelet.

My heart sank. This whole time, I'd been driving with a child in the back of my truck. A mere child. What kind of piece of shit—well, I *was* talking about Roscoe Skins here—did this of kind of stuff?

I took a tentative step forward. "Are you okay, honey?"

Nick snatched my arm. "Don't touch her. She's dangerous."

"This is really bad," the Muse murmured.

"Nick, we got a kid here. We can't just leave her in there."

His features darkened. "Do you know what she is? She's a fairy. And just as I suspected, she's one of the powerful ones."

Even though I hadn't known what she was, this was

wrong. I had a kid locked up in the back of the truck, and she was most likely cold and hungry. It wasn't right for us to keep her in there. Guilt struck me hard.

"She's dangerous," Nick repeated. "That's why the fairies came for her."

"Of course they did. Roscoe most likely kidnapped her."

He rolled his eyes. "I understand that. What I'm saying is, how the hell do we *give* her back to them without getting gutted alive. And do you understand what giving her back means to your debt?"

I hadn't thought about that. For a second, even more guilt soured my stomach. But my parents had taught me right from wrong. Pups should never be harmed when it came to the business of adults. This fairy wasn't a wolf, nor did she care about the Code, but as a child she should be presumed innocent.

Wasn't today a day of sacrifices? I had a moon debt, but I'd never forgive myself if I fulfilled the moon debt by sacrificing a kid.

The one in question hissed at us just then and stepped toward the opening.

I sensed movement around us. The fairies were circling, waiting for an opportunity to strike. "It's okay, honey," I said softly. "Don't be scared. We won't hurt you."

"It's not you I fear," the little girl said quietly. Her voice was high-pitched. Higher than most children's. Her eyes were focused on the Muse.

"Don't look at me." The Muse moved out of the way. "I mean you no ill will."

We all glanced at Abby. As usual, she appeared rather harmless. Why the fairy saw her as a threat, I had no idea.

A part of me wanted to rush away the cab. To back away from the disgusting edge of the dump truck. The interior had been cleaned, but gunk still clung to the walls. The poor thing had sat in there this whole time. I extended my hand to her. "Come on out. I'm setting you free."

She edged toward the doors.

From the corner of my eye, I spotted shadows inching toward us. Their eyes continued to glow brightly. Something told me not to look fully at them or they'd spring forward and attack us.

The child took one step. Then two. When she was a few feet from the opening, though, she slid back.

"I can't," she whispered.

"I almost forgot." Nick waved his staff against the truck and tapped the opening. A smooth sheen of iron disappeared.

The child leaped into my arms.

I expected to cringe. To cry out from the filth that crawled all over her. But she smelled of forever. Youth. The warmth of my babuska's blankets wrapped around me.

I cried out, but it wasn't in pain. It felt good to do the right thing.

My fingers touched her hair. Although it looked slightly prickly, it was soft to the touch. She didn't weigh anything at all, and I reveled in it. The blissful moment was lost when I turned to see endless forms standing around us. No imps. No monsters. Just fairies—wielding deadly weapons.

They should've swept in and tried to slit our throats. But they stood silent. Two of them stared at me with longing. One of them was a woman.

"Is that your mama?" I whispered to the girl.

She nodded against my neck. "Your life force smells warm and alive," the little girl whispered. The way she said it should have been sweet, but it actually kinda creeped me out.

"You need to go to them," I said. "No one needs to get hurt anymore."

She got down but took my hand. "What about you?"

I hadn't expected her to say that. Didn't most kids want to rejoin their families?

The woman gestured for the child to come to her, and said, "Don't linger with them, Lisbetta, come to me now." The lady was about my height, with the same black hair as the little girl, only much longer. The wicked blade in her hand shook.

"Don't worry about me. I'll be fine. We need to get that thing off your wrist." I moved my arm so I could guide the girl to her mother, but she refused to release my hand.

"You won't be. He'll kill you." She spoke casually, as if she were talking about some cartoon character she watched on Saturdays . . . in the same off-putting way, she'd told me my life force smelled appetizing.

"That's not for you to worry about right now." I tried to sound strong, even with my friends around me. None of them dared to move, thank goodness.

When the couple advanced on us, I again tried to let go of Lisbetta's hand, but the child wouldn't budge.

"I know of your moon debt. Of the price you must pay."

"Lisbetta," the woman warned. Somehow within the space of an inhale and exhale, the couple had come to stand before me. Lisbetta continued to cling to my hand.

I kneeled so we could be eye to eye. Werewolf or not, I had to face her dead-on. Power pulsed from her. Powerful enough for the wolf in me to want to escape. But I was in control now. This had to end. With no one dying, I hoped.

"I don't know what Roscoe did to you, or what plans he had for you. But what I do know is that it's wrong for you to be in that truck."

The frown on the woman's face deepened. Apparently I wasn't the only one who was eager to settle a score with Roscoe.

I continued, "I have problems, but they are mine to solve. Go to your family."

The child shook her head.

"Lisbetta, this woman planned to take you to those wolves. I don't think you should help her," her mother said.

"She didn't know I was in the truck. Roscoe told her nothing. Even the wizard couldn't see me." She thought for a moment. "She had a choice and could have used the wizard to help them escape from us. The wolf made a wise choice tonight."

While she talked, I tried to get a handle on how this child could speak so much like an adult. When she turned to face me, I almost fell into the penetrating gaze of her green eyes. "I heard what you said to the wizard when you spoke to him on the phone. To your family. You have honor, and I like that about you."

I was taken aback. It must've shown on my face.

"Don't worry, Little Wolf. I'm hungry to feast on wolves tonight—and I shall feast, at dawn—but not on you." She smiled, her teeth small and her face angelic. Yet her eyes revealed something far different.

She finally let go of my hand. "No one is to touch these people," she said to the gathered fairies. "Is that clear?"

The heads surrounding us bowed.

I looked at the girl again and fear sliced through me. What was she? Was she their leader? From the way they obeyed her orders, she had to be royalty of some kind. Which meant things had definitely gone downhill. No wonder the others thought I was nuts.

"We have work to do to fix what I have broken," she called out to the others. "Because it is winter, we are at our weakest, but that won't stop me from going after them. Prepare the truck. We have a pack of wolves to meet before dawn."

She had an exuberant grin on her face, but that didn't make me feel any better. It was the sign of impending doom, of a bloodbath waiting to come. Especially since the child queen was hungry.

The spindly woods of Jackson, Maine, folded over us, sending fear through me of what was to come.

Would the Jackson pack know about the trick we were about to tell them? They'd have no reason to suspect, and no way of telling. Or would they? It wasn't as if even I knew what was coming. Would the Jackson pack really take—and then kill—the decoy? Hell, how were the werewolves planning on taking their prize out of the truck safely in the first place? She was dangerous, just as Nick had told me.

The others sat next to me, quiet, focused on the road ahead. We'd been this way since the fairies had told Abby, Heidi, and I to climb back into the truck and wait while Nick worked out details with the fairies.

The truck and the deal was my affair, but they still told me to wait inside while they sorted out a replacement for Lisbetta. What I guessed was that while a replacement got inside, the fairies fixed the damage to the door and Nick resealed it with iron.

Everything felt like it was before. Only something had changed. No more attacks from the fairies. And what now frightened me the most were the Jackson werewolves. There's one thing wolves didn't do very well with other wolves. And that was lying. One's scent betrayed everything, and I was already on edge from this trip. A few words out of my mouth and they'd easily smell my deceit.

It didn't matter, though. I'd done the right thing, and

if I was lucky, the replacement would ensure that Lisbetta was no longer in danger. Grandma would be proud of me.

"Do I need to hold your hand again?" Nick whispered to me.

"Not unless you want it broken," I said after laughing a bit.

His words could hold other, hidden meanings, but I'm sure if he held my hand it would be merely to take my anxiety away.

I wished this was all over. I only had a bit more to go. Once there, we could do the transfer, then I'd return to Atlantic City and see Roscoe, ending the Stravinsky moon debt. It sounded easy enough.

The meeting place with the Jackson pack was a clearing deep within their territory, in a park not far from Frye Mountain. The area couldn't compare to Double Trouble State Park near my home, but this forest nevertheless called out to me. It begged me to explore its nooks and crannies. I asked Nick to roll down the window as we drove deeper into the park. Bits of light from the coming dawn filtered through the trees. The cold air blew into the truck, and I savored the scents of pine and ash. A few winter cottontails had emerged from their burrows. They'd be prey—*my* prey—if they didn't watch out.

Frost covered the windows in patches, but no one complained. The fresh air was welcome and allowed me to drift away.

Naturally, Nick brought me back to the present.

"Are you prepared for the possibility that they might figure out the ruse?"

"Not really. Maybe we could run?"

Nick rolled his eyes. "If my guess is right, we're dealing with spring fairies. They're a busy bunch—but they normally keep to themselves."

Questions instantly came to mind. "Why would Roscoe want a spring fairy?"

"For nefarious purposes. They're a source of magic just waiting to be tapped by any capable spellcaster. Of all the fairies, spring fairies have the most power. Moreover, they're most powerful in the spring; during the other seasons, they simply gather their strength in preparation for renewing the earth. So Roscoe picked the perfect time to sell Lisbetta to an interested buyer. That little girl is at her weakest right now, can't really defend herself—which might be why her people used dark elves to hunt for her, since the elves' magic isn't affected by the seasons."

"This makes no damn sense. It's wintertime. It's almost like that asshole's trying to sell an empty well with no water," Heidi grumbled.

"She won't be empty come spring," Abby said quietly.

Nick said, "Precisely. And anyone who's met a fairy or two knows they're not particular about how they renew their magic either."

My stomach flipped, thinking about how Lisbetta smelled my life force. But then again, I wasn't the one Roscoe wanted to sell. "What kind of werewolf needs a fairy?"

Nick stoically confirmed what I'd already guessed. "A werewolf who knows old magic."

Spring fairies. Old magic spell-casting werewolves. Russian mafia werewolves selling spring fairies to old magic spell-casting werewolves. No matter how I tried to piece it all together, this whole mess didn't look any better—and worse, I'd dragged all my friends into it.

"I should've dropped you two off," I said to Heidi.

She shrugged. "Not going to happen. And you can't drive this thing worth a shit."

"You know what I'm saying—things could get bad

with these people. I don't want you or Abby to get hurt."

She glanced at me briefly. "You know what I'm saying as well, so shut up and stop your hands from shaking. You need to look strong in front of those people."

I looked at my trembling fingers. How had I not noticed them? I clenched my hands into fists. A voice in my head repeated everything that could go wrong. They'll *know* the replacement isn't the child. It wouldn't *smell* right. It wouldn't *say* the right thing. What if they ask it questions? What if Roscoe's here waiting for the shipment?

"We're here," Heidi said.

"I need to get out. My legs are going numb."

The Muse followed the mermaid out of the truck, and I took in the clearing. Over the ridge to my right, I spotted smoke from a fire. Were they here already? Since we were downwind, my nose told me no wolves had walked here in a while.

Nick opened his door. When I climbed out after him, I heard the sounds of steps through snow. Broken twigs. So they *were* here, and they'd smelled us coming.

By the time I came around the truck, fifty or so pairs of eyes stared me down. A bunch of wolves, in human form, glancing from me to the truck.

A man—the alpha of the pack, judging from his scent—addressed me, his black eyes warning me not to look at him directly for too long. "Roscoe told us you'd never make it."

My mouth filled with glue. When I tried to speak, my words came out thick. "I've always been full of surprises."

"Who are these people?" He eyed my friends.

"They helped me drive the truck. I'm not too good at handling a big rig." So far so good.

The leader nodded to his cohorts behind them. "Secure the truck." He gestured at my friends. "Back away from it. Now." Since he was an alpha, his command snapped me to attention, and I quickly backed away. My friends didn't move as swiftly.

My heart raced as the Jackson pack approached the truck. One of the wolves, a woman with Eastern European features who appeared to be around my mother's age, checked the lock. She had a peculiar strawberry-colored birthmark on her olive-skinned cheek. It looked almost as if she'd been slapped recently. The wind blew at her brown hair and rustled the thin coat around her generous waist.

She sniffed at the lock and then ran her fingers along an edge while murmuring under her breath. I caught a faint whiff of ozone, the telltale sign of old magic. So she was one of the wolves who knew the forbidden magic.

"The lock's clean," she called to the Jackson pack leader.

He nodded, his gaze on me.

I prayed he didn't ask about the truck's contents, or the trip.

"Did you have any trouble along the way?" he asked.

Of course he'd ask me that question.

"As much trouble as you'd expect while driving a dump truck with a magical lock on it."

His smirk wasn't friendly. "Prepare for the opening, Tamara."

The woman growled. "Not with that wizard close by. I can feel the weight of the weapons he's hiding in his coat. He's been watching me this whole time. Tell him to back off."

The rest of the wolves closed in on my friends. Naturally, Nick's hand hovered near the edge of his coat. But the tricks within would get us into trouble. Fast.

"They'll back off." My hand went up, and slowly the three of them walked toward the forest line.

Nick suddenly stopped. "She comes with us."

"You're interfering in pack business, wizard. Keep your spells out of our affairs or I'll rip you and your coat to bloody bits." The warning slid black and bitter from the pack leader's mouth.

I mouthed to Nick, "Go."

Nick didn't move. Damn stubborn white wizard.

The Muse and the mermaid continued moving until they stood at the edge of the clearing.

"Don't fuck with me, wizard," the pack leader warned. "There's a lot more of me than there is of you."

"That might be true, but you must respect me enough to allow me to stand here." Nick put his hands up and placed them on top of his hat. Almost as if to allow a compromise, I hoped.

Satisfied, the Jackson pack leader nodded to the woman.

Tamara was leaning in close to the truck to examine the lock. I just about shuddered when she stretched out her palm to touch the door. It was still a dump truck after all—even if it had been repaired by fairies. They'd done a fabulous job making it appear as disgusting as it had before. Tamara rubbed her fingers over the lock—and then she put them into her mouth. Her eyelids fluttered.

What. The. Hell. I almost vomited in my mouth.

"I'm ready to open it now," the woman proclaimed. "It'll just take a few minutes to remove the binding spell."

The pack leader nodded. He motioned for the wolves to stand ready while Tamara did her job. The forest turned silent when she grunted, and then her voice settled into a deep hum. The sound reverberated through me and tickled the skin on my face.

Tamara's back hunched over, and her facial muscles twitched. Hair sprouted along her jawline as the change bubbled forth. Her limbs elongated. Memories of a night not so long ago with my grandmother came to mind. Back when the Long Island pack hunted the South Toms River pack, they'd sent the Burlington pack to hunt down my family in my aunt's home. They'd poisoned our food. I was lucky that I didn't eat it and thus didn't fall asleep. But I witnessed something I couldn't wipe from my mind. My grandmother had invoked the old magic, and her body had changed into a vicious creature to fight off our enemies. She'd saved my life—but at the price of losing a bit of her own.

Tamara's features turned hideous. Her clawed hands sizzled against the lock. Did she need to transform into that creature to fight against the black warlock magic securing the lock?

Nick had said the spell was strong, but any wizard could break it with a little help. Tamara wrenched at it, her hands turning red and blistering from prying it open. The act made the air stink with an acidic scent.

We waited patiently for some time before the lock finally fell to the ground, with a plume of smoke and an audible hiss.

I held my breath, wanting to look away, but I couldn't. I had to know that they were seeing the right thing. That they'd see the child and not the decoy—not some guy who'd forgotten to cast his "I'm-a-fairy-child" spell before the door opened.

To my relief, what appeared to be Lisbetta sat in the center with her legs crossed. She stared at us fearfully.

While Tamara clapped her grotesque claws and cackled with glee, the replacement cringed. My chest tightened when the wolves swarmed the truck. They climbed inside, and I wanted to spit on all of them. They had no idea that it wasn't Lisbetta in the back; in their minds, they were threatening a child.

"Be careful, boys. The bracelet she's wearing should

keep her subdued, but Roscoe told me she's got quite a bite on her," the pack leader said with a smile.

One of them, an older-looking wolf with the others in the back, said, "I've seen worse, Karl, but she'll be worth it." The wolf's speech then slipped into a tongue I didn't know. Most likely German, from the sound of it, but I didn't need to understand the words to recognize the need to pay attention to the collar they passed to the older wolf. It was small and, judging from the vibrations emanating from it, enchanted by black magic. So that was how they planned to further contain her.

These piece-of-shit bastards were just as bad as Roscoe.

The replacement hissed in the truck, but from my vantage point, I couldn't see inside well. The only thing I spied was a wolf flying through the air from the back. Then another.

Karl laughed, his breath sending mist into the air. "Now, this is the fight I expected."

The truck rocked and shifted. Growls and barks emerged from the back.

Not able to suppress my curiosity, I took a step forward. I tried not to think about how it could have been Lisbetta in there. If I'd never checked the back of the truck and found her, I would have been allowing a child to be treated like this. My family would have justifiably been ashamed of me.

"What are you going to do with her?" I whispered. I repeated it again when Karl didn't acknowledge me.

He snorted. "What do you care? In a few minutes, you can go back to Roscoe with a clean nose and be your family's savior."

I folded my arms. The chill hadn't penetrated my coat, but I felt cold nonetheless. "What honor is there in treating a child like that?"

Karl surged forward, grabbing me by the lapel of my coat. "Don't question me!"

I sensed Nick moving not far from me. I prayed he didn't strike. This wasn't the time.

"Get your hands off her," Nick warned.

I winced. No one gives orders to an alpha in front of his pack. No one. A *very* bad move on Nick's part.

With a tilt of Karl's head, five men stalked toward Nick.

Oh, shit.

"Hey!" The older werewolf leaned his head out from the back. "What kind of bullshit is this?" Something was shoved out of the truck a second later. It wasn't a wolf, or a little girl, but a bloodstained man with a large grin on his face. The man—actually, in reality, the fairy—laughed with a streak of black blood streaming from his mouth.

All hell had officially broken loose.

"What?" The fairy spat blood on the ground. "You don't like surprises?" Then he proceeded to say something in German. From the silence all around me, and the look of unabridged fury on Karl's face, he didn't *appreciate* what the fairy had to say.

I expected the alpha to grab the fairy, but instead he turned to me, his yellow eyes wide from his oncoming change.

"Betrüger!" His fist rose to swing at me, but the hit barely connected with my chin. By the time his fist encountered my flesh, something large and scaly had appeared to clamp down on his arm.

Karl, the imp, and I went crashing to the ground. Karl's heavy weight stole the breath from my lungs, and even worse, my ears rang from the jolt to my chin.

The pack leader snarled and swatted at the relentless imp on his back. He rolled off me to grab the creature. While he wrestled with it, many more imps jumped on him. His pack wasn't far away and rushed to his aid. Once I'd been hit, total chaos had erupted in the clearing. Imps scampered from over the ridge like a black tide. But the fifty or so werewolves weren't deterred. While some fended off imps, others initiated the change, to give themselves a fighting chance. Once the wolves had transformed, blood began to flow freely. Wolves snatched up imps, grabbing them like cottontail rabbits dashing through the snow.

At first, Tamara, the spell-casting wolf, hovered close by, but far enough away from the melee to avoid involvement. Maybe she was holding back long enough to regain her energy in order to cast her spell. Like Grandma, she knew the old magic of transformation. Suddenly, Tamara's form crackled and contorted to become what I didn't want to see, the ghastly form of a monster I remembered all too well. It towered over everyone, its mouth, full of jagged teeth, gaping wide.

I backed away, shaking my head.

A wolf tackled me, driving me into the present. He bit into my shoulder, shaking me violently. I clawed him and managed to kick him off. From behind me, Heidi surged forward with a trident, burying it in the wolf's side.

"Stop standing there!" she yelled at me. "Move your ass!"

She expertly glided forward, shoving back the advancing wolves while I trailed behind her, nursing my shoulder. All around me, the fight continued. I wanted to join in, but I was practically frozen with fear. Here I was in the middle of a damn clearing with blood spraying all over the place. With howls of pain coming from all sides. Not far away, even the Muse had somehow managed to join in, gutting a werewolf. What the hell?

The fairies provided support to the imps. The dark elves came first, wielding swords. Not far behind them came the fairies themselves. Their beautiful faces were marred by vicious snarls. Who would have thought someone who looked like Tinkerbell could leap on a wolf like that? It was almost like a nightmarish kids' movie where the good guys lost.

But where was the fairy child Lisbetta? Was she all right?

I would have expected the fairies to cast spells to fend off the wolves, but just as Nick had said, the fairies were right now at their weakest, and with every fairy the wolves viciously brought down, that weakness showed.

Five wolves moved to take down Heidi. I called out her name to warn her, but a man burst out of the woods not far away. He vaulted over scampering imps without effort. His white-blond hair was distinguishable from the snow only because it spiked out from the top. He wore nothing but a brown leather jacket and a pair of blue jeans. No shoes. He didn't even react to the cold around us.

A wolf was headed toward me, but I failed to notice. Instead, I was transfixed by the blond-haired man. Maybe it was the way he plunged his spear into one of the wolves, got tackled by the rest—and then didn't stay down for long. His attackers scrambled, and only he alone stood with his bloodied blade. Yet more wolves came at him. His movements were fluid. Graceful. Deadly.

He must have lost his natural mind to come here armed only with his pointy stick and a knife.

The wolf continued to come at me, his jaws now close and snapping. I watched in horror, begging my damn legs to move, until a hand clamped down on mine and dragged me backward.

"What are you doing?" It was Nick. He waved his staff in front of us. The spell only pushed them back temporarily, but he'd at least bought us some time.

We ran through the trees, not daring to look back. I sensed a few members of the pack at our heels, fighting to catch up with us. We'd made a mistake in running. That was exactly what wolves like me wanted. Blood for the hunt. Blood for the kill. We'd be dead soon if we didn't make a stand.

My shoulder throbbed. I'd been bitten deeply.

At my side, Nick panted, trying to keep up with me through the mud and snow. Under normal circumstances, I would have been freaking out at the *plop, plop* sound of mud on my shoes, but today the fight for my life took over.

Turn around and face them, the wolf in me begged. *Let me at them.*

I dared to turn around and noticed we had ten werewolves behind us, running in a tight formation. Three had separated from the pack to run ahead. They meant to slaughter us. I sensed their frenzied mood. My chest tightened, and I wheezed painfully. My legs, which had once yearned to run, now turned to rubber. This wasn't the Long Island pack or the Burlington pack. They didn't want to take me prisoner. They wanted to end me—and it wouldn't be pretty.

I should have seen the tree coming as soon as I turned around again. But instead I plowed right into it while Nick managed to dodge it. With an *umph,* I landed painfully on the ground.

Ehh, they would've caught us anyway, I tried to tell myself. I stood up slowly, dizzy from the impact. My fingers brushed against the underside of my nose and came away wet with blood. *Well, there'll be more of that when they get done with me.*

When Nick urged me to run, I shook my head. The three wolves had circled around, and now they ran at us.

I whispered, "You got an atomic bomb in that coat?"

He faced me, fear in his eyes. "Not today, I don't."

Mountains of terror crushed me. Enough to make every breath horribly painful.

Yellow eyes glowing and bright closed in. With claws out, ready to slice us to ribbons.

Our backs touched—maybe for the last time. "It's been good knowing you, Nick." My voice came out hoarse.

"Oh, I'm not done yet."

I managed a short laugh before the first one leaped at us. Nick swung his staff. I expected fireworks, light, something magical to back up his words. It spurted a few times and then went dark.

The wolf howled in pain and scampered away.

Still, I groaned. "Is that it? I've seen sparklers that are hotter."

Nick bit out, "If you can do better, you're more than welcome to try. I'm a *white* wizard using a warlock staff. A rather shitty loaner staff, actually, and if I'm alive afterward to complain, I'll do so to the guy about it."

"I told you what I was up against, and you showed up with a borrowed staff?"

Before I could get out another snide comment, the other wolves came at us, much sooner than I'd expected them to. There was power in numbers and with their count, we were done for. I saw the next sequence of events with each blink of my eyes.

The first wolf swept in, mouth wide open.

Nick grabbed my hand.

A second wolf came at my feet.

A third surged toward Nick, prepared to gut him.

My mouth opened to call Nick's name.

Suddenly, the dark greens and browns of the forest around me lightened and then turned gray. The air disappeared and my ears popped. I faintly heard a grunt when another wolf struck my leg. Pain blossomed, but it was nothing compared to the emptiness I felt. That raw feeling after someone punches you in the gut when you weren't expecting it. Your eyes roll back and your body shifts forward to protect yourself. I wanted to look at Nick one last time. To see the slight tilt of his smile. To see the lips I'd never kiss. To see the look of finality in his eyes before he was taken away from me.

But all I saw was the wolves around us faltering. Tilting wildly. Then I realized the tilting was me as well. Falling with the wolves—Nick's hand locked around my wrist. He kept me from slamming too hard into the ground.

When I finally hit, my eyes fluttered closed.

Chapter 14

I woke up to the worst hangover I'd ever had in my life. Mind you, I've only been drunk once. At most, like anyone who drank wine on occasion, I'd experienced a light buzz. But this was insane.

Every inch of my skull throbbed. Especially when my head moved forward.

"Don't move," a voice whispered.

I squirmed slightly and then winced when my shoulder protested. I was lying in the backseat of a car. A rental, if my nose was correct.

Rentals should always have that lovely clean car smell. Until I'd rented that SUV with Thorn in Atlantic City, I'd yet to meet a rental car I didn't adore. But that wasn't what I should be focusing on right now. How the hell had I gone from the middle of a life-and-death situation to feeling like utter bottom-of-the-pan-burnt-on-couldn't-be-scraped-off crap?

"What time is it?" Even my voice sounded jacked-up. It had that kind-of-gravelly sound of a person who had a sore throat. My fingers brushed against my face. Even that action made the world flip upside down, and I wanted to purge my already empty stomach.

From the front seat, Nick said, "It's about two. You've been sleeping for a while."

I blinked a few times. I never slept in. That was unusual—unless I'd been hurt badly.

"What happened? Is everyone okay?"

I shifted my head to look at the opposite seat, but the movement made me nearly black out. The pain was that bad.

"I told you not to move."

"I won't if you tell me what happened," I grated.

Slowly, I felt around to make sure I wasn't missing any body parts. I counted all my limbs and fingers. Everything was accounted for. So why did I feel like I'd been tackled by every NFL team in existence?

"Heidi and Abby are okay. They got out of it just fine. The fairies and some big guy protected them from the wolves."

I wanted to nod, but I'd learned my lesson the first time the pain came.

"Who was that guy?" He wasn't someone a person could easily forget.

"I don't know, but I sensed he came from the sea, like Heidi."

I rested for a few minutes, and then spoke again. "What happened after that?"

Nick replied, "Well, you and I didn't fare as well. The Jackson pack's short several members today, but the ones who came for us hit us pretty hard."

"How are you holding up?" I managed to ask.

"With spells. I'm also forcing my eyes open with imaginary toothpicks."

"Why aren't we in a hotel right now, imitating a rock formation?" With nice, very clean sheets for me to lose myself within.

"You were in pretty bad shape. And I didn't want you in their territory in case they had other ideas." He sighed. "I fended off our attackers, but you collapsed in the process. Not long after, I regrouped with the fairies, along with Heidi and Abby."

Memories bounced around my head. "I think I saw the child fairy again. But all I remember is her voice."

"She came to us, and her people guided us through the forest. They got us back to civilization so we could find a way out of town."

I tried to string together what happened when those wolves attacked us, but my mind couldn't wrap around it.

"Did you cast some kind of spell? On the wolves? 'Cause it got me, too."

He didn't speak for a bit. "Yeah, I did something. Something I regret."

What did he have to regret? What was bad about *saving* us? I did my best slight shrug. "I'm alive. I guess I should be happy about that."

"Should I take you home? Let the pissed-off fairies take care of Roscoe?"

The name made the pain come back with renewed force. "Absolutely not! Are we on the Parkway yet?"

"We'll be there in about an hour."

"Then keep going south to Atlantic City. You're not taking me home."

A groan from the front seat. Even though I couldn't see his face, I naturally guessed he was angry. His next comment confirmed it.

"I can't do it, Nat. You're not well."

"If you're my friend, you'll take me where I need to go."

"What good will it do you if you can barely walk?"

I fumed from my seat. He had a point. He also hadn't mentioned healing me, which meant I was in *really* bad shape.

"I've got about two hours or more before we get there. I'll be ready to stand when you open that door."

He shook his head, and I waited for him to say more.

To give me a million reasons why I should just go home. My dad had to have healed himself by now. But how could I face him? I'd given my best. I'd sacrificed everything. Or had I? Especially if I went home. I could see Auntie Yelena now. She'd have a thing or two to say about how defective I was.

A familiar *beep* from the front seat caught my attention. Nick leaned over and grabbed my phone. Using one hand, he flicked through the screens. From my angle, I couldn't see them.

"It's for you."

He placed the phone in my hand, and I about melted. It was the picture of a baby. A perfect child.

"Ya tyotia," I murmured.

"What?"

A rush of emotions went through me, and all my tense muscles relaxed for a moment.

"I'm. An. Aunt." Although my voice was weak, there was a full smile in the words. The child was wrapped in one of Grandma's blankets. Snuggled perfectly in her crib. The text message with the picture read, *Svetlana Mina Stravinsky, six hours old.*

"I was wondering if that was your brother's baby."

I wiped a tear from my cheek. He'd named the baby after Grandma Lasovskaya. I was sure she was overjoyed at the news. She'd spent so much time fretting about Alex over the years. Now she had a new great-grandchild to enjoy. A new half-werewolf, half–wood nymph baby, of course, but a beautiful baby girl nonetheless.

Alex had sent an additional text message, one that had me release a sigh of relief, but also saddened me: *dad's healing well. how u holding up, sis? u need help?*

Thank God Dad was okay, but the truth of the matter was, I wasn't doing well. This wasn't the time to focus on my problems or bring my brother into them, though. He needed to focus on bonding with his daughter. And, well, I had a baby picture to savor and enjoy.

Nick said, "Congratulations."

"She's so perfect," I replied. "Although, I wish I knew if she had any hair under her cap."

Every Stravinsky child had been born bald and bawling, according to my mother. It took at least a year before our true hair color was revealed. Maybe it was a good thing for me not to know. It would be something to look forward to.

Then I realized that Svetlana wouldn't have a pack to belong to when I returned. Even after the trials, the Stravinskys wouldn't have a formal relationship with the pack. That's what happened to families with an unfulfilled moon debt. We would have no honor, and with no allegiances, we'd all be considered rogues, unless another pack took us in. And all of this was because of me. I'd failed my family. I'd failed little Sveta.

The tears came quickly, and since I couldn't even manage to cry quietly, a hand reached back to touch me. "Are you okay?"

"Perfectly fine." I sucked at sarcasm while crying.

"Do you want to talk about it?"

I wanted to shake my head, but that would hurt too much. Instead of revealing my worries, I turned away.

Time passed, at least an hour, before the dryness left my mouth. "If you stop driving, I'll find the strength to cover your staff with the grossest thing I can find. And I'm resourceful."

Nick chuckled in the front seat.

Sleep called to me with promises of fat rabbits and spotless forest floors. I whispered, "Promise me you'll take me to Atlantic City."

When my eyes closed again, I wondered if it was sadness or pity I'd seen on Nick's face.

* * *

The lights of Atlantic City should've given me a bit of comfort. I was back to face the moon debt. To be truthful, I had fulfilled part of the payment, I'd delivered the truck to the Jackson pack. Of course, the contents weren't what the pack expected. But you can't win them all, can you?

Nick continued to drive, not speaking to me. Maybe he was letting me rest up for what was to come. After all, he wasn't a fool. I'd been asked to transport a truck across New England with a fairy child imprisoned inside. It wasn't your average trip to Coney Island with the family.

I wanted to sit up, but just the effort of stretching out my legs pained my stiff muscles. As a werewolf, I usually healed quite quickly. I could sense my shoulder muscles reconnecting, my tendons snapping back into place. And Nick had made a drive-through pit stop to give me a nice meal of sub sandwiches. But even a full belly did nothing to take away the heaviness that weighed down my every limb.

Something was very wrong with me.

I extended my hand, and it brushed against the window. The surface was cold against my fingertips. My mind drifted to Thorn. I held back a laugh, wondering if he'd be waiting at Roscoe's place. Maybe leaning against the wall outside of the door. Like he always did.

The car pulled to a stop, Nick shifted it into PARK, turned off the ignition, stepped out, and handed the keys to a valet. Then he opened the back door and waited.

"Couldn't you have gone to the parking garage? So I'm not rushed?"

The valet stood there, focusing his gaze on the distance, as if looking at a faraway place. He was obviously trying not to listen to us.

Nick slowly leaned into the backseat. He was close enough for me to make out the details of his face. His long nose. His strong chin. Nick was a handsome man at any angle. He reached out and gently tucked his arms around my waist. With minimal effort, he lifted me from the car.

"If you would've given me some time . . ." I whispered.

"A few hours' time maybe?"

"More like forty-five minutes, give or take."

He carried me up the entrance stairs, and I snuggled in his arms. He said, "The only thing you seem to be moving is your mouth."

"Well, it doesn't take all that much work."

"So I noticed." But when Nick reached the final step, he stumbled.

"Okay, that's what you get for your jokes."

A few people around us glanced in our direction. *We must look like the most embarrassing couple ever,* I thought. Then, still slightly sagged in Nick's arms: *Do we look like a married couple? A girl with her newlywed husband?* The very thought warmed my face.

That dream was squashed when Nick nearly dropped me again. "Okay, hero. You're not doing too well here."

"I'm not the one who ate five, I repeat, five deluxe sandwiches with all the fixings."

We were barely into the lobby, and Nick's strong strides had turned into a shuffle.

"Really, are you sure you're okay?" I asked.

"I don't know. Something's wrong."

He let go of my legs. They hit the ground painfully but managed to hold me up.

"Are you sure you want to walk?" Now that I was standing, it wasn't so bad. My legs were a little wobbly, but I didn't stumble when we continued forward. My stomach was still sour, but I definitely didn't look as pale as Nick. He usually had the lack-of-melanin thing going for him, but now he looked ghostly.

"I'm so tired, but you look pretty bad too," I said.

"I can sense the wards now. Pretty powerful ones." He laughed softly. "They paid someone to put these in place. Most likely a warlock."

"Will they hurt you?" We were at the end of the entrance and still had to go through the casino to reach the doorway to the facilities. A long way at the rate we were walking.

"It's like tiny threads holding me back," Nick said. "And it's not just one or two, but millions of them, pulling at every muscle in my body." He appeared thoughtful. "It's a well-crafted spell."

I took his arm to urge him forward when he slowed down further.

"So, it's not hurting you—just slowing you down."

"Yeah."

We continued, but stopped to laugh when a bunch of slow-going elderly people passed us. Or should I say, left the building and then came *back* again.

When we arrived at the middle of the casino, I knew this couldn't go on any longer. "Nick, you need to go back."

"After all this effort? I promise the weekend won't be over by the time I make it to the door." Even under the difficult circumstances, his smile was infectious.

"If I were the warlock who made this spell, I wouldn't construct it to keep people from leaving. Take a step toward the door."

"You're not getting rid of me, Nat."

"Just do it!" I pushed him toward the lobby.

He took a step and then another, much faster one.

I gave him my most smug smile. Ever.

He stared at me. And I wished I could take a picture

to preserve how wonderful it was. He'd done so much for me. He'd saved my life numerous times. Yet this was my journey to take alone.

"Don't worry about me. I'll head in there, talk to Roscoe, and then come back. A quick trip."

He continued to stare for a bit, then said, "You're lying."

"Why would you think that?" My damn tears betrayed me again.

Nick reached up and wiped one off my face.

"You don't have to go in there. People like Roscoe never show mercy."

I shuffled a bit. What could I say? "I know—but I'm not doing this for me anymore. I'm doing it for my family now."

"I could keep you safe," he offered softly. He took a step closer to me. "Hide you away."

"In your never-ending wizard pocket."

"If you like."

A grin snuck on my face.

"I'd really like to show you more than what's in my pocket, but perhaps that's a bit too forward."

I rolled my eyes. Even his dirty wizard jokes needed help.

"Either way, you don't have to go to Roscoe right now. You'd be safer if you ran away." He took my hand, but all I felt was warm skin—no racing pulse.

"Hiding seems to be what you're good at," I mumbled. "I can never truly sense you. It's like you protect yourself with magic so nothing can touch you. I wonder if you ever follow your own advice when it comes to me."

Frustrated, I pulled him back toward the entrance. With each step, his stride became stronger. By the time we were outside, he was the old Nick again. When I tried to direct him down the steps, he yanked back.

I turned to look at him, but I wished I hadn't. He was right next to me—with an expression I wasn't ready for. When I didn't speak, he took a half step closer, ensuring that the mist from his breath brushed against my nose. "You're right."

He immediately interrupted me when I tried to speak.

"Can you see it now?"

"See what?" My voice had grown small for some reason.

"My heart."

Something inside his body pulsed. Where before there had been silence—now I heard a sound, both soft and familiar.

His fingertips traced a path along my chin, and I couldn't look away. I fell into his eyes. A light flashed like starlight. So beautiful. So hypnotizing. Yet I knew I had the free will to look away. What power did he have over me?

In the reflection of his eyes, I saw myself. From my brown hair to my chin, back up to my cheeks. My small smile grew to a full-blown one. But I didn't just see my face—I sensed what he felt when I smiled at him.

His heart fluttered. *For me.*

"Now can you see me as I see you?"

I was speechless. That white wizard had rendered me speechless.

He laughed and then slowly leaned closer to me. His hands brushed against the sides of my face before he brought his lips toward mine. Our noses lightly bumped before we kissed.

Pure warmth came from the kiss. Not a burning fire, but an exquisiteness that was both gentle and precious. My body hummed, but since it was in a weakened state, it didn't do a very good job to help a gal out.

My damn knees buckled when Nick tried to deepen the kiss.

No romantic moment for me tonight. His lips ended up making out with my nose, and I got a mouthful of his chin.

Yep, it was as awkward as it sounds.

Nick wiped off my nose while I tried to keep from laughing. Nick had just kissed me—our first kiss— and here I was laughing as if two friends had shared a joke.

Were we just friends? My smile faded for a bit. For some reason, I regretted that I still saw him as one.

"Sorry about that," I said.

"Don't apologize." He took my hand again, his lips twitching.

What more could we say to each other? What hadn't been said with the kiss?

"You should go now," I whispered. "I need to see Roscoe before I change my mind and decide to hide in your pocket—as tempting as the offer appears."

He opened his coat. "It still stands." He was silent for a moment. "I don't want you to go," he said.

"I know."

I took a step back, and he released me. The warmth of his palm lingered in mine.

After taking a deep breath, I turned and walked back into the casino. Then I realized I hadn't said good-bye and glanced over my shoulder, hoping to remedy that. He'd already left.

The trip through the casino into the basement should have been easy. I'd made it just twenty-four hours ago, with Thorn and my brother at my side. But this time it was different. I'd failed, and now I'd come to beg for mercy.

Briefly, I thought about how easy it would be to let Nick protect me. He'd keep me safe. I wouldn't have to face Roscoe or any of the consequences of the unfulfilled moon debt. But none of my problems would be resolved. I paused for a moment, then kept going. Turning back wasn't an option anymore.

When the guards outside the door saw me, they almost shot me a look asking me why I'd come. I guessed I had that I'm-dumb-enough-to-come-back-for-it appearance about me. My feet shuffled outside the door. They suddenly felt heavy again. Was that the relentless exhaustion, or my fear finally coming into play? A sheen of sweat built along the nape of my neck, and the racing of my heart threatened to turn into a full-blown panic attack.

With each deep breath, I stepped back into Roscoe's den. This time, he was entertaining guests instead of playing games on the computer. Men and women dressed in fine clothes stood among the black lounge chairs, sipping drinks. From the state of their clothes, they'd been partying for some time. A few of the men had undone their shirts, while two of the girls had discarded their shoes.

None of them stopped talking when I approached Roscoe. The strong stench of the rum from his rum and Coke drink hit my nose. He was chatting with a lady who needed a few inches added to the hem of her minidress.

When the guard leaned over to tap his boss' shoulder, the girl gave the guard a dirty look. Evidently, he was messing with her chances of turning into Roscoe's scantily clad tramp-of-the-night.

Roscoe looked at me and blurted in Russian, "You've got to be kidding me. Who brought you here?"

"No one." Why say otherwise?

"Most people who don't fulfill their moon debt don't come sauntering back to the debt owner."

"I'm not most people." I swallowed twice, hoping to make my voice stronger.

Roscoe's date frowned further. Maybe she hated not knowing what we were talking about. I, for one, wished I didn't—no matter the language.

"I've come to ask for mercy. Maybe another chance to repay my father's debt." My hand itched terribly. I wanted to ignore the desire to scratch it—to keep my eyes on Roscoe and his men. But it was damn difficult when all I could think about was the likelihood that I had millions of ants crawling over my digits.

Roscoe snorted. "Moon debt doesn't work that way, *devushka*. Do you know what happens to debtors who don't pay?"

He'd told me earlier, but a thousand other ideas ran through my mind: death, slavery, many others that would be the end of me anyway.

"Baby, you told me no business tonight," the woman whined.

Roscoe's hand shot up, and she went silent instantly. "I told you they die, *devushka*."

I shuddered as a chill ran down my spine. I managed to mumble, "Couldn't they make a few payments and then die of old age?"

The prickling intensified in the palm Nick had held. Enough to make all the hairs on the back of my neck rise. Had he done something to me? Sweat lined my brow, and when I wiped it, my hand came away with a sheen that sparkled in the light.

I stared dumbfounded while Roscoe motioned to the guards. "You know where to take her and what to do."

Now the shimmering sweat coated both my hands. And when I unzipped my coat, I found more along my neck. *What the hell?*

The guards approached me. I opened my mouth to

ask for more options but stopped when I noticed their shocked expressions. One backed away rather than moved forward.

I glanced over my shoulder to see three people standing behind me: Lisbetta and her parents.

Chapter 15

I think I could count on my hand the number of times I'd felt like a mosquito waiting to be squashed by a gigantic eager hand. Thank goodness, this time I was no longer the mosquito. And the hand behind me was a rather big one, even if it came in a little package.

"Your wards are much stronger now," Lisbetta said. "Quite a clever set of spells to keep spellcasters like me out of your little hideaway." She was dressed in clean clothes now: a bright red coat with large buttons down the front, a pair of white tights, and black Mary Jane shoes.

In her hand, she held the iron bracelet I'd seen on her wrist. Somehow the fairies had managed to remove it. The bracelet was partially wrapped in a white silky handkerchief. With a flick of her fingers, it flew across the room, landing in Roscoe's lap.

All conversation in the room died.

Lisbetta stepped around me. Her parents followed. She gave me a brief smile, which would have charmed any grandmother, but made my blood run cold. Pain on the sides of my face warned me I'd locked my jaw. My chest tightened again. Tight enough for me to gasp a few times. My hand found the seashell around my neck. As usual, it didn't bring me comfort.

"Don't be afraid, Little Wolf," Lisbetta said to me.

"I'm not here for you. You've done your part to help me, serving as my vessel." She turned to Roscoe. "Mr. Skins and I, however, have some *business* to settle."

The guests stared in shock. All of them were were-wolves, and most of them suspected this visitor—who stank of magic—wasn't a welcome one.

"After I deal with you tonight, I'll hunt down the warlock who helped you trap me," Lisbetta purred. "Would you like to tell me his name before I pull out your lying tongue?"

"Let me *slit* his throat," Lisbetta's father said. The word *slit* came out like a serpent's low hiss. Compared to Lisbetta, he was less reserved in his anger. His pale fingers jerked madly.

One of the guards in the corner hunched over. His face bulged from the approaching change. Other guards followed suit. A fight was coming. I felt it stirring in the air, and it drew me in to join them.

Instead of giving in to the urge, though, I contemplated a question—*Why the hell was I standing where I'd surely get mauled?* My weak legs finally moved, and I backed toward the nearest wall.

Roscoe's date trembled in her seat, and then she bolted for the door.

Lisbetta's hands flowed through the air. The crates slid across the floor and slammed in front of the exit. Sparks danced across her fingers, filling the air with the tang of acidic spring fairy magic.

Roscoe's date yelled for help and banged her fists against the barrier, while the wolves crept up on the fairy trio in a standard attack formation. Lisbetta's parents continued to hold their ground with their weapons.

Wolves crept toward them from the front and the back. Roscoe continued to sit comfortably in his seat, while his guests all stood. At first I thought the wolves would be the ones to come for the parents. But it was the armed guards who moved.

The men with AK-47s opened fire.

I gasped, expecting the fairies to fall bleeding—their bodies contorting—to the floor. But they stood there, unmoving, as if the guns had fired blanks. Bullet shells rained down, and the fairies continued to just stand there.

"Are you done yet?" For a moment Lisbetta appeared weakened, but then I realized she was merely bored. Her hands rose again. When they fell, the guns smashed to bits.

"No more metal toys. No more games." Her normally high-pitched voice sounded strange. More guttural. More primal.

Roscoe glanced at the wolves behind Lisbetta. They rushed at her. I couldn't tell how many. I saw only the pack leaping forward again, now toward Lisbetta's mother. She moved deftly. The first attacker didn't even touch her. The second flew straight into her blow. Its belly opened as if her blade were slicing through butter. The rest of the wolves went for Lisbetta's father, but he was just as deadly. These fairies definitely knew how to use their weapons.

Another wave of werewolves came for them—a larger and much faster one. From their approach, these wolves were far more experienced. The first one approached Lisbetta's mother from the front, while the second came from the rear. A dark wolf grabbed her by the arm with an elongated snout and snapped down. The fairy screamed. Another one clamped down on the back of her neck. Now everything sped up, happening too fast. Lisbetta's father had a wolf on his leg while another disarmed him.

Lisbetta finally moved. And I wished I had closed my eyes at the sight. Her tiny form swarmed the wolves, leaping on one, then another. When she touched them, something strange happened. They folded in on themselves and withered away. Skin grayed and wrinkled. Hair turned white. Bodies convulsed. I couldn't help but remember her young voice when she whispered at my neck, *"Your life force smells warm and alive."*

What kind of damn fairy drained the living? But drain them she did. With each touch, she moved faster. Lisbetta showed no mercy to the wolf that attacked her mother. With one lingering touch, it shrank to dusty bones.

The once-bold guests slowly backed away from the carnage in front of us.

Roscoe flipped open his cell phone and yelled into it, "Primus, get your ass down here right now!" Then, as Lisbetta advanced toward him, he inched backward. "I'll have your sorry ass for every piece-of-shit spell you failed to cast. That girl got in, and she's fucking pissed."

I just about laughed, watching Roscoe squirm. A line of sweat formed on his brow. His fancy jacket had sweat stains under the armpits. Wow, she'd worked on his psyche pretty fast.

Lisbetta took several bold steps, then froze in place. Her face showed effort as she tried to move. The scent in the air changed. A faint whiff of cinnamon grew strong—and became overwhelming. A powerful spellcaster had arrived.

The man in question materialized in a black suit with a dark green shirt. His hair was long and dirty blond, with a trace of gray along the edges. He stood between Lisbetta and Roscoe, in the fifteen feet or so that separated them.

I glanced around for her parents. Her mother perched on bended knee behind Lisbetta, nursing her bleeding arm. Her father lay on the ground, unmoving.

"About time you got here," Roscoe said with a visible pant.

From the wave of magic around the newcomer, I suspected he was the warlock Roscoe had on speed dial. The man approached Lisbetta with a smug grin. "Now, how did you get out of my little cage?"

He stepped forward. I wanted to speak, but I only growled instead.

When the warlock glanced my way, I dropped closer to the ground and tried to look insignificant. Rather difficult with all the madness around me.

"If you had only stayed put, your family never would've been hurt. But look what you've done." The warlock continued to smile at her. "You've brought them right to me, so now I have two new playthings."

Lisbetta spat in some language I didn't recognize. But I doubted she was reciting a nursery rhyme, from the way a bit of spittle clung to her chin.

Primus placed his palm up and another bracelet materialized in his hand. "Once I put this little lovely back on your arm, we'll hold another auction, to see where you'll be useful. It's a shame the Jackson pack won't be interested buyers again." He strolled toward her. "They paid a lot of money to assist Tamara's spell-casting. I'm sure it would've been worth it in the end."

He fingered the bracelet. Lisbetta stared at it, but her expression didn't waver.

Primus glanced around the room. "So, who wants the honor of putting this on her?"

"Why not do it yourself?" Lisbetta said with a smirk.

Primus' eyebrow rose and he shook his index finger at her. "I already know your range, sweetheart. I know your touch is a lot more powerful than most."

Lisbetta laughed. "I'll slaughter any of these dogs you bring my way. Why not feed me more of them before I feast on you?"

"Why don't you have one of your boys take care of this?" He turned to Roscoe.

Roscoe shook his head vigorously, then he spotted me. "Her! Make her do it!"

Fear sucked me in, and I wished I could melt into the wall.

Primus shifted his gaze to me, and then he pulled at me. At first I sensed it as a slight tug on my midsection. But then it strengthened, until I was shuffling across the floor. I tried to fight it. To use what little strength I had to propel myself in reverse. Nothing worked. My hand snaked out as if I were an eager child coming for candy. I heard whimpers and thought that perhaps Lisbetta's father had awoken. But something inside told me that the whimpers came from me. That I knew this would be the end of me, either by Lisbetta's hands, Primus's, or Roscoe's.

I never should have returned here. For once, I should have taken advice, Nick's advice.

When I came to a halt in front of Primus, I noticed that, up close, he was a handsome man. His skin was flawless, without a single wrinkle. He continued to hold the bracelet out to me.

With everything I had, I willed my hand to my side. After I closed my eyes, I finally felt it move. It shifted downward, as if something powerful, something besides my will, was pulling it there.

Was it Lisbetta?

Someone else?

From my side, my hand moved to my pocket. It twitched as it tucked inside the fold of my jeans, then rested on something warm—something about the size of a pocketknife. I searched my thoughts frantically, trying to remember what the hell was in there. A pack of gum? A tissue box? Hand sanitizer? I'd gone daft standing there waiting for my demise. Now, when my hand emerged, I opened my eyes. I was holding something golden and rectangular. It vibrated.

Primus whispered, "Most unexpected."

Then the lights flickered.

Primus waved his hand toward the box, but nothing happened. His confident smile broke.

Lisbetta blinked and then she took a step toward him. I just about shit my pants.

What happened next wasn't pretty. Whatever tricks or spells Primus had, the golden box had sent them flying south for the winter.

Lisbetta came at him, leaping through the air. She landed on him, clamping down, refusing to let go. The stench of cinnamon overwhelmed my nostrils. Sparks—bright red and orange—flew from her hands, while the essence of Primus's life force flowed into her. It was rather comical—for a moment anyway. Here was this little girl hugging a grown man. All the while, Primus screamed again and again—punching and flailing while Lisbetta drained her prey.

Not far from us, Roscoe was cursing in Russian, running to join his floozy at the blocked door. "Shit! Shit! Shit! Oh, God, help me!"

The whole time, I stood there like an idiot, holding the golden box in the air. I had no idea what the hell it did, but if I just had to stand there to save my ass, I'd do it.

Dust covered Lisbetta's hands. She even had a few handprints on her pretty coat. I found it creepy that my first thought was to offer her something to clean it off.

Lisbetta walked slowly toward Roscoe. His girlfriend now tried to get help on her cell phone, but who the hell could she call at a time like this? Another warlock? Roscoe turned to face Lisbetta, his face ash-white.

She briefly turned my way, winked, and then *skipped* toward him. Talk about a mind-fuck in the making.

Like a cockroach caught in daylight, Roscoe tried to scamper away, but Lisbetta trapped him with her tiny clawed hands.

"You almost won again tonight." She threw a quick glance at Primus's corpse. "Your warlock's dead, and you'll soon follow. But—" Her head whipped in my direction. "We have business to settle for the Little Wolf."

She ran one clawed hand down the side of his face while the other one gripped his windpipe. "What is it you need to do to clear her moon debt?"

"I need to call her pack leader," Roscoe moaned.

"By all means." Her hands flicked, and a phone snapped out of his pocket into his hand. "Make the call."

Roscoe choked as he tried to take a breath. He squirmed, and I saw Lisbetta's grip tighten.

His hand barely held the phone while he dialed. I heard a familiar voice over the speakerphone.

"Roscoe, you dumbass. You know what time it is, boy?" Old Farley Grantham grated.

"Yes." His response was so low it barely sounded like one.

The other end of the phone went quiet.

Roscoe's voice was wet and weak when he said, "I . . . release Fyodor Stravinsky from his moon debt."

The cell phone was silent for a bit. "Are you sure about that?"

I rolled my eyes. Of course Farley would say some bullshit like that.

"Yes," Roscoe choked out.

The spring fairy queen spoke next, in the voice of Roscoe's girlfriend. "Honey, you need to come back and give me attention. Tell him you're busy." Lisbetta's free hand shot out to crush the cell phone.

With the moon debt lifted, my hand lowered. Instead of gripping a box, I now held a blade. The goblin's blade. Well, who would've thought it'd come in so handy?

Lisbetta flicked her fingers, and the crates moved out of the way. Roscoe's girl beat a hasty retreat.

"It's time for you to go home, Little Wolf," Lisbetta said softly.

I took a tentative step toward Roscoe. Here was the man who'd taken my father. Called him a bastard, had him beaten to near death, plotted to have Thorn and me captured by the goblin. Seeing tears streak down his face, I almost wanted him released—so I could beat the shit out of him myself. But I knew our ways. If he was caught by anyone from my family, they'd slaughter him without an afterthought. Since he had no honor, he never would have agreed to release my family from the debt.

My voice wavered, but I spoke true. "I want to see his punishment."

Lisbetta slowly grinned. "No, you really don't. There's a part of you that's human—and that part isn't ready for what I'm about to do to him. What I did to Primus is *nothing* compared to the punishment Roscoe shall receive."

The little girl was gone. Only the bitter spring fairy remained. She yanked harder on his neck. "Just think of it this way, you'll have your revenge tonight. And so will I."

As I turned and walked out of the room, I pondered the Code and what it meant to be an honorable werewolf. Who was the strong one now? I wondered if Roscoe would be thinking the same thing before he died.

Chapter 16

The first thing I did when I entered South Toms River was find my dad. I was practically gnawing at the bit to snuggle with my niece, but that could wait. I'd have plenty of time to get acquainted with her and play babysitter.

Werewolves usually don't need medical care, since we have the ability to heal rapidly. But sometimes—like when a wolf is at death's door—we must turn to a werewolf who knows the healing arts. Most healers were pack members who have had training as veterinarians. The pack offered them additional money on the side to provide care as needed.

When I arrived at the healer's home to see Dad, he had a look of shock on his face. His wide eyes told me everything. He hadn't expected his daughter to live through fulfilling—or not fulfilling—the moon debt.

After what I'd experienced in Maine, and at Roscoe's place, and finally with Nick's kiss, I felt like I couldn't experience anything crazier. Even taxes in April seemed a welcome trial to have to go through.

"You're alive," he said with relief. "Farley called not too long ago and told me I was free."

"Looks like I don't get to be the one to share my good news."

Dad's large hand stretched out and pulled me into a

warm hug. I might be a grown woman now, but hugs from my dad still felt good. Especially after how things had been a few months ago. We hadn't spoken to each other much after I'd been kicked out of the pack.

"How did the trip go?" he asked.

I gave him the blow by blow. Minus the details of what had occurred between Nick and me. When I got to the part where Lisbetta manhandled Roscoe, Dad feigned disgust. But he didn't have to hold back his anger from me anymore. I knew more about his dirty little secrets now.

"You never should've been involved in this. I never wanted you to see such things," he said. "My daughter should be married with kids. Not rescuing her old man in Atlantic City."

He left out the fact that I'd also seen him beaten to near death. That was something I really hadn't wanted to see. Even after my family had turned me away, I never would have wished for something like that to happen. My father was irreplaceable.

When tears threatened to come, I rolled my eyes and tried to look cheerful. "Dad, it's all over now. You can forget Roscoe and all the bad things about him."

"He was once another man—in another time. When he saved my life, his intentions weren't malicious back then."

Well, time had done a really bad number on Roscoe, then. My father hadn't seen the look on his face when Roscoe'd told me he wanted to kill me.

"Would you have given him mercy even after what he did to you?" I asked.

Dad sat for a bit, thinking. He scratched the bald spot on his head, like he always did when he thought deeply. "I think I would have—unless he threatened to hurt my children. Every man tries to do the right thing, but that ends when another man hurts—or attempts to hurt—one of his own."

His voice lowered. "Did he threaten to take your life?"

"He wasn't happy I'd failed . . ." My voice trailed off, and so I changed the subject. "Your color looks good, Dad."

"Yours doesn't." He chuckled and patted my shoulder. The bad one.

"Easy there." I cringed and couldn't stop from making that noise best described as something between a sheep bleating and a bear groaning.

The healer came in to investigate. At around five foot one, Pearl McDowell was smaller compared to most wolves. In a way, she reminded me a bit of my grandmother, if you rewound the clock a century or two. Pearl was around my mother's age and had the same brown hair and soft brown eyes as Grandma. Maybe one could even say she had gentle features that would've offered a nice smile. But that's where it all ended. She wasn't as gentle as Grandma, and I'd learned the hard way she believed a firm hand was needed with ornery werewolves.

"In the examination room," she snapped with her hand on her hips. "Now. You stink of death and blood, so I'm curious to see what you've broken."

After a quick exam, the healer wasn't happy. "You've broken your shoulder. The healing's coming along nicely, but it's *much* slower than it should be. You're also barely awake right now."

She examined my eyes and checked my pulse. "Way too slow. Rather weird."

"The fairies somehow hijacked my body to reach the man who held my father's debt. Maybe I've got a few residual signs." I didn't dare tell her about everything else that happened during the trip. Especially since it involved a wizard. It wouldn't take long at all for the news to go from my father to my mom. She's always had a personal vendetta against spellcasters.

"I honestly don't know. In all my years, I've never heard of such things before." She shrugged. "Magic's not something I deal with in my trade so anything could be wrong with you. It could very well be exhaustion."

"But I've been exhausted before and it's never been like *this*."

"Could you be pregnant?" She knew very well by my scent that I wasn't knocked up, and I didn't find her joke funny.

"I'd need to have sex first for that to be a possibility."

She snorted. "Magic might be behind all this, but either way, I want you to come back to see me in a few days. At least I can make sure you're bouncing back."

I nodded and said my good-byes to Dad and Pearl. Now that I knew he was well, I could go home and face the next day. With the trials coming soon, I'd need as much recovery time as possible.

Like any excited aunt, I rushed to visit my niece—but only after a thorough shower. It felt so good to get back into my regular clothes. There's nothing like a black pencil skirt and a crisp blouse to make a gal feel clean. Most folks don't wear business casual where I'm from, but the way I see it, I'm always prepared for most occasions. Aggie wasn't at the house, so I headed to my brother's alone. Karey had given birth at home—which was now Alex's house—so my destination wasn't far from my parents' place.

My brother had never thought much in terms of decorating his house, so his starter home used to blend in with the rest of the colonials in his subdivision. Karey had changed that. I walked up to a house where happy hands had landscaped the lawn to perfection. There wasn't a sprinkle of snow on the sidewalk. Hell, even the barren trees looked like they'd had makeovers.

The driveway was full of cars, and judging by the earthy scent coming from the house, I suspected this place was full to the brim with nymphs and other woodland creatures.

I knocked on the door, and Karey actually answered it.

"You made it!" Alex's wife was a tiny little thing. I'd met many wood nymphs in my time. They had a strange come-frolic-in-the-woods smell that always seemed to brighten my mood. But unlike Karey, most woodland creatures preferred to keep away from werewolves. Our kinds just didn't have much in common. While the nymphs protected the forest and its creatures, the pack hunted and *ate* its inhabitants. A rather awkward situation, if one thought about it.

I presented Karey with the gift bags I was carrying. Thank goodness I'd bought this stuff a few weeks ago. I always tried to plan ahead. As much as I shopped for holiday stuff, you wouldn't believe the deals I got on holiday baby stuff as well. While stuffing my cart, I'd looked like I was a holiday crack addict with a look of wild glee on my face.

"Oh, thank you." She directed me through the living room and into the kitchen. Most of her guests were in there. A few scrutinized me with disdain, since I was one of *his* relatives.

"Natalya made it back from Maine safely." Karey pointed to the empty chairs. "Have a seat. I'll go get Alex."

Right after Karey left, one of the girls gave her an oh-that's-so-nice look. I hated those looks. Anyone with a brain cell that fired correctly knew people eyeballed you that way when they didn't give a damn if you'd gotten lost in the woods and had to gnaw your arm off to escape from under a rock. You were just another person interfering with their inner circle of friends.

To show I'd been raised well, I waved at everyone and introduced myself. No one waved back.

I glanced around the room and spotted my niece right away. A nymph, who had to be around my age (I think), held the baby close. When she spotted me coming, she angled the child in my direction.

"Isn't she pretty?" the nymph said.

"Absolutely gorgeous." I put down my purse on the kitchen table and pulled out some antiseptic gel. After cleaning my hands, I'd be ready to hold Sveta.

When I approached the baby, I said gently, "Auntie Nat has been waiting so long to see you."

"I bet you have," the nymph holding her said. She eyed the faint bruises along my wrists.

I kept the smile on my face—this wasn't the time for snide comebacks.

All the nymphs continued to stare me down. Their conversation had abruptly ended, probably so they could make me feel even *more* self-conscious. How nice of them.

"Could I hold her?" I asked.

The nymph pursed her lips. I could almost see the hamster turning its wheel in her brain before she replied. "She's just gone to sleep. I wouldn't want her to wake up."

"I won't wake her. I've held babies before." I offered my hand and curled arm to show I knew what to do. "Besides, I'm her aunt."

The nymph's reply came fast. "I'm her aunt as well. So are most of the women in this room."

My smile froze on my face.

One of the nymphs on the other side of the room said something in a foreign tongue to the nymph beside her. Probably Greek. The other laughed.

My hands threatened to clench into fists. But I kept on smiling. I really did.

Alex thankfully showed up before I won a nomination for the Nobel Peace Prize.

"Nat." We hugged briefly. "Dad called me and told me about what happened. You okay?"

"As much as I can be. I'll be better once I cuddle with my niece."

Alex's forehead scrunched. "You haven't held Sveta yet?"

My brother marched right up to the nymph who held the baby and plucked her from the nymph's arms.

"Now, Alex, Karey just got her to sleep."

Alex grunted. "I'll rock her if she wakes up, Fiona. Don't worry. Sveta needs to know the smell of her pack."

The nymph gave me a dirty look when my brother turned away, but I didn't care. I was caught up in seeing my younger brother with his firstborn. He was so gentle with her. My chest swelled, and I couldn't help the sigh I released. Alexander Stravinsky had come a long way, from man-whore to responsible dad.

"Here's your *tyotia, princessa.*" He placed her in my arms.

Pure happiness filled me to the brim. A tear hit my cheek and wetted her blanket. She barely weighed a thing.

"She's perfect." I ran a finger down the side of Svetlana's face. So soft. The child didn't even stir when I pulled back her cap to reveal a head free from hair. Not a single strand.

"I guess that answers that question," I murmured.

I rubbed my nose against her cheek and inhaled. She was a mixture of scents—the forest at dawn when a mist covered it, the light musk of fur when you rubbed your nose on it. Both her mother and father lived in her.

"How are you doing? Really?" My brother's face was serious.

"Very tired. Like I've been hit below the belt so many times that I wonder how I'm even standing."

"Do you need anything? Money?"

I shook my head. "I need time to forget what's happened to us. Time to prepare for what's to come."

Alex laid his hand over mine on his daughter. "Just let me know if I can help. I want to make sure you're ready for the trials in two weeks."

"Thanks, Alex."

I really was grateful for his offer, since I'd need all the help I could muster to recover in time.

After visiting with Alex and Sveta, I stopped at my parents' house to check on my mother and grandmother. I had plans to work the Wednesday shift tomorrow and wanted to make sure they were doing well.

I expected my grandma's caretaker, Aunt Olga, to answer the door, but Auntie Yelena answered it instead.

The fun just never ends, does it?

"Can I help you?"

My ears told me my mother wasn't home—so I had no one on my side today.

"I've come to check on Mom and Grandma now that everything's settled," I said respectfully, averting my eyes, as she expected. Somehow I managed to slouch my shoulders as well. Hopefully she'd noticed my effort.

"Your mother isn't here." She continued to block the door and keep me out in the cold.

"Then may I see Grandma? I'd like to tell her personally that I've returned with father's *honor.*"

Her jaw tightened, and I suspected I'd said the right thing. Especially since she hadn't lifted a finger to help or advise my brother and me during this difficult time.

"Natalya, is that you?" Grandma called from upstairs.

"Yes, Grandma." I wanted to look Auntie Yelena in the eye so badly. I practically itched to stand up to her. But I didn't.

I took an uncertain step forward. A slight movement of my leg. Anything more would've been an open act of dominance.

My grandma called my name again.

Yelena stared at me long enough to make a point: She was in control here. Then she reluctantly stepped aside.

Even with Auntie Yelena's virulent presence, my parents' home smelled of fine food: freshly baked *rogaliki* filled with strawberry jam. My mother enjoyed cooking for anyone with an open mouth. My auntie Yelena, on the other hand, detested doing any manual labor. As a so-called retiree—who shouldn't be called one, by the way, since she's never had a job to retire from—Yelena had enjoyed running her household as the wife of a fur trader. At a height barely reaching her chin, her husband, Uncle Kolya, often traveled to Europe and Russia for business. He'd made a brief appearance at my brother's wedding, offered the glowing couple their dead animal fur gifts, and then promptly returned home. Only to have Yelena come back here. Perhaps all his time overseas was meant to make his heart grow fonder of his lovely wife. *Yeah, right.*

As usual, Yelena wore a garment with fur on it. My nose told me her expensive cashmere sweater had rabbit along the collar. It appeared fluffy and expensive. At least she didn't wear wolf fur. The Code forbade us from hunting them.

I headed into the kitchen and prepared two cups of tea, along with a plate of baked goods. Grandma entered the room not long after to join me at the kitchen table.

"I'm so glad you're all right," she said. "I prayed you and Sasha would return home safely."

She took the tea I offered, then said, "A new baby and a new start for our family is a blessing."

I grinned, thinking of little Sveta. "Could you ever imagine Alex married with a baby?"

She seemed thoughtful for a moment—the lines on her elderly face made her look serene. "Yes, I could. With time, naturally. Eventually everything flows forward to its rightful place. Someday, even you will get married to a good man and have children."

Her eyes had that playful glee she usually hid from others.

"I don't see that happening, to be honest. Not with my track record."

"Give yourself more credit, Granddaughter. Sometimes the runt of the litter can have the biggest bite."

While we sat drinking tea, I briefly told her about my trip to Maine. She nodded at the appropriate times until a question came to mind. "When I delivered the truck to the Jackson pack, I encountered a woman I'd never met before. She looked to be around Mom's age. No more than one hundred years or so." Visions of the woman's transformation flashed before my eyes as I spoke.

"She knew the old magic. I saw her undo a warlock's spell on a lock. And she . . ." I tried to find the words, but fear bit into me. Just the memory of what my grandmother had become made me uncomfortable. "She knew some of the magic you know."

Grandma was quiet for a bit. "What did she look like?"

"She had dark brown hair. Brown eyes. What I remember the most about her was a bright red birthmark on her cheek—about the size of a closed fist. The pack leader called her Tamara."

My grandmother burst out laughing. "So Tamara's

her name now? She couldn't transform her way out of a burlap sack. I've met her before. Back when your mother was around your age. Your father came calling to see your mother quite often around that time."

"They courted in New York, right?" I'd finished the tea and poured another serving. My stomach growled, so I next dived into some kasha. A nice bowl of porridge would warm my belly.

Grandma nodded and continued, "Tatiana, as she called herself then, had emigrated from Romania to America to find someone to teach her the old magic. She had her eye on your father until she learned my daughter wanted him as well. She had the worst Russian accent I'd ever heard. She kinda sounded like a cat in heat every time she spoke."

I just about choked on my tea.

"She thought she was doing my family a favor by not standing in the way of their courtship. That I'd be so grateful to her for allowing my daughter to fetch a good husband, I'd teach her my old magic." Grandma leaned toward me. "Do you know what I told her?"

"Based on the fact that she didn't complete the transformation like you did, I'm assuming you told her to have a nice day."

"And more! Old magic isn't a bag of tricks to be bartered or sold to the highest bidder."

After selling goods to other supernaturals at the flea market, I'd learned a great deal. But none of the awe of learning something new compared to right now. It was like discovering a hidden part of one's heritage. "How did you learn? From your mother?"

Grandma made a sour face. "No one in my village had the memory for such a thing. Old magic isn't about strength. It's about the power here." She tapped her forehead. "I'm centuries old and hard of hearing on most days, but I remember my house, my village, even my old friends, as if it were yesterday. That's my gift, and why old magic settles well within my bones."

I chewed on this information as Auntie Yelena came into the kitchen to get some coffee. Or to eavesdrop more closely. She made a rude noise. "It isn't good to teach this girl such things. She doesn't have the mind for it."

Grandma didn't say another thing until Yelena left the room.

"Don't listen to her," she said. "Anyone who speaks to you like that just envies what you have."

My grandma always had nice things to say about me. Too bad this particular one wasn't true. "I don't have anything she wants."

Grandma offered me a half smile. "I'd tell you what you have compared to her, but then you'd never learn for yourself why you are so powerful."

I tried to nod and smile. That's what grandmas were supposed to do—make their grandchildren feel good about themselves.

Since my grandmother seemed open to talking about old magic at the moment, now seemed like a good time to ask a couple more questions. "If only a good memory is required for old magic, then why don't more wolves know how to do it?"

Grandma's eyebrow rose. "Most wolves obey the Code—also, most don't want to pay the price that old magic requires. They are unprepared for the even exchange that must be given for a spell."

After Grandma had saved me, she'd slept for several days. I'd thought we'd lost her. She'd told me later that she'd given up a piece of her life to save mine. Which might mean that old magic requires an exchange of one's life force—like the magic used by the spring fairies. Lisbetta took the life force of those wolves and used the magic in other ways.

I sighed deeply. Everything I'd learned so far should've been a warning, but I wanted to learn more. Old magic was like this forbidden fruit I wanted to pluck and collect. Any wolf could do it, so that meant even someone low on the totem pole, like me, could cast a spell.

I chewed on my thoughts until Grandma spoke.

"I tell you what," she said. "If I wanted to teach you something simple, do you think you could learn it?"

A simple spell? Old magic was never that simple, but I was game. "Of course. Would it make me invisible? Fly?"

"I'm not that foolish, Natalya. You memorize the words. If you can do that, then at the right time I'll teach you how to invoke the power behind them. Deal?"

"Of course."

"Just remember. With everything there's a price to be paid. For this spell in particular. But then, you know us Lasovskaya women love to break the rules, no?"

This sounded too good to be true. "What price will be paid? Will I grow older faster every time I do it?"

Grandma rolled her eyes. "Just listen and trust your grandma."

For the next twenty minutes, Grandma chanted. As to the tongue she spoke or what the gibberish might've meant, I couldn't place it. All I knew was I sat across from my grandmother, holding her hand and feeling at peace. The phrase she recited was about fifteen syllables, and it rolled off the tongue with the guttural reflections of a Middle Eastern language. I clung to the words and cradled them close, saying them with my grandmother. Each inflection, each clip. The words flowed off my lips, and before long I spoke alone.

When I looked up, Grandma chuckled. "Not bad for your first time. You still need to clean up a few words, but you didn't butcher too many."

"Are you sure you won't tell me what the spell does?"

"You keep trying and see if you can convince me to tell you."

I laughed. Like Grandma had said, her eyesight might be weakening, but I suspected she'd see through my attempts to get the information from her from a mile away.

"I'm glad we had this time together. Did Mom ever show an interest?"

"None of my daughters did. Your mother the most of all. You know how she feels about magic."

I didn't need my grandmother to tell me about the bitterness my mother felt toward old magic or anything having to do with spellcasters. If I brought a man like Nick home with the prospects of marriage, my mother wouldn't be happy about it. Not even a Russian white wizard with money would be welcome.

"Why is she so angry?"

Grandma tapped the rim of her coffee cup. "My Anna hasn't told you about what happened to her not long after she married your father, has she?"

I frowned. "No, she hasn't."

"Back when your parents were young, in the early 1940s, we all lived in New York. They were a young couple back then. We lived in Brooklyn, settled with the European immigrants on one side and groups of witches, warlocks, and wizards on the other. Back in those days, the immigrants had brought more than their individual cultures over the pond. The supernaturals arrived with them as well.

"We were a happy lot." She frowned. "Except for the warlocks and wizards. They fought all the time, like a bunch of unruly kids."

"Why?"

"Ehh, the story is a long and never-ending one. The warlocks got into trouble. The wizards would have to clean it up.

"Anyway, I'd hoped for Anna to have children immediately, but she told me she wanted to work hard to make money to travel with your father. She wanted to see the world."

My hand played with the chain holding the seashell while she spoke. I could picture New York in the early twentieth century. All the clothes and smells. None of them like the old country.

"Anna worked as a housemaid for a family in one of those nicer neighborhoods. She'd come home late in the evenings. Most folks worked long shifts back in those days, but us werewolves could work double that time without tiring.

"One night, she didn't come home. Fyodor came to my place to check to see if she was there, but I hadn't seen her. Anna didn't come home for three days. When she returned, she wasn't the same."

Grandma grabbed the napkin, and then her voice lowered. "Compared to other girls, Anna was breathtaking. We'd suspected she'd been raped, something like that. She was barely alive. So weak and pale. A milkman had found her in an alley and brought her to us. Anna wouldn't speak for weeks, and when she did talk about it . . . well, we learned it had been far worse."

I watched her swallow slowly, obviously searching for a way to tell her tale without crying.

"A wizard had captured her on her way home. He'd been following her for over a week, apparently. He took her that night and caged her in his home. Over days, he stole her life force from her, for his healing magic—for a spell to save his dying witch wife."

A gasp escaped my mouth, and I couldn't help but think of Nick. Of what he'd said to me about what had happened at the battle: *"Yeah, I did something. Something I regret."*

It couldn't be true—yet suddenly, deep inside, I knew it was.

My weakness. All that pain and my slowed healing. Nick had done something to me to save us. He'd used my life force. I finally found the words to speak to my grandmother, feeling numb inside. "No wonder Mom has such animosity against them."

"Yes. Your father never found the wizard who took her. He searched for years and never found that man, or his wife."

"So you think the spell worked?"

"We don't know for certain. But your mother said it most likely did, since the wizard set her free."

My throat was painfully dry, but I managed to speak, to say what was on my mind. "What would Mother think if I ever wanted to be with a wizard?"

"You know the answer to that question, Natalya. Even I know she wouldn't take the news well."

I didn't need to ask any more. Still, my relationship with Nick felt like something I needed.

"What if this wizard made me feel good about myself? Even with all my quirks. What if this man is the perfect friend and makes me forget, albeit briefly, about what I can't have with Thorn?"

She patted my hand. "Then you need to make a choice, depending on what makes you happy. I know you love your mother and wouldn't want to do anything to disappoint her. But you shouldn't give up a good friend."

I shook my head. "If I had a choice, I would've chosen Thorn a long time ago. But I can't have him."

She snorted. "Who says so? I've been through enough to know that the path before any woman makes unexpected turns."

I took her words to heart, and I wished everything could be that simple.

"Of course, having the attention of more than one man is *never* a bad thing for a woman. Especially if one of them has deep pockets and a good nature. A strong back doesn't hurt either, if you know what I mean."

"Grandma!"

"You think I didn't have my share of admirers before I married my Pyotr?" Her old eyes danced mischievously. "Since you're young, you don't see what I see quite clearly. One of them was made for your heart, and the other was made for your soul."

I opened my mouth to ask her what she meant, but Auntie Yelena entered the kitchen again. When she didn't leave, I knew that, for now, I wouldn't get a clear answer from her.

Chapter 17

An evening at home to recover should have been the best medicine. I was exhausted and I'd had a revelation about Nick that knocked me down so hard, I wondered if I'd ever get back up. But, naturally, with a family that lived on celebrations, my hot date with my bed didn't happen.

Not long after walking through the door, Aggie took me right back out.

"Hey, what are you doing?"

Aggie snorted and dragged me back out to the car. "Oh, stop grumbling. Something good is about to happen, for once."

My best friend took the wheel while I sat on the passenger side with my arms crossed. Visions of my fluffy pillows and stacks of ornaments came to mind as the scenery passed by. This *trip* better be an improvement over stroking a nutcracker, drinking hot cocoa, and staring in a trance at the wall.

Ten minutes later, I noticed we'd reached South Toms River's main street. We pulled up along the curb—right in front of Barney's. I hadn't eaten here in a while. Before Aggie started bringing home leftovers from here on the days she worked, I used to grab a fresh sandwich and supersized green pickle. I took in the familiar green awning over the windows, the festive lights around them. The place brought back fond, yet sad, memories of how I used to always be alone.

"Hey, time to get some chow."

I stepped out of the car and followed Aggie inside. This place seemed to make her more comfortable than it did me. Especially since she was a part-time manager here. Not long after she arrived at my doorstep, Aggie had quickly run out of dough and found herself needing a job. As the daughter of a socialite with a college education, she'd expected to get some kind of white-collar position. But thanks to an application I'd submitted for her, Aggie happily became the newest employee of Barney's Pickles.

I took no more than a couple steps inside before I heard the ruckus of laughter and conversation from inside the private party room.

We walked past the main dining area, filled with dark wood tables and country blue chairs. The place hadn't changed since I'd last been there—it still had the rustic feel of a countryside kitchen. Even the staff behind the counter had a welcome-home-dear smile on their faces and freshly pressed aprons that matched the color of the chairs. The flashing Christmas lights just added to the ambience.

The noises from the back room grew louder, drawing my attention.

"What did you do?" I asked with a feigned groan.

"Your aunts and I just planned a little something, that's all."

As we walked into the private dining room, I whispered to her, "Be careful, you might start looking responsible to them."

She laughed. "Way too late for that."

The room was filled to capacity. All around me were smiling faces—except for one. When I caught the gaze of Auntie Yelena, I wanted to frown back at her, but I smiled instead. Why not enjoy this moment and show her I was happy?

"Good to see you came home, Nat." Uncle Boris was the first one to reach my side, giving me a pat on the shoulder. The bad one—again.

"I'm glad to be home," I said, smiling through the pain.

More family members approached me, nearly all with hugs and kisses. I'd never before experienced such a display of affection from them. Each looked me in the eye and addressed me with respect.

Then one of my young cousins stepped up to me and asked, "What was it like to kill Roscoe?"

Huh?

My mouth wobbled, and I looked around for help. His father took the boy and directed him back to their table. "Sorry," my uncle mumbled, "rumors have been spreading around pretty quickly."

"That one definitely isn't true," I said.

My aunt Olga, a former Russian beauty queen who always knew how to dress for a party, stood decked out in a gorgeous yellow knee-length dress. She directed me to a free seat at one of the tables. "Let her eat, everyone. She has plenty of time for us to show her how grateful we are."

Of course, they didn't listen to her. While I sat munching on a turkey and Swiss sandwich, every relative who hadn't already greeted me—except for Auntie Yelena—came by to say hello. Most thanked me, while others wanted more details about what I'd experienced. At first all their attention seemed nice, but it didn't take long for it to get overwhelming. The weakness I'd experienced earlier hadn't backed down that much.

Just when I thought I'd had enough of the party, a new pair showed up at the doorway: Thorn and Erica. Thank goodness I didn't have anything in my mouth. The giant green pickle in my hand plopped down onto my plate, hit the floor, and then proceeded to roll under the table, however. I moved to retrieve it, but one of my aunts came to the rescue.

Ever the well-mannered lady, Aunt Olga spouted, "Greet your guest, Natalya."

With Erica standing there, her arm clenched around Thorn's, I didn't even want to offer them a potato chip. My legs also refused to react, making it difficult to take action. Since I didn't move, Thorn and Erica came my way. As the consort-to-be of the next alpha, Erica actually just trailed after Thorn—even when he shrugged her arm off.

Once they were up close, I saw that Thorn's smile was warm—but Erica's presence dampened my happiness. Out of respect for Thorn, my gaze went to the floor before it shifted to look at his face. And suddenly I felt bitter. What kind of man took advantage of my moment to further remind me of what I couldn't have anymore?

From my line of sight into the main dining room, it didn't take long to spot the culprit. A pretty brunette in an expensive coat sat at a table with a man I didn't know, eating her dinner. I knew the woman's face quite well, since I usually spied it whenever I saw Erica: Becky Knoll. The two made quite the pair of money-spending-no-job-having chicks. And now that Erica wanted to be on Thorn's tail all the time, Becky acted as lookout to make sure her best friend stayed by his side.

"Hey, you," Thorn said.

The words bounced around my head before slamming into my heart. We used to greet each other like that a long time ago. Even though we weren't together anymore, hadn't been for a long time, they still had meaning to me.

Thorn continued. "I heard from Will about your party and thought I'd stop by."

A quick glance at the smirk on Erica's face told me her wordless greeting, *And I tagged along, since luckily I heard about it from Becky!*

Well, isn't that *swell*.

Most people would've shrugged any negativity off and invited the couple to sit down and enjoy the festivities. But I'd been bitten on the shoulder, attacked by imps, and threatened by the mafia. Colorful bruises kept popping up on my body. So, now, after all this drama, the only thing that came out of my mouth was an incoherent stutter. "H-hi . . . W-welcome."

Thorn frowned. "You okay?" He took a step toward me.

Erica's hand snapped out faster than my eye could follow it. "She's fine, Thorn."

Finally, I found my voice. "Thanks for coming. Go ahead and get some food."

There, that wasn't so bad. Even though I did sound like a damn robot. But the others around me didn't seem to care. I'd done the polite thing and greeted my new guests.

When Thorn moved to the long table with the food, I'd hoped he'd take some and just leave. That he wouldn't claim the free spot not far from me. That his date wouldn't need a seat and force one of my aunts to move to accommodate her. And finally, that his presence wouldn't turn such a great night into a painful one.

After Thorn and Erica sat down side by side, the food didn't taste as good. Barney's had the best quality deli meat. But now the turkey had gone bland and the bread had a staleness that wasn't there before. When a cousin came by to chat, I wondered if I was truly paying attention to her. Or was my mind somewhere else? Even though my head was turned away from Thorn and Erica, I could still see them from the corner of my eye. Erica's subtle move to shift her arm near his. Her left leg crossed to bring her right one closer to his. All the while, Thorn ate his food and engaged in conversation with the men at the table. They seemed like a regular couple enjoying a meal together.

Thankfully, my dad soon distracted me. He stood and tapped his fork against his glass to get everyone's attention. I smiled. His bruises had faded a bit, and he appeared to be in a good mood.

"I'm glad that everyone could come today to congratulate my daughter," he said. His powerful voice quieted everyone. "A long time ago, back when I was courting Anna, I remember seeing her standing at a flower shop. The place was run-down—not in the best neighborhood, since this was the Brooklyn from the days many of you weren't alive to see."

As expected, my aunts and uncles nodded with understanding.

"My Anna told me she always stopped there to try to find a particular flower she favored—lilies. Since I was a man who was willing to work to find a good wife, I showed up as early as I could to buy her all the lilies she wanted, but what I found at the shop wasn't what I expected."

I turned to see Mom, quiet and smiling shyly from her spot not far from me. I'd never heard this story before, but the look on her face made me feel good.

Dad continued. "From the front counter, I saw Anna in the back, cooking dinner for the owner's family. I didn't say a word for a few minutes as she tended to their children and cooked the stew. Later that night, I returned. After I cornered her outside of the owner's house, I learned she'd been working nights to pay back a moon debt for her late Uncle Vladimir. That she'd made her own sacrifice after hours of long work scrubbing floors to help her family." Dad waited for everyone to absorb the meaning of his words.

Not a single person looked away from him.

"It was at that moment I realized she'd make a good wife, a good mother. My daughter Natalya is the same. She has the same tenacity. The same fire for her kin. She bravely left with her brother and made a stand to protect the Stravinsky name. Even after Sasha was called home, Natalya made the choice to think of her family first. All you young pups should remember this day and know that you too can be honorable for your family." He raised his glass of water toward me.

"To Natalya!"

Cheers of congratulations came my way. Thorn stood and began to applaud. Erica reluctantly joined him with a halfhearted clap. Soon everyone was on their feet, cheering me. By the time they'd settled back into their seats, I was heady from their kindness. I didn't have the respect and admiration of all the South Toms River pack, but the Stravinskys would make do just fine.

The pleasant vibe in the room lasted for a little while. Then Erica Holden opened her mouth and spoiled it.

"Are you sure we can't have a real wedding?" Erica asked out of the blue.

I kept my focus on my food, but I immediately detected the flick of Thorn's eyes in my direction. He'd just finished a bite of his sandwich, so he wiped off his mouth with a napkin and then tossed it onto his plate.

He tried to keep his voice low, but every wolf in the room could hear him. "This isn't the time or the place, Erica. I already told you no."

"You can't keep avoiding the question." She leaned forward, and her voice rose a bit. "My father has business associates who are expecting an invitation of some kind. To an expensive event at a nice place. After all, they've worked hard with Dad to pay the pack's debts."

From the way Thorn sighed, I suspected this wasn't a new conversation. She must be rubbing salt in his wounds every day, reminding him of his obligation to the pack.

"Just because this is an arranged marriage doesn't mean I should get shortchanged. I'm just as exasperated as you are." She reached out and touched his hand as if to console him. It was like a hungry snake comforting a mouse. "It'll take time, but soon enough we'll be able to show our true feelings."

"Okay, you've had your fun. We're going now." Thorn stood—leaving Erica looking dumbfounded. She hadn't touched a single thing on her plate. Before standing, Erica shot me a heated glare and then hurried to follow Thorn. For me, their retreating backs were both a welcome and disappointing sight.

At the doorway, though, Thorn turned briefly. He didn't look my way, but I heard him say faintly, "See you 'round, Nat."

I closed my eyes. Heard their footsteps walk out. Heard the restaurant door open and close. Beyond that there was nothing else.

The temptation to stand and follow them was overwhelming. How long had it been since I'd seen Thorn? A few days? How much longer will I be such a sad, lovesick fool?

I got up and started to march right out of the dining room. I'd made it no more than five steps before a hand grabbed my wrist.

"Let him go," Aggie whispered.

A lump grew in my throat. There was no sign of Thorn or Erica through the restaurant windows. It was too late for me to watch them leave. Maybe that was for the best.

Aggie wrapped her arm around my shoulder—the good one. "I think you need some alcohol. Your aunt Vera's holding back the good stuff under the table."

I snorted and followed her back to our table. "I should drink while on medication?"

"Not a lot." She offered me a mischievous smirk, and her blue eyes twinkled. "Just enough to make you forget for a little while."

A few minutes later, I sat back down and enjoyed a beer or two. But I couldn't help thinking, wasn't this *my* victory dinner? Wasn't this the night when I should have felt triumphant over my enemies? But it didn't feel that way now. It seemed like for every two steps I took up the mountain, I always fell back one.

Chapter 18

Concentrating today was near to impossible. A part of me hummed from seeing Thorn, but another part hated myself for enjoying it. Soon enough, this yearning—this never-ending draw to him—would be severed. And then I'd be free to move on with my life.

Thank goodness I had therapy today to help with that, 'cause those beers I drank last night hadn't done anything but sour my stomach.

Once I arrived at Dr. Frank's office, I immediately noticed Abby wasn't there. Heidi walked up to me, a sullen expression on her face.

"You look like you survived okay," she said. Instead of coffee, she gulped down some water from her ever-present bottle.

"As well as I can manage. Where's Abby?"

"She's still in Maine. She'll be there for a while. I don't know how long."

"I guess if she's with her new author, she's stuck there until the book's done."

Heidi appeared thoughtful. "I guess so." Her eyes drifted to the window. Even though it was afternoon, the overcast sky had darkened the skyline.

To lighten her mood, I asked, "Did you ever figure out why Lisbetta was scared of someone like Abby? She's a pretty good fighter, but I haven't seen her cast powerful spells or anything."

Heidi shrugged, barely looking my way. "Abby said a thing or two before I dropped her off. Something about her being favored by the gods—a bunch of stuff I barely understood about how her powers of persuasion could be extended to defend herself in a dire situation."

Based on the last time I discussed Abby's powers with Heidi, she'd told me the Muse could only influence mortal writers—not supernatural creatures. I wanted to pry further, especially since it shed new light on our quiet friend, but something was wrong with Heidi herself right now. On most days, she was so exuberant she made me look like a recluse.

"So." I shuffled from one foot to the other. "When are you going to tell me about the guy who showed up in Maine?"

Heidi blinked a few times and continued to stare out the window. "I've been busy lately."

"He looked like you . . . in a way." How could I describe him? He'd been a blur of movement across the forest. But my quick eye could still spot the telltale features humans couldn't see on Heidi. Water magic stirred under the mermaid's skin. I didn't need Nick's magic to see that.

"He's my best friend from back home."

My eyebrows lowered, and I stepped closer to her. The obvious question came to mind. "What was he doing there?"

"He followed me—to deliver a message."

Not long after she spoke, Dr. Frank walked in, followed by Nick. Just one look at his smiling face made me think about what had happened between us. How could he smile, knowing what he'd done to me?

Nick was in the process of walking over to me when

Dr. Frank turned to him. "Have a seat, Nick, it's time to start."

Heidi left my side. I opened my mouth to invite her over, but she sat down between Raj and Tyler. Lilith the succubus sat next to Tyler and me. The clear air told me we had another obvious absence: The nymph wasn't here.

"So far this season, I've noticed many changes in my patients." Dr. Frank glanced at each of us briefly. "Most of the changes have been positive, while the other ones have been setbacks."

As he gave his introductory speech, I had to admit it: I was kinda hoping he'd get to the point where he gave us a dose of his happy magic. I needed it. At least enough to get my mind off Nick. I knew he was staring at me, but as my irritation rose, I refused to return his gaze. I'd yet to receive a single phone call or text message about the matter. Even smoke signals would've been nice—

"Natalya? Did you hear my question? You can do it, right?"

I looked up to see Dr. Frank, as well as everyone else, looking my way. Based on the wide smirk the succubus wore, I'd missed something important.

"Of course. What do I have to do?"

"I was just telling everyone that the holidays often present challenges, both social and physical. For you, this time of the year is difficult in terms of self-control."

I nodded the whole time, feeling *slightly* guilty. At least I hadn't bought anything lately—in Manhattan anyway.

Dr. Frank continued with a sly look in his eyes. "The best exercise to face your demons—the figurative ones—is to go to a post-Christmas sale and leave with *one* purchase. You can do that, can't you?"

I returned his gaze with confidence. Over the past few months, I'd made progress. My late-night Home Shopping Network buying binges had gone down. (After Aggie blocked the channel.) I'd been clipping fewer coupons in preparation for the holidays. (The Sunday newspaper with the ads kept disappearing.) And I'd even cut back on arranging my ornaments in their boxes. (Since the flood a few months ago I actually had fewer ornaments to arrange.)

Dr. Frank said, "You'll be doing this exercise with Nick."

Thanks a million, Dr. Frank, for dropping your bucket of reality on my fragile sandcastle.

"Will that be a problem?" Dr. Frank asked Nick.

"None at all." Matter of fact, Nick appeared pleased to be my buddy again.

Once again, I wondered if Dr. Frank had mind-reading abilities he hid from his patients. He further exhibited that possibility as he managed to convince Tyler to attend a dwarf ritual. Tyler was all about protesting naturally.

"I'd stand out in front of all those people."

"You will—but you'll have the coping mechanisms we talked about. What are they?" Dr. Frank asked.

"Confidence. Stand straight, like a man. Charisma. I'm a nice guy anyone would want to meet . . ." Tyler faltered for a moment but then kept going. "Character. I have to believe in myself before someone else can."

"That's right," Dr. Frank said with a smile.

I couldn't help but smile as well, hearing Tyler say those words. During the last couple of sessions, he'd reached a new low with his self-deprecating speeches.

Next, Dr. Frank opened the discussion to some other suggestions for Tyler, then he switched to Heidi. "How have things been going for you, Heidi? Did you get that part-time job on the pier, like we talked about?"

"No, I didn't," she snapped.

Everyone quieted. Heidi had not only folded in on

herself, but she was trying to cover the side of her face. Her perfect skin now marred all over with splotches of blue.

"Heidi, are you okay?" I mouthed.

She sucked in a sob, and I immediately walked over to her.

With her boots and army jacket, she would've looked tough any other day, but the mermaid's now tear-streaked face appeared vulnerable. I knelt in front of her. On her other side, Tyler placed a concerned hand on her shoulder.

I tried again. "What's wrong?"

"I d-don't w-want to go." Her voice quivered, and she shut her eyes tightly.

"Go where?" I asked gently. Tentatively, I pushed her red hair behind her ear.

"Back there."

I glanced at Nick. Everyone else looked on with concern.

Nick said, "Why did he follow us? To take you home?"

Heidi's gaze looked far away. She lightly rubbed the hives she'd told me were called blotchies. I dreaded what she had to face almost as much as she did. She hadn't set foot in the ocean in many years.

"I need some air. I don't want to be seen like this." Heidi slowly stood and then went to the door. I moved to stop her, but Nick shook his head, silently telling me to give her space. Heidi rarely cried in front of anyone.

Before she left, she said a few words, keeping her back to us. "It's kinda crazy, huh? No matter how much we run away, what we fear the most always catches up to us."

Chapter 19

Heidi didn't return to the therapy session. Chasing after her wasn't an option since I didn't even know where to start in a city as big as New York. The best thing to do was go home and hope she'd turn up to say good-bye before she had to leave.

Time passed too quickly. Just a few more days until Christmas, and not long after that I'd face the trials. This ticking clock bothered me the most.

Dinner plans with the Stravinsky clan should have brought nothing more than the prospect of a full belly and time for me to reconnect with my family before the trials. But after the past few days, I wasn't excited about it. I hadn't seen Sveta for a while, but I dreaded seeing Auntie Yelena. When I reached my parents' house, I had even more of a reason to hate her guts. Seated next to her on the couch was Rex. The minute I walked through the door, he glanced at me briefly with his dark eyes and then acted as if I weren't there. *Great.* That suited me just fine.

Unlike Thorn, Rex only had the good looks thing going for him. As a good-looking bachelor with a half-way decent rank in the pack, my aunts must've brought him here to look him over for matchmaking purposes. But didn't they know my past history with him?

A few months ago, Thorn's return brought back the painful memories I had of Rex—the day I'd lost it in front of the whole pack. Right in front of Old Farley as he and my father attempted to pair me with Rex. Thorn had left a few months earlier, and my wounds had been too deep to take another man.

So I had the panic attack from hell and lost my family and pack in one day.

With my appetizer in hand, I marched up to my grandmother and greeted her. I tried to concentrate on how warmly she said my name instead of thinking about Rex behind me. He continued to chat away with Yelena.

"I don't have much here—but at least I've got my own place and a job over at the mill." He sounded all confident and smug. Too bad Auntie Yelena didn't know he had that rampant asshole disease going around on the East Coast.

"You have just enough to take care of yourself." Yelena sounded all bubbly and nice. She even sounded excited when she said, "My youngest daughter, Clara, is nineteen. I think you'd really like her."

"I'd love to meet her," he replied.

I dodged around a card table where my uncles and Aunt Vera played poker. If the men weren't careful with their pocket change, she'd go home with lunch money for my cousins for weeks to come.

I ventured to the kitchen to drop off the food I'd brought. There wasn't as much space in here. Since the nymphs were here tonight, Mom had prepared both vegetarian and meat-eater fare. To most cooks, this would've been an interesting challenge, an opportunity to try out new recipes. For a woman like my mother, who always served meat, the look on her face told me this had been an exasperating affair.

"Do you want help?" I asked.

"Check on the marinated mushrooms. I have no idea what I need to do to them."

"Mushrooms? That's new for you."

"Yeah. I made some sauerkraut and some potato salad, but I can't have our guests eating side dishes all night."

I went to the sink to wash my hands. She hadn't asked, but like a good daughter I should try to assist her. And anyway, helping her would keep me out of the living room.

For the next half hour, I helped my mother figure out a delicious way to cook the marinated mushrooms. She'd gotten the recipe from Karey, but the new mother's handwriting was as cryptic as a three-year-old child's drawing of their family. You kind of had to guess the different parts and hope you got it right without offending them.

"Have you washed your hands enough times?" a voice from the entrance to the kitchen asked.

I turned to see Auntie Yelena in the doorway. When I looked at my hands, I noticed I had them under the water again. But I was in the kitchen handling food. I'd only washed them once before. Hadn't I?

My mother grumbled from the pot she was stirring, "Go bother someone else, Yelena. Just because your husband abandoned you for the winter again doesn't mean we need to deal with your sour mood."

Auntie Yelena simply leaned against the nearest wall and stared me down. Mom's words had bounced right off her.

"Have you seen the baby yet tonight, Anna? Karey's done feeding her."

Mom shook her head. "There'll be plenty of time after I get dinner finished."

"Oh, stop it." Auntie Yelena took the spoon from Mom's hand and thrust in mine. "Mind the kitchen, Natalya, while your mom gets some quality time with her grandchild." To my mother, she added, "You'll have to share her with everyone else after dinner, and you might *never* get another chance to experience a grandchild while she's so young."

My blood pressure rose enough to pop a vein. *Now, what the hell did she mean by that?*

I prepared to follow, but they left me in the kitchen all alone. Jealous and fuming, I heard the baby cry for a bit as she was handed over to my mother. All the women cooed and had words of wisdom to rain down on Karey. Even though I had no prospects of getting knocked up anytime soon, I definitely wanted the same treatment someday. I'd been raised to be excited about getting married and having children. With all these women around rubbing bellies and holding hands with their husbands, it was enough to make me ask the valuable question most women my age often contemplated: Would it ever be my turn? Would I be worthy enough to find a man who'd come here with me, so I could have my aunts give my baby endless attention?

I probably would someday . . . but it wouldn't be Thorn at my side.

Auntie Yelena came back into the kitchen while my back was turned yet again. Naturally she found me at the sink.

"Don't your hands ever get dry from washing them so much?"

Yelena knew very well what she was doing. I had washed my hands excessively tonight out of stress, but she didn't need to be evil and rub my nose in it. Just like Dr. Frank had taught me, I'd tried most of the coping mechanisms: focusing on the task at hand, recognizing when the repeated activity took place, and most of all, avoiding stressful situations that induced coping behaviors. It was too damn bad that the person who brought on my current compulsive behavior stood right next to me.

"Lotion works wonders on a night like tonight." See, I could forgive and forget.

"Don't you worry you won't do well in the trials if you're like this?"

"I'm sure I'll do just fine, if you're not at the trials riding my ass." Whoops, I remembered why I *didn't* forgive her. How unfortunate. I wiped my hands off with a dish towel.

She smirked and folded her arms. I was probably in for it now. "Even if you were half the wolf that everyone in this house is, shouldn't you be part of the pack? Do you honestly think you can succeed? Don't let your little victory party give you false confidence."

With a snort for good measure, she added, "Look at yourself. A perfectly good man like Rex out there isn't interested in you anymore. Neither is Thorn."

I gripped the towel instead of biting through the skin on the inside of my mouth. It'd be so easy to march out of the room, away from Yelena, but my mom's food would be left unattended.

Her voice lowered. "You walk around as if no one notices that you're *flawed*. You're alone, with no man and no future. It makes me wonder what you're still doing here, why you even bother."

I slowly turned my head to look at her. That mean bitch was dead serious. She meant every vicious word that came out of her mouth.

And that's what hurt me the most.

"So what if you make it through the trials?" she reasoned. "What will you have after that? You'll have a place in the pack, and your family, most certainly. But what else? Do you think anyone would want someone like you?"

I took a step back from the sink, but she closed in like a barracuda that had scented blood.

"The days of dragging you along are over, Natalya. You need to move on, allow this family to rise up again in the ranks."

I sucked in a breath. Should I be surprised she went there?

"Stop it!" I hissed.

"You think people respect you? They only *pity* you—especially after you lost your belongings in the flood." Her sinister smile grew. She'd hit me below the belt with a sucker punch. "You think I don't know what happened to you at the park five years ago when your father tried to pair you with Rex?"

This couldn't be happening right now.

"Rex told me about your little panic attack. About how you flipped out in front of the pack leader and affected the Stravinsky family's position among the South Toms River wolves. Do you want to continuously remind us of what you did? Have you ever thought about more than yourself?"

She tapped the counter to drive her point home. "You think about it for the next few days. I know you'll do the right thing."

After she left to join the rest of the family in the living room, I had the quietest panic attack I'd ever had. The room spun, but I didn't move. I thought I'd suffocate, but I didn't move. My knees buckled, but I didn't move. Everything that could go wrong went wrong, but I refused to interrupt my family in the other room. I wouldn't give Yelena the satisfaction of seeing me break down in front of everyone.

My mother didn't abandon me for long, and since I knew her kitchen well I managed to finish the food. Even after my panic attack. Auntie Yelena knew what she'd done to me was wrong. She had to. My mouth felt sealed with glue for the rest of the night. I didn't speak unless spoken to—and only when the other person wanted an answer. When anyone asked me if something was wrong, I feigned exhaustion over training. I just had to get through the dinner, and then I'd be able to go hide away at home.

While I ate, my head turned to the side, and a part of me expected to see Aggie there. She'd always been my supporter and best friend. But she was with Will, having a movie night at his place. She'd made a life for herself here, and soon she'd pass me by as well. Wasn't that what Auntie Yelena said would happen?

Well into dinner, Karey passed Sveta to me. Holding my niece gave me my own moment of peace. I didn't even care that I had to wash my hands again to hold her. (Even if it was the thirteenth time of the night.) Sveta snuggled next to me. Only an innocent face that looked back at me with love and gripped my finger without prejudice.

But my blissful moment didn't last long. One of her nymph aunts swept in to take her away after only a few minutes. On any other day I would've protested, and thrown a fit, but tonight I'd been beaten down. Why bother when even the nymphs didn't respect me?

The dinner eventually came to a close. Ever the dutiful daughter, I went to the kitchen and cleaned up. There were endless pots and plates waiting. The dining room table had bits of food ground into the nice tablecloth. Someone had even spilled sauerkraut on the floor and their lazy ass didn't bother to wipe it up.

The other families had left for the night. Gone was my moment of glory at the victory dinner. None of them had volunteered their kids for cleanup duty. As I filled a bucket with water, I couldn't help thinking the obvious: No one complained about the outcast picking up other people's messes all by herself.

Things had changed, yet somehow some still remained the same.

Chapter 20

When I wasn't running in the mornings—all alone—or working during the day, I tried to feel like I had some kind of a normal life. Which wasn't easy, since Nick was still trying to maintain a relationship with me. After figuring out what he'd done, it was rather hard to agree to anything. But he had saved my life multiple times. Totally giving up on a friendship over that didn't feel right with me.

Since Christmas was tomorrow, Nick had asked me to eat dinner with him in New York and exchange gifts at his place. It was definitely a compromise on my part, as his place wasn't exactly the cleanest.

"Are you sure you want to have dinner with me?" Nick asked as we walked through Brooklyn. "Doesn't your family have big plans?"

I nodded. Our hands brushed briefly, so I tucked mine in my pocket. "Mom always cooks a Christmas Eve dinner, but I'm not in the mood this year."

Nick groaned. "You've worked so hard in therapy. You should be with your family tonight, continuing to patch things up."

Auntie Yelena's words bounced around in my head. Now that I'd had time to dust myself off and cover the gaping wound she'd created, I remembered that her remarks were just words. But who could forget if someone made you feel like you're worthless garbage that dragged one's family down? What kind of person did that to family?

"I've made progress with them," I blurted. "Nothing's wrong."

"Your face doesn't say that."

"My face says that we need to get to your place and you better give me loads of ornaments to add to my collection."

Nick groaned again. "You really need to work on your diversion tactics."

"I made an *effort* to change the subject—there's a difference."

We walked a ways before we reached a stretch of brownstones. Nick lived in a nice neighborhood that I enjoyed walking through. I didn't look forward to seeing his apartment, of course, but a promise was a promise: We were going to eat dinner and then open gifts at his place.

We reached his door and I told myself that I'd ignore his mess. That I'd brush aside any claustrophobic feelings that might sneak up on me. So when he opened the door, I was pleasantly surprised.

Nick stepped inside and gestured for me to join him. He had the smuggest smile on his face.

The main room had been completely cleared out. Where I remembered once seeing an endless stack of books, I noticed a set of bookcases. In the former place of an overrun coatrack was a nearly barren one, a single black coat on it. And Nick actually had furniture.

A light from a small Christmas tree illuminated a corner. I took in its meager number of ornaments, promising myself I'd try to share something from my collection with him.

The room wasn't large, with the kitchen combined with the living room, but now that everything had been organized, the place was actually cozy. Nick headed into the kitchen and pulled a large casserole dish from the oven. When he lifted the lid, I had to hold back the urge to tackle him for the food.

"Whatever's in there smells wonderful!" Only slow-cooked meat would generate that kind of drool-worthy reaction.

"Well, if you're hungry, there's plenty to go around."

With all the stuff Nick usually had everywhere, I wondered how he pulled off the cleanup.

The food piqued my attention as well, since I'd never seen him cook. With hardly any kitchen space, how would he have an opportunity? I didn't want to offend him, but I had to ask. "Did you perhaps cast a spell or two to make this food?"

Nick feigned a hurt face. "I can't believe you'd think I'd use magic to cook."

I continued to stare him down.

"Okay, I picked up a prepared roast at the deli down the street after work. Then I left the food in the oven on low heat."

The expression I gave him should've been of mock distaste, but I couldn't keep from laughing. "At least I know it won't kill me. I trust your food source choices."

Nick put the dish back in the oven. He fumbled through the kitchen as if he wasn't sure where everything was.

"Do you need help?"

"I'm good." He searched around the meager counter space. "When I cleaned up the apartment I didn't really use a system when I put everything away."

My eyebrows lowered. "And where did you put it all? Your coat?"

"Even my coat pocket wouldn't hold all the junk I've got."

I took a step out of the kitchen toward the two other

doors. One of them was to the bathroom—while the other one had to be his bedroom. Would it be too forward of me to look behind curtain number one?

With a wicked giggle, I raced to the bedroom door and whipped it open. Behind me I heard Nick's protests.

"What do you think you're doing—"

His voice cut off as I stood gaping at his bedroom. Or should I say the wall of junk blocking the entrance into his bedroom. So that's where all his stuff had gone.

"It all had to go somewhere," he said quietly.

With my index finger, I tapped on a set of books protruding from a tangled mass of clothes. The books didn't budge an inch. Somehow he'd crammed everything into the room.

I shrugged. "As long as you can shut the door, no one will be able to tell you stuffed half of Brooklyn in there."

"True." He appeared a bit embarrassed, and I felt kind of bad I'd teased him.

"You did a great job. So, when are we going to eat and open presents?"

He sensed my graceful change in subject and pointed over into the living room. "Have a seat and I'll serve."

Dinner tasted great. Nick turned on the radio to some light jazz music. Since it was only the two of us, I got as much pot roast as I wanted. The sides had been picked up from the local deli as well, but I couldn't complain. We finished the food quickly.

I'd bought Nick's gift long before Christmas. Even though I still felt a bit awkward with him, the gift seemed appropriate.

"Lady's choice! You get to open yours first." I shoved the bag into his hands. I could've received mine first, but I just wanted to see his reaction to my gift.

He opened the box and chuckled. "You can't be serious."

With a smirk he held up the lime-green T-shirt, socks,

and slacks I'd bought him. A matching hat would've made him the twin of the Jolly Green Giant—so I threw in one of those suckers too.

"You like?" My eyebrows danced. I could be bad when I wanted to be.

He continued to shake his head but then stood. In a few deft movements, he took off his black shirt and donned the green one. "How does it look?"

"You look nice and normal."

After I said it, we both laughed uncontrollably. We were *so* far from normal, it was hilarious.

Next, it was my turn. His gift to me left me breathless. A beautiful crystal ornament of a wolf with a string of woven gold. Far too expensive to give to a friend. But then again, maybe he didn't see me that way.

"This is too much." I put the open box on the coffee table. I was afraid to touch it. It probably wouldn't be as pure afterward.

"A new ornament for . . . hopefully a new start." He picked it up and pushed it into my hands so I could examine it closely. "Don't worry about the cost. A friend owed me big-time, and his skills produced the work of art you see before you."

He gazed at me with those midnight eyes as if he expected something. My chest tightened. Forgiveness maybe for what he'd done? It wasn't as if I didn't think of him as attractive. I knew that underneath his green shirt lurked wide shoulders, a set of washboard abs, and a narrow waist. But the truth of the matter was that no matter how hard I tried, I couldn't find space in my heart for him when images of another constantly flashed in my mind.

All I managed to say was, "Thank you, Nick."

I felt nothing more. I couldn't give him any more. Not with Thorn in the way or the events from the fairy battle. Just not right now. I had to tell him as much.

"Nick, there's something we need to talk about." I held the crystal wolf in my hand, hoping my grip wouldn't crush it. "I can't give you what you want. We can't be more than friends."

"Can I ask why?" he asked softly. "Is it about what happened in Jackson?"

I immediately replied, "No, it isn't." I'd said it far too quickly not to sound guilty.

Nick looked toward the tree, then his gaze shifted to his hands. "I was wondering when you'd figure everything out."

"Did you plan to ever tell me?" There was no anger in my voice—only concern that things had progressed to this point. I should be used to Nick hiding things from me. But the whole life-force-draining thing was something else entirely. It was on the level of hey-I-should-tell-you-I-used-you-and-you-almost-died kind of thing.

Here we were, having a quiet dinner between friends, but after what had happened in Maine, could we move on to a *real* relationship? One where we walked hand in hand down the street, among other wary shape-shifters who avoided wizards? One where I took him home to meet my parents? And finally, could I ever trust him again?

Nick spoke first. "To be honest, I'd hoped I'd never need to tell you, since I didn't want to lose you. I don't want to. I am sincerely sorry."

My heart dropped, and my voice quivered when I said, "Would you do it again? If we were in the same situation?"

"To save the life of the woman I care deeply for, I'd do it even if she'd never want to see me again."

I didn't look at him, but I knew he gazed at me with an expression in his eyes I couldn't run away from.

"Things would be difficult for us," I managed to say. "Especially with the way things are between our people."

Nick offered a bitter snort. "Not all wizards and war-locks are bad, Nat. A few rotten apples on the tree shouldn't spoil the whole bunch. Has what people said about you stopped you from doing what you wanted? I never took you for a person who only saw someone's race, instead of who they truly are."

"You know I'm not that way."

"Then stop giving me excuses. If you don't want to be with me, then cool, but don't tell me we can't be to-gether because you're a werewolf and I'm a wizard. You and I know very well what's between us right now."

I was quiet for a while, then finally replied. My fingers ran back and forth over the ornament while I tried to find the word he'd pushed me to say. "Thorn."

He smiled briefly, and then his shoulders sagged a bit. "I'm not blind. I know you still think about him. But the way I see it, if he's marrying someone else, then all you need is time to forgive me for what happened back in Maine. And I'm the kind of man who has all the time in the world. Whether you need me as a friend—or some-thing more."

Damn. I thought he'd say more to press the matter—maybe even fight me a little, like a wolf would, but he simply sat next to me on his couch, humming lightly under his breath while Miles Davis's jazz trumpet played a lonely song on the radio. Miles's music had been a part of my past with Thorn. A past I'd never recapture. Every haunting note was pure torture.

I set the crystal wolf on the coffee table. My hands were far too shaky. My heart tore. Ripped over poten-tially hurting Nick, angry I couldn't let Thorn go.

Five days. I just needed to make it five more days. Then I'd stop holding out the hope that Thorn could be mine.

Chapter 21

After such a rough evening with Nick, I hadn't expected to come home to find Thorn waiting for me.

"I thought you'd be home." He sat on the bench on my back porch.

"I was out for the evening."

"I know. I can smell the wizard all over you."

I didn't have any other seats on the porch except for the single bench so I had to sit next to him. On the farthest side anyway. As much as I wanted to be next to him, I didn't feel strong enough to be seated beside him. The words I said next surprised even me. "What I do with Nick is none of your business. Whether he rubbed himself all over me or I rubbed his shirts all over my face is my affair."

We'd done *none* of that, but why not let Thorn feel a bit jealous?

He didn't respond for some time. Long enough for the cold to seep into my coat. What made things even worse was I didn't detect anger or any other emotions. Just his stone face staring at mine.

"You're right. I don't have a say in whether you see him or not. But you can't stop me from wanting to protect you."

"That's another thing. I'm rather happy right now that your fiancée hasn't stalked me since we don't see each other anymore. Especially since she threatened to knock me on my ass a few months ago. You're pretty much handing me an Erica-should-kick-my-ass card with your little visit tonight."

Thorn leaned forward and sighed. "When will you get it through your head that I don't care about what she thinks about us?"

"You're here. We're alone. Her imagination could go nuts coming up with the array of sexual positions we're plotting on this porch."

Thorn grunted and stood to lean against the wall. "Is that better?"

It didn't make a damn difference. I could practically smell his skin—enough to feed my imagination. Feed it with thoughts of running my nose from his neck down to his chest. My tongue wanted to take the same path. *Good Lord. How the hell did my mind go there so fast?*

"It doesn't matter." I looked away from him to focus on the forest behind my house. "The point is that I'm moving on with my life. You *left* five years ago, and now that you're back, I can't assume anymore that we'd have a chance."

"Just because we can't be together doesn't mean I can stop caring about you."

I harrumphed. "After you left I didn't expect as much."

"I've only given what I have to give."

Which should've been everything, but couldn't be.

He sighed. "Right now it feels like you've already left me behind to start something new."

"I've left? You left me a long time ago when you ran away in the *first* place. Better yet, you seem to have easily forgotten that I'm not the one who left this town. You ran away from *me*. Not the other way around."

His face tightened, but he waited for me to finish.

"You could've come back, but you didn't. You had a

chance to be with me, but you chose another life. Which was rather shitty of you, by the way."

"I already apologized for that. I can't say sorry enough."

"No, you can't."

"You also don't know the whole story." He sat beside me. Close enough for me to feel uncomfortable.

"I don't need to know, since the memory pretty much stabs me repeatedly in the brain stem every time I think about how a guy—who I thought loved me—could just leave, and then stay away for five years."

"I did run away, but—"

"After you left, I had to pick up the pieces of my life, which I still think are pretty much scattered up and down the Parkway."

He blurted out, "Can I speak for a minute?"

Blathering helped me focus on anything except for having to deal with what I faced right now. Everything between us had fallen apart way too quickly.

"When I left, I had every intention of leaving New Jersey and not coming back," Thorn said. "My dad had made plans for me for years. And I'm not just talking about marriage. He wanted me to be the pack leader after him. That maybe I'd build up the pack to become bigger and stronger than it was now. While we were in college, my father had accrued monetary debts for the sake of the pack. And only the Holdens could save us from losing valuable pack land.

"When I graduated, I thought he'd consider another successor. Maybe one of his right-hand men. My brother wasn't ready, but there were plenty of prospects. I at least expected Rex to be one of them, but he'd chosen me instead." He frowned bitterly from the memory.

"Most men would step up to the challenge and do what they had to do. For a while there, I was ready to give my all. Wasn't I the son of the alpha? But then I learned I had another obligation. I also had to marry a woman I didn't love. Through Erica I had to sire the son her father had always wanted." His voice grew more and more quiet. "At first I flat-out told him no. Especially since I'd have to break your heart. Here I was—with my family honor and the Code on one side, and on the other was you. My father told me that perhaps he should make you disappear if I couldn't make the *right* choice—"

"So you left," I interjected.

"To protect you, I left."

"Why didn't you tell me all of this a few months ago when you came back?"

"Would it have taken away the pain you felt?"

I shook my head.

"I tried to *immediately* come back. I *knew* I was wrong, so I packed up my things and I prepared to return . . . but I ran into trouble."

I turned away from the view that had held me steady to look at his profile. How many times had I wished I could be sitting next to him like this?

"Trouble for five years?" I whispered.

"The kind of trouble where I moved every mountain to get back home—but someone else didn't see things the way I did."

"What happened to you?"

"Do you remember the night of the battle? The night when Luther stabbed me?"

I nodded. Who the hell could forget when a madman stabs someone else three times in the chest?

"I'd used old magic that night. Old magic I'd learned from another werewolf."

"But—"

"Let me finish." He sighed. "For the longest time, I'd always been fascinated with it. Studied it. But because of the Code, I kept the knowledge to myself. Not long after

I'd arrived in San Diego, I learned of a woman who was willing to teach old magic. I saw it as an opportunity to satisfy my curiosity. It was a big mistake. Mira taught me a bunch of dime-store tricks, but never told me about the consequences for werewolves practicing magic. Even worse, she'd only used me to get her former warlock lover jealous."

I licked my lips. I had a question bubbling in my mind and if I thought about it too much, I'd never get up the nerve to ask. "Did you sleep with her?"

He touched my knee briefly. Only rubbed his fingertips along the curve. "No. I'd never do something like that willingly. Although she offered, I still belonged to you.

"In the meantime, her former boyfriend got jealous. When he caught sight of me, his only plans were to use me for his own magic." Thorn's voice roughened. "I almost got away. It was the fight of a lifetime, but I was no match for him. And he knew it. For five fucking years he held me captive. When he wasn't gloating, he used me for his best spells."

I took his hand. When I tightened my grip, he didn't respond.

"But I had the upper hand. I wasn't some dumb rogue who circled its cage waiting for a split-second opportunity to attack. I learned from him to figure out his weaknesses. Wizards and warlocks might not play with the same kind of magic, but they sure as hell both draw their energy from the same source: me. If I waited for the right opportunity, I could use myself and apply what Mira had taught me.

"By the time I'd entered my fourth year, I was plenty ready to play. You'd be surprised how easy it is to go stir-crazy in a cage. When all you have are your memories and time to recite the old magic spells. Spellcasters believe that since werewolves follow the Code, they have an advantage over us. But we're the ones with the power. We *are* a source. When I killed him, I showed him just how powerful that source could be."

"But at what price?" I whispered.

"Everything has a price, Nat. But to escape servitude, I thought the price was worth it."

The cold crept deeper into me, and I clutched his hand tight enough to hurt him. What had he done? "What are you saying?"

With his other hand he brushed his fingers through a few strands of my hair. "There are some spells you shouldn't whisper in the wind. Very black ones. On that day, I invoked a death spell, and its poison entered my system."

I sucked in a breath and then couldn't breathe anymore. Everything in me clenched. He kept going. I wanted him to stop. I didn't want to hear what he had to say next.

"Black magic doesn't affect warlocks like it does werewolves. They play with it differently since they aren't the source, merely a conduit of its power. I learned from Mira that once a wand or staff is blackened, it's tainted. Once its magic is used again, it won't be of use anymore."

The pain in my chest expanded further. Driving a knife of agony into my brain as it begged for air. The wolf in me whined, and then forced me to suck in air. But the inhalation resulted in an exhale of anguish. Anguish in knowing that to save my life, Thorn had sealed his own doom by using old magic to win his fight with Luther.

I saw the scene again and again. The knife in Thorn's chest. The chanting. The rising blade. The sealing flesh. All of it was a mistake. *For me.*

"You shouldn't have saved me," I managed.

Thorn picked me up and cradled me in his arms. The

heat of his skin warmed me. Not from magic, from his body. "After what I've done to you, it was worth it."

For a while I sat there. For how long, I wasn't sure. All I knew was sitting here with him felt *right*.

"What's going to happen to you?" I finally asked.

"I'm not sure. All I do know is that I'm not as strong as I used to be. And not as fast. Maybe in five years I'll be dead. Maybe less." He shrugged. "But we all can't live forever, can we?"

I detected his smile. Nevertheless, my heart broke.

He shifted me slightly. Enough for his face to look down on mine. He stared at me, but I couldn't look at him. I couldn't face him when I felt like everything was collapsing all around me. When I didn't glance at him, he leaned forward to rub his lips against mine. Not a real kiss, but a touch, one that made my belly quiver in anticipation of something I'd *never* have again. Something I wasn't worthy of having.

A few agonizing seconds later, he turned to look at the woods again. We settled into the silence and didn't speak anymore.

What was there to say? Things could've played out differently. He could've asked me to leave with him. But would I have left my dream job in New York City for him? My hearts says yes now, but what about five years ago—when I'd been more confident and happy? The scenarios rolled through my mind, but none of them brought me comfort.

I fell asleep in his arms on the porch, but when I woke up the next morning, I was tucked safely in my bed. All alone. I sat up, my mind racing. My gaze shifted to the empty spot next to me on the bed. The blankets hadn't been moved, but the pillow had been used. He'd briefly lain next to me while I'd slept.

If Thorn had asked me if he could stay the night, would I have said yes? Even under the circumstances? I knew the truth now about why he'd stayed away, and I still wanted him.

Then I remembered Grandma's words: *"One of them was made for your heart. While the other one was made for your soul."*

Out of the two men in my life, Nick was my kindred spirit—my kindred soul. The man who had quirks similar to mine. We could surely sit together for hours talking. Content with each other's company. But that wasn't enough. I yearned for Thorn, with every breath I took, every beat of my forever stubborn heart. Grandma didn't need to tell me which was which. After the talk with Thorn last night, I knew the answer.

The revelation didn't ease my pain. Matter of fact, it made it all the more powerful. I lightly banged the back of my head against my headboard and wished I had some grand scheme to escape this place. To escape this feeling: *regret at what might have been.*

I didn't want to face Nick, but I still worked up the bravery to ask him out for some coffee.

Even after what happened during our Christmas dinner, he was still willing to hear me out.

"Sure, I got the scoop on Mike's Magical Cart if you're interested," he said.

I couldn't resist chuckling. Nick always knew how much I loved cart food in New York. The stuff was practically a food group to any New Yorker, but for the supernaturals who roamed here, Mike's cart offered the best.

"Not today. I'd prefer a quick coffee."

We walked through the snow to the nearest deli. We didn't have to go far. Nick offered to teleport us there, but I declined. My feet worked just fine. Even though I was still sore from training every morning by myself.

After we sat down with coffee, he spoke while I wiped down the table.

"You look really distracted today."

I shrugged. "We all have our good days and our bad ones. Today, mine isn't of the good variety."

He reached out and touched my hand as I wiped off the creamer. When I paused, he withdrew.

"Do you want to talk about it?" he asked.

Would talking about it make it any better? "There's been some developments." I searched my frazzled brain for the right words. When they grouped together, I recounted to Nick what had happened to Thorn five years ago. Every little detail. It felt great to get it out—to lay my pain out to someone else, someone who listened without interrupting me.

Instead of immediately telling me everything would be all right, he said, "You must hate me right now."

"No, I don't hate you. It's rather hard to hate someone so nice."

"What I did to you wasn't what happened to Thorn. You know that, don't you?"

I prepared my coffee as I spoke. Anything to keep my mind steady. "Didn't you use me?"

He swallowed visibly. "Yes, I did. But it wasn't like what that warlock did. He didn't care about Thorn."

"So then why did you do it? Couldn't you have saved us without using me?"

Nick had abandoned his coffee to rub his fingers together. It seemed our hands told the world so much about how we were feeling. "With more time, I could've thought of something. But I had to make a split-second choice. It wasn't the best decision, but I had to protect us."

He was silent for a moment, then added, "Do you believe me?"

I nodded, although part of me wished things could've

gone differently. How could I forget about it when Thorn and my mother had been through something so similar? Could wizards and warlocks just go around doing that kind of thing to anyone?

"I want to ask you something." I leaned forward in my seat. "Based on what happened to Thorn, would it be possible to reverse the damage? He compared himself to a tainted wand."

Nick thought for a bit. "I don't know. I've never owned a tainted weapon before. The most I've heard is that blackened wands and staffs are turned in to the Warlocks' Guild to be disposed of. Whether they can be cleaned is a matter they'd handle."

"The Warlocks' Guild. I've never heard of them. Would they see me?"

"No," he said. When I frowned, he spoke quickly. "Don't even think about seeing those guys. If you think the warlock who captured Thorn was bad—well, you haven't seen the worst of the lot. They're a bunch of thieves and con men who keep the wizards busy cleaning up their messes with the humans."

My disappointment must've been evident.

"I'll ask around for you, see what I can find. But I can't guarantee anything. Warlocks and wizards haven't gotten along in a very long time."

That wasn't new information to me about their little fights, but I nodded and left it at that. We sat for the longest of time, silent and staring into our coffee cups.

By the time I finished mine, we said our good-byes.

I hoped Nick didn't think I hated him.

Not long after I started cooking dinner that evening, Aggie asked if she could have company over.

"Would you have a problem if I had a guest tonight?" she asked.

I gave her a sly smile. "You mean would I have a problem if you and Will had hot monkey sex tonight in your room?"

"It's not what you think, Nat."

"Oh, yes it is."

"I actually like him. I think he likes me, too."

I couldn't help revealing a cheesy grin from looking at Aggie's very serious face. "You really do like him."

"Yeah, I talked to your grandma and aunt Vera, and they said he'd make a good match for me."

"Ehh, I wouldn't listen to Aunt Vera when it comes to matchmaking. She's a barracuda who'll hook you up with one of my cousins when you least expect it."

Aggie stole a mini-tomato from the salad I was preparing. "Give the woman a break. She means well. Your grandma says Will and I would make pretty pups."

"Anything the Grantham brothers produce would be pretty." The statement immediately made me pause and cringe. Why had I said it?

Thankfully, Aggie missed the connection, and continued. "My dad would never approve of him, but it's not like he has a say in my life anymore."

"That's true." Aggie's overbearing father stopped calling here looking for her. At first, this had bothered Aggie, since she'd expected her dad to show up to take her back to New York City, but then she relaxed a bit when Will came calling more often. He'd been good for her.

"So when's Will coming over?" I asked.

"I have to ask him."

"Aggie, when's he coming over?"

"You just assume I made the arrangements without asking you?"

I stared her down in a way that said, *Did you really expect me not to know?*

She sighed. "Midnight."

I took the pan-seared chicken off the skillet. "Good.

You'll have plenty of time to clean up before he gets here."

I sensed her smirk behind me. Let her fume for a bit. At least one of us will wake up tomorrow morning with an I-got-some-and-it-was-good smile on her face.

"Did you get the message from your grandmother?" Aggie asked.

"What message?"

"The one I left you by the door."

In my current state, Aggie could have left a message on a billboard and I would've missed the damn thing.

"She wants you to stop at your parents' house. She wasn't specific when I pried." Aggie winked when she mentioned how she'd tried to call Grandma and get more information from her. "The note says she wants to show you something."

More old magic, perhaps?

I placed both chicken breasts on one plate and handed it to Aggie. "Enjoy!"

"Hey, where are you going?"

"To see Grandma real quick."

"What about the food?"

"I'll pick up a burger at Archie's on the way home. Save it for Will, for all I care."

By the time I got to my parents' place, they'd already eaten dinner. Everyone was settled in front of the TV, watching some Russian-dubbed soap opera. Dad was snoring on his La-Z-Boy while Mom helped Grandma with her knitting. From the pink-and-white blanket I spotted, Grandma and Mom had another gift set planned for Sveta.

"What are you doing here, Nat?" Mom asked.

"I came to talk to Grandma about a few things."

Grandma motioned me over. I kissed her cheeks and gave her a warm hug.

"I want to take a walk, Anna. Can you fetch my coat?" Grandma asked.

A few minutes later, I journeyed with my grandmother through the subdivision. She asked me how I was doing, but she primarily wanted to know if I'd been practicing.

"Do you still remember?" she asked.

I chanted the spell slowly. When I made mistakes, she corrected them.

"Not bad," she said.

By the time we were almost back at the house, I expected to learn something new, but she didn't offer.

"You seem distracted tonight," she said.

We chatted at the back of the house. I offered to go inside, but she declined, saying she wanted to enjoy the cold air like she did when she was back in Russia.

"Everything isn't going as planned, Grandma. First, it's Nick and now it's Thorn." I sat down on the old swing set while she sat in the bench across from me. I kicked at the snow and it drifted slowly back down.

"What's wrong with Thorn?"

I told her everything. About his imprisonment. About the price he'd paid for me. Just speaking of it left me feeling empty again.

"That isn't good at all. Such a shame." She tsked.

I gripped the ice-cold railings that held up the swing. The glacial sensation seeped through my gloves. "And I can't help feeling bad for Nick as well. He's very sorry about what happened between us."

"Is that your wizard friend?"

"Yes." I tried to find the courage to say everything. I had to tell someone or it would drive me crazy. "Nick helped me when the Jackson pack attacked us from all sides. He saved me, but he had to use me—like that wizard used my mother, like Thorn's kidnapper used him."

I stared at the ground and made circles in the snow with my shoe. A heeled boot was the worst thing to wear out in the snow, but it was part of my standard wardrobe during the wintertime.

"Did Nick apologize for what happened?"

"Of course he did. But it doesn't change that it happened."

"Does Thorn know?"

I gulped. "No, and I'd never tell him. I don't think Nick should have his throat torn out. But I also feel like what he did has made our friendship awkward."

Grandma nodded. "I'd imagine so."

The back door creaked open. We turned to see my mother poking her head outside. Had she heard anything?

"Natalya, don't let your grandma stay in the cold like this." My mother frowned for good measure, then smiled. "My mother might be a polar bear, but she's bound to get sick if she plays outside too long."

Grandma rolled her eyes. Thankfully, Mom wasn't at an angle to see her mother's expression. Folks tried to take care of Grandma much more than she'd prefer at times.

"Let's go inside, Grandma."

She placed her arm through mine, and we walked into the house. As I got her settled, I heard a knock at the door. "I'll get it."

I unlocked the door and opened it to see Alex.

"What are you doing here?" he asked.

"Talking with Grandma. Is everything okay with the baby?"

He pushed off my concerns. "She's fine. Karey needs some spices, and I knew Mom would have them. What did Thorn want?"

I froze. "Thorn was here?"

"He was just outside the door. It looked like he was leaving. And boy, was he pissed."

The synapses in my brain choked and then fired to connect point A to point B in mere seconds. Outside. In the backyard. Oh God, I'd told Grandma about Nick and me. I'd told her everything about how Nick had used me.

Oh, shit.

Before I could grab my keys, Grandma sputtered, "Find Nick, *now.*"

Chapter 22

I'd never driven so fast in my life. Driving at night wasn't my favorite activity, especially when my mind couldn't stop thinking about every cop along the Parkway waiting for someone like me to donate the cost of a speeding ticket to their department budget.

My mind then kept twirling around two questions: How far ahead was he? Did he know *where* to find Nick?

To be safe, first I drove by the Grantham cabin, but Thorn's SUV wasn't there. Driving past his usual haunts also came up with zero results.

My heart sank to think about what could be happening right now. Thorn, furious and bitter, ready to open a new bloody pocket in Nick's coat. Nick, forced to defend himself, having to hurt Thorn.

This whole situation would go down the crapper faster than I could snatch an ornament at a post-Christmas sale.

While one hand held the wheel, the other one tried his cell phone. It rang, and rang, and rang.

"Pick up the phone, Thorn Grantham," I hissed.

I tossed the phone in the passenger seat. Why *would* he pick up? He was probably too busy sharpening his hunting knife while he drove with his knees!

A normally one-hour drive to New York took me forty-five minutes. I still had to cross Manhattan to reach Brooklyn, where Nick lived, but the evening traffic wasn't cruel to me.

By the time I reached the Greenpoint neighborhood, I was happy to see everything looked intact. There was hardly a place for me to park, though, so I decided to walk to Nick's place to investigate.

Then I spotted a line of smoke in the air from the next street over. I rolled down my window, and the smell hit me. Burning gasoline and burnt cinnamon in the air.

"Damn it, Thorn."

Screw the car. I'd been towed before. I double-parked and sprinted around the corner. If I didn't have to worry about the poor humans who might get in the middle of a fight, I might have freaked out from the possibility of no way home or having to pay an exorbitant fee to retrieve my vehicle.

By the time I ran down the block a ways, I heard the fight. Or should I say, I watched as a four-door Buick came flying down the street. From the haphazard way it landed, I suspected it was Thorn's handiwork.

I caught up with them, after I thankfully entered the veil of a magical masking field. Nick must've painstakingly tried to keep humans out of the mix. (Which would be rather difficult with cars flying all over the place.)

The overwhelming stench of burnt cinnamon made my eyes water. Many spells had been cast here.

"Face me, wizard!" I heard Thorn snarl. "Or do you hide behind your cowardice?"

Thorn stormed toward me. Which meant Nick was somewhere in front of me. Among all the cars parked along the street.

"Thorn, don't do this." I held up my hands. From the rage that shadowed his features, I knew the wolf was in control now. Thorn rarely looked like this: claws out, eyes dark yellow with hunger for blood.

"Nat." A faint whisper from my right. Along the wall of one of the brownstones. "Get away from here."

Thorn surged forward. He'd caught Nick's scent. Before he could close in, I watched the street light up so bright, I couldn't help but turn away for fear of being blinded. But Thorn didn't need his eyes to see. His nose and planned path led right up to Nick.

The thudding sound of his footsteps got louder. A growl emerged as he charged. When I expected him to ram into Nick, I felt the impact.

And so did Thorn, as he bounced off an invisible wall of some kind.

Dazed, he yelled with a hoarse voice, "You'll fight me for what you did to her."

The lights around me dimmed. When I spotted Nick standing not far from me, his staff aimed at Thorn, I whispered a plea. "Just go. Don't force him to use old magic to hurt you."

"I haven't done anything to him except defend myself."

"I know. I'm asking you to look the other way. Teleport out of here. Do what you always do. Just give him time to cool off."

Nick took in my face for a few seconds. All the while, Thorn paced in front of the barrier. When Nick touched my cheek, Thorn banged against the wall holding him back.

"Please?" I put some distance between Nick and me.

"I could end this now," Nick said. "He'd never remember tonight or what he learned."

The barrier disappeared. Thorn moved, closing in fast.

"But I'd never forgive you if you did that," I whispered.

"That's why I won't." Lights shimmered around the edges of Nick's form. By the time Thorn reached for him, Nick had blinked away into the night.

Chapter 23

*M*ost women didn't have to drag their ex-boyfriends to their double-parked cars after breaking up a fight. I guessed I was the lucky lottery winner tonight for that particular ordeal.

"Why did you do it?" Thorn grumbled.

"I didn't do anything."

Thorn refused to open the passenger door. "You know damn well what I'm talking about."

Fury rose in me quickly. "I'm not the one throwing around cars in a fit just because I got angry after *eavesdropping* on a conversation." I rolled down the passenger-side window. "Now get in the car before I throw you in it."

Thorn got in and slammed the door.

"Feel better now?" I quipped.

Thorn was beyond furious, so I let him stew while I drove. We'd been through long drives together before. Back in college, Thorn had driven me to all sorts of parks so I could run as a wolf. But tonight was different. Thorn had raced all the way here to defend my honor. And I'd denied him justice in order to protect the man who was my friend.

At last we made it to the Grantham cabin—thankfully in one piece. When I pulled up to the house, I expected him to flat-out leave me.

"Come run with me," was all he said.

"What?"

"Take off your clothes and come with me to the forest."

When a man like Thorn Grantham spoke words like that, he demanded enough attention to make any woman remove her breeches. But I didn't want to run tonight. Snow continued to fall. Some of the roads were slick with slush and mud. After all the running *after* Thorn, I didn't want to chase him anymore. I'd had enough.

But then I looked at him. His eyes blazed with need that made my heart ache. He didn't touch me, but I felt the invisible tug nonetheless. It had a hypnotic effect on me that I couldn't resist. The wolf within urged me forward. I took off my coat first. Unzipped the back of my skirt. My boots followed not long after.

We abandoned the car to sprint out into the woods. Once we ran a bit from the house, the rest of our clothes came off. The change took over, and the wolf inside me reveled as I surrendered control.

Like carefree pups, we ran through the snow and bushes into the night. I didn't care where we went. Or what we hunted for. Only that this moment lasted where Thorn and I were together.

After a few miles, he took me to an abandoned house. From the outside the structure appeared dead: broken shutters, boarded-up windows, and a slightly caved-in roof. The scent of the fire that had burned part of the roof remained. But the years of sunshine and cold weather had dried out the wood.

I switched back to human form once I was safely inside. Even with walls, a bone-cold chill swept through the room.

"Where are we?" I asked.

"A quiet place. The old Taggert house. We can hide away for a while from the others." By "others," I knew he meant Erica. I suspected she'd call him pretty soon to check on his whereabouts.

"I should go home."

He grabbed and shushed me. "Do you want to go home?"

I wanted to protest. But the feel of his strong arms wrapped around me left me heady with happiness. Instead of running tonight all alone to vent his anger, he'd chosen me to join him.

He tucked me into a safe spot next to the stone fireplace. A few pieces of wood remained inside. Thorn had been here before—alone. His scent lingered in the blankets stowed away in a corner.

Why did he hide away here? As the future alpha, he should stay in his father's cabin. Was it to hide from Erica as well?

"Everything will be nice and comfy once I get the fire going." He left my side to light the fire with a set of matches. When the flames danced in the bitter wind, he added two bits of hay to bring the fire to life.

"Why did you bring me here?" I asked. Why not head straight for the truth?

"We need to talk." He didn't speak for a minute or two, and then blurted, "Are you happy with that wizard who used you?"

I'd hoped, at all costs, to avoid this conversation. Thorn knew about Nick, but I'd never meant for him to learn about what happened. "Nick's harmless. No matter what's happened, he only wanted to protect me."

"I don't like it when you're with him."

A smile crept to my lips. "And you think I like it when Erica rubs her relationship with you in my face?"

"That's different."

"How? I'd love to know."

Thorn's face reflected both pain and anger. "I don't want her. I want to be with you."

Slowly, the fingers of his right hand crept along the floor. They lingered close to my thigh before they flexed and contracted. I read hunger in his brooding eyes, the tension stretching the muscles on his shoulders and neck. The fingertips brushed against my skin briefly, then retreated. For seconds that stretched into eons, all I could hear were his rapid breaths. The rapid beating of his heart. Finally he surrendered to his need without words, pulling me closer. The hard lines of his heated body drew me in, stirring my blood. I tried to fight the rising desire, but, hell, the man was naked.

His body was mere inches from mine as his eyes took me in. Even though we faced each other, he didn't speak for a few minutes. "I could kill that wizard. But no matter how much I hate him, I can't deny that we've *both* wanted to protect you. Even if you didn't want it that way." He tilted my chin up and possessively brushed his lips against mine. Our gazes locked again. The heady scent of his desire increased. His desire to be with me instead of Erica.

"Do you remember the night when I came home with your father?" he asked.

I nodded and tried to rub the chill from my arms.

"Erica asked me point-blank why I couldn't let you go." He pushed my hands away from my arms and caressed my skin. "She said you were flawed. I told her you were perfect. Perfect in all the right places."

I sucked in a deep breath. Then snickered to hide my elation. "I bet she took that well."

He rubbed his nose against my cheek and inhaled. Deeply. "I won't bore you with her response."

His hands descended down my arms, then drifted to my face. He left a trail of pleasure that heated my skin.

Something inside begged for me to go home, but I couldn't resist. This moment, this second, Thorn Grantham belonged to me. From his smooth lips to the tips of his toes. I breathed in his essence and filled the empty space in my heart with its warmth and love.

I had to speak. He'd called me *perfect*. Perfect, for God's sake. Even if this man truly didn't belong to me, his words brought sunshine to a ship cast adrift on turbulent waters.

"You're the love of my life, Thorn."

He opened his mouth to reply, but I placed my fingertip against his lips. His mouth moved to speak, but I didn't want to hear his words. Even if he wanted to say the same. I knew where things stood. My trembling hands moved to place his hands on my hips. The cold air, from the hole in the ceiling, brushed against my shoulders and hardened the tips of my breasts.

A smile touched my lips. Was I imagining this whole encounter? His lips placed kisses from my forehead down to my nose. Then they met mine. At first tentative, then possessive. The urgency grew to a fevered pitch as our tongues touched. The chill in my bones turned to fire.

Thorn continued to head southward, to nip at my neck. The blond whiskers on his chin rasped against my skin.

"I've hungered for you," he whispered against my skin. "For so long." He reunited our lips. Light kisses melded into a hungry embrace, where we reached for each other again and again—fervently trying to keep the momentum going. From my position in his lap, my body responded to his every touch. He reached under my arms to pull me upward so he could kiss my breasts. I became heady with each stinging bite. Each tug of his lips as he sucked, each pull of his mouth tightened my body until I shuddered with need.

But he wasn't done with me yet. His rough hands roamed over my back and then cupped my bottom.

For years I'd imagined us together like this. All the

elaborate positions we'd do. How we'd make love and then sleep for hours curled next to each other. Like we used to do when we were together. I refused to hold back anymore. No one would come for us tonight. We wouldn't stop this time. The length of his arousal pressed against my stomach told me as much. More kisses from him turned into my moans and pleas. He'd touched me everywhere . . . except for where I truly needed him.

But Thorn Grantham had limits as well. Teeth clenched and eyes churning with need, he grasped my waist and pulled my hips up. The whole time we couldn't break our gaze from each other. I swam within the pools of his golden eyes, waiting for him. Then he united our bodies, releasing a satisfied growl as he wrapped my legs around his waist.

I gripped his shoulders, an exquisite pressure building in me while I rode him in his lap. Every sensation left me wishing, hoping, our lovemaking wouldn't end. He held my hips and ground into my body, whispering my name in my ear. "Natalya." Additional words tickled my neck, but I couldn't hear them. What words did he whisper?

After so long without him, the urgent need for release came fast. When I reached the peak, I held him close and sighed. Thorn continued to move inside me, gently now. Contracting and pulsing with each thrust, I expected him to grab my hips to find his release, but he seemed content to wait for his moment.

When our breathing had slowed, he led me to the blankets. Thorn unfolded them and pulled me down beside him.

He explored my body again. Kissed calves. Nibbled inner thighs. For the longest time, he teased me with his tongue, licking my belly button and then descending southward again and again. When I thought I'd climaxed too many times—as if that's possible—he claimed me between my legs. While before I'd set the pace, now Thorn took control. I reveled in his heat, his passion.

The energy built between us. His eyes turned from gold to burnt amber. So dark. So strong. He adjusted his position to grasp my buttocks. The deep strokes left me begging.

"Please, Thorn . . ."

"Soon, baby, soon." His warm breath against my neck turned into soft growls. Then his body stiffened, his pleasure found. I followed him a second later, gripping his waist. He collapsed against me, and I welcomed his weight. The feel and scent of him surrounded me like a protective cocoon. I missed this feeling so much.

Eventually, he settled himself at my side, my back against his chest. With a worn wool blanket pulled over us, I drifted off into a peaceful slumber as the lights of the fire danced against the walls.

When I woke up, I could see the lingering dark of the night sky through the hole in the roof. I stretched and couldn't resist smiling. I'd spent the night with Thorn. He lay next to me with his arm protectively over my hip. The fit was perfect—as if his arm should be there every time I woke up.

Yet, it wasn't meant to be that way. Especially once we left this house.

The sting came fast, and it seared me deep enough to bring tears to my eyes. An ache that was painful enough to churn my stomach. This place. This moment. This hideaway had been stolen, and *I* was the one who took it. I'd put Thorn in this position.

I didn't know how I managed to do it, but I pulled his arm off me. Oh, God, it hurt *so* bad to do it. I made it a few steps and stopped at the open doorway. The freezing cold flowing through the forest nipped at my skin. It was the punishment I deserved for putting myself before the pack.

Hands snuck around my waist and pulled me back against a warm body. "Hey, you," Thorn whispered.

He attempted to kiss my ear, but with a stiff back, I turned away. I shook my head. "I shouldn't have come here with you." My heart beat painfully, but I had to do it. I knew the Code. The pack and its debts came first. Not me.

With a fiery sword, I had to let him go, had to pierce his heart to do the right thing. "All these feelings I have for you—I knew I wouldn't be able to resist. Hell, I didn't want to resist. And so I came here. And I touched you. But I shouldn't have."

He cursed under his breath as I took a step away from him. He continued to hold on to me.

Tears wet my cheeks, lingered on my upper lip.

He touched my back, but I shifted away. This couldn't be happening—how could I just let him go? He tried to pull me back again, but I refused to budge.

Why was it that I could still taste him, that it took *everything* I had to not turn around?

"I'd be willing to give up everything for you. We could try to make it work," he whispered. "You don't have to do this."

After an awkward amount of time passed, I managed to reply. "But you'd have to abandon the pack for me. It comes first, Thorn. You have an obligation to it."

"Nat . . . We both knew the moment we first kissed that I had an obligation. I want you to come first this time."

I was crying now, but the words came easily. "I've fought so hard to put my family and the pack first. I can't just turn my back on them. No matter how I feel."

"Did my *obligation* to the pack stop me from making love to you?"

I tried to bury the increasing pain in my chest. To ignore the bitter taste of the bile at the back of my throat. Even though I moved to leave, I wished I'd heard the words he'd whispered into my hair before they left with the wind. Perhaps he'd told me he loved me back.

"Did it?" he repeated, his voice vehement.

"We need to stay away from each other from now on." The pain returned, and I accepted it. Just as I accepted our lovemaking couldn't be shoved under a rock and forgotten. Every werewolf who encountered either of us would know. They would smell him on me, and me on him. Anyone would know we'd made love.

He let go of me and walked around me to leave the house. He didn't turn around. And he didn't reply to what I'd said.

It was a damn shame no one was around to hear me say, "I love you, Thorn."

Chapter 24

The next morning, I still didn't feel any better. My belly ached, and since I'd wronged the universe, my morning just went to hell. My best blouse had a tear. My skirt had a wrinkle that just wouldn't *die*, even after I steamed it to death. And on the way to work, I got a lovely flat tire.

No one stopped to help me either.

While I hauled out the spare, more dark thoughts weighed down my shoulders. It was the shame of my late-night tryst being out in the open. No matter how many times I doused myself in body wash, I couldn't scrub Thorn's scent from my body. The next couple of days would be pure hell. I cringed as I finished changing the tire. I'd brought all of this on myself. I was the *other* woman. The one that wasn't good enough to actually be his mate. Whatever happened to me today, I pretty much deserved it.

Like I'd promised, I'd packaged that treacherous goblin's enchanted blade to ship it back to him. But when I got to the postal service drop-box by The Bends, I noticed that the damn weapon had morphed itself again, this time into a stupid broadsword. (As to what was lurking nearby that would require me to need one, I really didn't want to know.) The sharp blade protruded out of the metal box. Somehow it had "cut" through the metal, and now I had something I couldn't ship without violating several safety laws. *Swell*.

It didn't improve my mood, of course, when Bill had something to say about my tardy arrival.

"What happened to you? You're *late*." He spied a customer who let her kids wander too close to some glasses. Any closer and he'd have to show his true colors and be an irate business owner. "Just because your trials are coming soon doesn't give you an excuse to show up looking all tired and old—"

"Good morning to you too, Bill." With a sour face, I waved at him and kept walking. He had no room to talk about people looking old. I'd seen what his species really looked like. Even though he was a few centuries old, his age was the *least* of his problems.

Work that morning was blissfully quiet. That is, until the customer service desk bell went off. I didn't want to look to see who it was. Especially if it was Erica. With one whiff of Thorn she'd be pining for a bitchfest of epic proportions.

When I couldn't take the ringing anymore, I left the business office and noticed a witch around my age playing with the ringer on the desk. I didn't recognize her, but she had a casual air about her. She flipped her chestnut bob back and smiled as I approached. Not too much perfume, but a pleasant dab of something expensive and tasteful. I wondered if she'd been around werewolves before. Most folks bathed themselves in the stuff without thinking about the noses around them.

"Hi," she said. "I corresponded with someone regarding an item I found online." She whipped out her Black-Berry and typed furiously on it. My goodness, I had a phone, but the most I did with it was place calls. She swiveled her hand around to show me a picture of the ornament she was referring to.

"I called about the Santa's Big Breakfast Christmas ornament. I saw it on your website a month ago, and I thought it'd be a perfect present for my friend. She goes crazy for anything related to breakfast."

I grinned and thought, *She isn't the only one crazy for that thing.* I knew exactly where it was on the floor. I'd ogled it every time I passed it. In fact, I'd almost bought it, until an e-mail from a Tessa Dandridge up in New York City inquired about it. I could have said no and hoarded the thing like that Golem from the *Lord of the Rings,* but my customers came first.

She leaned forward and smiled. "It's still available, right?"

Willpower, could you kick in right now, please? Customers needed to come first. "Of course. Isn't he cute? Let's go take a look at him." Part of me screamed, *Santa's Big Breakfast should be mine!* I've had a bad day, and he should be part of my collection at home to make up for the hell I was about to endure. Would she appreciate him? Or should I ask, would her breakfast-crazed friend protect his wooden table with a plate of pancakes stacked in a precarious manner? I didn't think so.

We walked over to the display case for small trinkets. I blurted, "Are you sure she'll like it? I have plenty of shiny wands I'm sure she'd love."

"Oh, no. She gets wind-witch wands from her family in Chicago for her birthday every year. She donates them to charity all the time. I mean, who'd want a wand simply because it's shiny? For all you know, the thing could cast spells to make mud pies." Then she slowed down as she spied the ornament.

"There it is! So adorable." Her face wore the same expression as people do when they saw a cute baby. She had great taste in clothes and ornaments, but I didn't see myself tolerating her presence for hours on end.

Of course, Thorn would pick this time to walk in. My

body softened, and I hoped he wouldn't look my way. *Especially after what I'd done.* The witch's eyes left the display case to follow my brief glance. She gave a short assessment. "Not married. And quite attractive."

I eyed her and tried to fight the surge of jealousy. Had she set her sights on him as well? "What kind of comment is that?"

"I'm a matchmaker. With your eyesight you would've caught it as well if you looked for such things. He's not my type, but I can see he's yours." She leaned against the display case with a wide grin.

"He's a friend from a few years ago."

"I beg to differ on that one."

"You just met me. What makes you think you can stand here and figure out whether I find a guy attractive?"

From across the room, I heard Thorn whisper a few words to Bill and then walk out the door. But before he left, he paused. I almost waited for him to turn around. To at least glance my way. But it was best to at least *try* to be strong under the circumstances. So I focused on my customer.

"Should I scrape you off the floor now or later?" the witch matchmaker asked with a knowing smile. She pulled an imaginary piece of lint from her mauve-colored coat.

"I just glanced at him—that's all." I had no plans to broadcast my pain to some stranger.

"Look, I've been matching people for several years now. I can tell you like him. You might've thought you stood there, but you didn't. While you were trying to play coy, he got an eyeful of you that would've made me want to check out his wand if he had one."

Damn. So he had looked at me. I tried to pull myself together, but the woman read body language like a sharp-eyed werewolf.

"Th-there's nothing between us—not anymore."

She snorted. "Yeah, and you're just good friends. Isn't that what you said?" She tapped the display case. "Is the price the same as what was advertised on the Internet?"

I wasn't ready to let the subject die. "We're just friends."

Tessa stood up and rested her hands on her hips. "Can you stand there with a straight face and tell me you wouldn't say yes if he asked you out right now?"

"He's engaged." I reached for reasons, and they came quickly. "Her name is Erica, and I'm sure they'll have a happy life together with lots of kids."

She tilted her head and waited. Damn, she was good.

"Yes, Thorn and I have a history, but we're not in a position to act on it." I glanced at the door and hoped she didn't see it. "We can never be more. Not ever."

"Is that what you want? Is that what he wants?"

I bit my lower lip and pushed a tray of fake costume jewelry on the counter two inches, into its proper place. "What I want doesn't matter anymore."

"Who says so? Someone important?"

The Code said so. The pack's well-being said so. Didn't she have a purchase to make? I may have desired Santa for my collection, but this intrusive witch scratched my hide the wrong way, and I wanted her to leave.

"You deserve happiness like everyone else." She flashed me a bright smile, and I couldn't help but return it. "You should grasp the bull—errr, wolf—by the tail and go after what you want."

I shook my head. I'd already made my choice and couldn't go back. It was time to focus on the store. Where was the incessant stream of customers who bothered me all the time? Of course, for this brief moment in time, the witch had me on the spot without interruptions.

"Do you want to be alone?" she asked me. "Is that the

way you want to live? 'Cause if I had a man like him around, I wouldn't want to be alone." She opened her pocketbook and retrieved a card. "Look, you may not want to do it, but even shy people can connect with others. Here's my card. Give me a call at my office and we can talk. You seem like a nice woman. A bit eccentric—but as a witch, people could say the same about me."

"Thanks." I traced my fingers along the glossy letters of the card.

"No problem. And keep your head up! You need to go after him if your heart's in it. Or at least start dating. Happiness these days is yours to have, if you want it. Life's a journey that's meant to be shared with someone else." She peered into the display case again.

I tucked her card into my pocket. Time to buck up, think about taking her advice for the future. The trials would pass, and I'd need to reevaluate my life after that. "Would you like the ornament gift-wrapped?"

"That would be fabulous. Danielle will love it!"

The trip home from work was a quiet one. There was no need to hurry. Tomorrow I'd have enough to stress about, what with the trials. Why rush to meet my doom?

When I reached my house, Aggie had already come home and left. I didn't see a note either. I guessed she'd make an appearance after spending some quality time with Will.

I ventured outside to get some firewood. Might as well start a fire and make some s'mores like I usually did.

With all the quiet around, I never saw the strike coming. Like Thorn often does, she seemed to appear out of nowhere, a blonde wraith with bouncing curls—and a solid swing of her iron crowbar against my thigh.

Chapter 25

For the rest of my life, I'll never forget the sound of my bones breaking, my flesh tearing open from the splintered bits. The choked sounds from my mouth as the agonizing pain shuddered through me.

Erica stood over me, her eyes venomous. "When burned, a lesson learned," she purred.

To add to the fun, that evil, vindictive bitch lit a match and burned my hand with it. I guessed she had to back up her little "lesson" with the real thing. She circled around me before tossing her crowbar in the snow. Then she kicked me in my ribs. Her steel-toe boots hurt like hell.

I tried to suck in a few breaths, but she grabbed my hair and brought me up to look at her. "I told you over and over again to stay away from him. I guess you're too stupid to figure it out."

She was silent for a moment, but that didn't last for long. "Since you've *fallen down,* I don't expect you'll show up at the trials. And if you tell Thorn about our little *talk,* I might just have to visit your brother and his family after I become Thorn's mate." The sneer on her mouth grew. "Perhaps all the Stravinskys deserve my special treatment?"

Something in me snapped. "If you touch them—"

"Shut up!" She placed her boot on my shattered leg, and daze-inducing white pain arched through me.

I yelped like a wounded pup.

She released my hair with a vicious jerk and then retrieved her crowbar. Shocked and dizzy, I stared at the growing red spot on the snow. The pool built—all of it from me. I could almost feel the pull of my body attempting to close the wound. To keep my lifeblood from seeping out of me.

"If you know what's good for you, you won't show up." She tapped the crowbar in her hands a few times. "Though, with that nasty break, I don't think I'll have to worry about you, will I?"

I didn't look at her as I slowly shook my head. The wolf inside wanted to lash out at her. To scratch that self-serving smile from her face. But the human part of me had been broken. Erica had finally won.

She stared me down and then left. I should've watched her walk away, so I could glare at her, but the only thing that came to mind was my new burden. A much-deserved one.

Another sacrifice. Another price to be paid, and another secret to be kept.

My trip to my car to retrieve my backup cell phone could be better described as a shuffling, zombielike motion. Every hop hurt enough to make black dots dance in my peripheral vision.

I had to give that woman credit. She knew exactly where to hit me and how much force was necessary to break—or should I say splinter—my tibia. How studious of her!

Out of all the bones in the body, she chose to injure the one that would take the longest to heal. A break that would've killed a human, due to excessive blood loss. She'd made a solid hit to the largest bone in the leg—a blow that would debilitate *any* wolf for about a week.

Unfortunately, I didn't have a week to recover.

A strange laugh escaped my mouth. I never expected things to end like this. Not in this nauseating manner, as I limped to my car, barely able to breathe. I was supposed to have a fighting chance to enter the pack.

My hand shook as I fumbled the door open. My breath came out in wet gasps. A dampness I didn't want to think about soaked my pant leg. It was just more evidence for me to clean up. Using my arms, I precariously tried to lean into my car while not touching the inside with my filth. The very thought that I'd get blood all over my seats was enough to make me start panting faster.

Normal people wouldn't care, I tried to tell myself. Normal people just let things go. (Especially when they were dying, damn it!) But I couldn't reason with the rising anxiety or the painful whimper from my indecisiveness. The pain of knowing I needed serious help versus that incessant reminder of the consequences of my actions.

Do you know how much you'll have to clean? (Screw the cleaning!)

Are you thinking about the germs? (I'm dying here!)

Blood draws vermin. Vermin bring disease, they cause infection. (To hell with infection. To hell with the vermin. Pick up the damn phone.)

I closed my eyes and snatched the phone. My fingers flew over the keys to dial a number. But I stopped before I hit the CALL key. When I opened my eyes, I realized the number I'd dialed and knew what would happen if I talked to him. Nothing good.

Somehow, I cleared out the number and dialed the person I should've called in the first place.

"Nat?"

I could barely hear him over the sounds of music and a crowd. All the external noise bled into me, and I held the phone away from my ear. Or maybe my grip had faltered. I wasn't sure which.

"Help me . . . Please." My voice sounded dry.

"Where are you?" The music sounded softer. His voice farther away.

My lips moved, but nothing came out.

"Don't move," his voice was urgent. "I will find *you*."

My legs wobbled, and then the ground came at me fast. Face-first. The last thing I heard was Nick's voice.

"I will find you. I promise."

A warm hand caressed my cheek. Then it traced a curved line over my eyebrow.

I heard a voice mumbling something. A phrase on rapid repeat.

"It's all dirty. It's all dirty. It's all dirty."

The hand moved from my eyebrow down to my lips. The voice was silenced. Mine.

A sensation—like the warmth of fresh honey for bread—coursed over my leg. It was strange compared to the cold of the snow. I felt the warmth of the body that wrapped its black coat around me.

The heat turned into a smoldering fire that blanketed me until I couldn't feel the pain anymore. I swam within it. Reveled in the comfort of forgotten pain.

"Open your eyes, Natalya."

I blinked twice and then opened them. Nick sat next to me on the ground. His coat was over me, protecting me from the cold snow that fell. One of his hands rested on my thigh, while the other brushed against my face.

"What happened to you?" I didn't answer. His next question came a bit later. "Who did this?"

"I was attacked. But you don't have to worry about that—I managed to get in a few hits." Even as I said it, my voice croaked a few times. I wasn't fooling him.

"Was anyone else hurt?"

"No," I said quickly. "Just me."

"Who did this?" He said again. This time more forcefully.

"Please don't ask anymore."

His mouth formed a thin line. "I could force you to tell me."

"You could, but you'd hate yourself afterward."

Should I feel bad that I'd used his valor against him? Perhaps so. Perhaps not.

Nick was silent for a while, and I assumed I'd won. Then he ended my happy moment by saying, "I don't know if I'll be able to heal this break."

He'd healed me over and over again. Just like the other times, beyond the feelings of healing and protection, he always made me feel like I was the most important thing in the world. Even after I'd turned him away on Christmas, he'd come for me. My mind flashed to our time in the truck when he'd held my hand. How he'd always found a way to make the impossible . . . possible.

"Can't you just use more magic? Another wand?" Wasn't that what those spellcasters used when they were in a bind? It wasn't as if he could use me to boost his magic. I was as useful as a broken can opener.

I sort of knew the answer to my question, but he gave it to me anyway, "Magic doesn't work that way."

"So how does it work?" I whispered. Every time I'd whispered the spell from Grandma, I'd wondered what the trigger was. What did the spell do and how could I make it happen?

"Magic comes from within or from another source. If it's from another source, they must be touched by magic as well—like the transformation magic that shape-shifters have."

I nodded. "So my source of power lies in my ability to transform."

"Yes, but even if you do have that ability, you must understand that to harness it, you have to put in what you expect to get out. An equal exchange." He sighed. "I don't have any staffs and what I need from inside of me isn't enough."

Inside of him? What was he sacrificing?

"What are you saying, Nick?"

"I'm saying that magic isn't a simple formula. It isn't like a chemistry set you can put together and expect the same results every time you combine ingredients. It comes from here." He placed his free hand on my heart. "When you have the right tools—the right words—and you believe without a doubt, magic can happen."

But I'd said the words. I'd chanted until I felt like I could say them backward, forward. Hell, I could've been saying "I like cheeseburgers" in ancient Sumerian all day. But if nothing happened and I didn't know what to expect, what good would the words do me?

I settled for something I could see ahead of me. Something I couldn't avoid. "Is there any way I can be ready tomorrow? For the trials?"

"There's only so much I can do. Whoever did this to you messed up your leg pretty bad."

So my celebration for how well she'd hit me hadn't been mistaken.

"I want to know who did this to you."

I sensed the bitterness behind his words. He wanted to take my pain away and satisfy his anger by finding out who'd hurt me.

Silence was my answer, so he resumed healing me. When he spoke again, he sounded cheerful, as if he was trying to distract me. "Hey, do you remember our first exercise together?"

A small laugh snuck out of my mouth. "The drunken satyr—I mean, shape-shifter."

"I ran into the fellow over a week ago."

Memories of our first exercise from Dr. Frank made me feel good. I hadn't expected to learn this white wizard had an affinity for fine furniture, or that he had the messiest home I'd ever seen in my life. (He even had my brother beat.)

"What form was he in this time? Or maybe I should ask if he was sober?"

"He was only *slightly* drunk, and he was in the shape of a dwarf . . . and a pack mule. But I was at a bar at the time."

I giggled at the thought of a dwarf sitting slumped at a counter—barely able to hold his form between the two. But then another thought came to mind: Who ordered the drinks, the dwarf or the pack mule?

"Did Mike and his Supernatural Drunk Bus service have to come and pick him up?"

"Oh, I think the shape-shifter put in a call somewhere else when a female centaur came by to show him a good time."

The very thought of it made me want to scrub my mind with bleach to rid me of the awful image of a mule/dwarf/shape-shifter doing the nasty with a half-horse, half-human creature.

When the laughter dwindled, I closed my eyes and clenched the seashell. It never worked, but I guess giving up on its magic was rather difficult.

I lay quietly, thinking about the spell Grandma had taught me. Eventually the words emerged from my lips.

Nick chuckled softly beside me. "You did it."

"Did what?"

"I felt it."

My eyebrows lowered.

"Do you feel any different now?" He had a knowing look on his face. Almost like a smug teacher.

"How did you know I did something?"

"Magic's a part of me as much as it's in you."

"So what did I do to you?"

"The spell wasn't meant to affect me."

I was calm. Blissfully, wonderfully calm. The kind of calm I only got from my pills. I laughed. The perfect gift from my grandmother for an anxious human and her wolf.

"Can you move the leg?" he asked.

I shifted slightly—only to feel pain sharp enough for me to inhale with a hiss.

"Like I said before, I can only do so much."

The pain radiated up my leg. How long had I lain here on the cold ground? My hand crawled along my leg until it encountered the tear. The bones weren't protruding anymore, but even the slightest touch spoke volumes: I wouldn't be 100 percent tomorrow.

"Can you help me stand up?"

"You need more time."

"Vulnerable wolves just lie there. I need to get up, Nick." I shifted to show I was serious, and he finally got the idea.

With the amount of pain I felt, standing wasn't the smartest idea. But the gesture had a point. Erica may have beaten me down, but I could still stand. The whole thing didn't have that "Here's my middle finger" kind of feeling, but it was close enough.

With Nick's help, I walked a few steps toward the house. Even though we were outside in the cold, I was drenched in sweat. Every step was another nail sealing my coffin. When I cried out, Nick stopped me.

"Just rest for a second."

A half hour later, I'd made it to my porch. By then I was walking on my own.

Nick laughed. "Do you have a high tolerance for pain or a death wish?"

"Both." I ran my hands through my hair. It was filthy from the ground—I tried not to care. The urge to cry suddenly came out of nowhere. Maybe it finally hit me that I wouldn't be able to rejoin the pack. Maybe it was pain from the price I'd paid to put the pack before myself—for Thorn.

I cried quietly.

Nick didn't speak, nor did he reach for me. He simply let me get it out, like a good friend.

When I composed myself and cleaned up my bloody leg in the house, I returned to him. "I want to feel happy right now."

"Huh?" was all he said.

"We're going to the store to do our post-Christmas sale exercise."

"This isn't exactly the right time."

"Yes it is." I had money, and my fingers were itching to spend it on useless post-Christmas crap. "I need to maintain mobility to keep my body healing."

"That's a lame excuse."

"Just shut up and drive."

The post-Christmas sale at the local shopping center looked like the North Pole had blown up and left the remains of Santa's cheery innards scattered everywhere. Discount signs had been hung here and there, hoping to draw in shoppers to pick up decorations for next year.

I didn't need the signs to make me feel less guilty tonight.

Nick had offered to get me one of those motorized chairs when we went in, but I'd ignored him and grabbed a cart.

"Are you sure you want to do this?" he asked while I browsed the aisle.

"They have really nice fake Victorian lamps here. You might find one you really like."

"Trying to tempt me won't help. I have a lot more self-control than you do, apparently." He watched me toss a Santa hat filled with candy into my cart. It was followed by Christmas coloring books. Sveta was *far* too young for them, but I'd kindly hold on to them for her for the next two to three years, like a good auntie.

Nick's cell phone buzzed. "I'll let you get off on shopping for a bit while I answer this. Once I get back, though, you're done with your little binge."

He stalked off and left me to my cart of goodies. I continued down the aisle, examining anything that caught my eye. When I reached for an ornament in a torn box, I paused. Where was the pleasure? That feeling of unadulterated excitement that I felt when I shopped for my treasures? I patted down my pockets as if the excitement were something I possessed in physical form. I picked up the box and waited for the bubbling feeling, but it didn't come. The box was like others at home. The contents, a golden Rudolph ornament, promised something pretty to hang on a tree. But when I fingered the box's smooth surface, I felt . . . *nothing*.

"Are you gonna keep that, honey?"

I turned to see an old lady staring at the box in my hands. She wore a heavy brown overcoat that smothered her tiny frame. She smiled at me, wearing a shade of red lipstick on lips that were far too thin for it. A golden stocking cap completed her post-holiday ensemble.

"It's seventy percent off," she said. "That's a good deal. Are you gonna keep it?"

"No." My voice was quiet as I handed it to her.

"Are you sure? It's really pretty." She tossed it onto her massive pile of Christmas purchases. She'd even grabbed the broken candy I'd skipped when I first walked in.

"You find anything good?" she asked, pulling me further out of my reverie.

"Not really."

"Those mothertruckers here need to reduce the prices some more. My son of a bucket husband doesn't give me enough money to buy the expensive stuff."

My head tilted to the side. Had she just referred to her husband as a *son of a bucket*?

She thrust a set of Christmas doggie shirts into my now empty hands. "Honey, you need to grab this stuff fast before someone else takes it."

The aisle was very empty. No one came scrambling to snatch my stuff away.

"I don't really see anything I want."

"Oh, shake and bake!" She leaned across her cart and shook her finger at me. While she berated me, I wondered if she really had told me "bullshit" or if she actually needed to find a box of Shake and Bake.

"You can never have enough Christmas supplies. Especially at these cheap ace prices."

Now that I had the pattern of her cursing down, all I could do was chuckle. She cursed like a sailor—a clean one anyway.

I watched her pick out selections for a while, and my heart sank as she joyfully added her choices into her cart. She had a bright smile on her face, even when she groaned while stretching for something beyond her reach. I grabbed the item for her, and she thanked me.

By the time we were at the end of the aisle, it became crystal clear: It was time for me to find Nick and go home. I had things to do, and I was wasting my time here trying to use buying things as a crutch when I had real problems to face. But as I walked slowly down the aisle, dread filled me. I had a healing injury, and I wasn't fully trained yet. What the hell should I do?

Night came and ate away at the remains of the day. Thankfully, Aggie was spending the night with Will. She'd called briefly to check on me.

"Are you doing okay?"

"I'm fine. Nick stopped by and plotted our next exercise. Right now I'm just hanging out."

"You should get some sleep for tomorrow."

I sat straighter in my seat to try to come off as normal. "I'm too nervous to sleep. You know me. I'll watch TV and then doze off." Or maybe I'd cry in the corner over how shitty things had become in my life.

Aggie sighed, and then the sounds of enthusiastic chewing came through the phone. Probably fried chicken from the spacing between breaths. "I wish sleeping pills worked on you. When you stay up late your credit card mysteriously pops out."

"There was this nice china I saw on an infomercial—"

"Useless junk."

I heard a voice whispering in the background. Aggie giggled, and I could tell she'd placed something over the phone to muffle the sound. As her friend, I was genuinely happy for her. But I was jealous too. Here I was, resting for the night all alone.

After Nick got back to NYC, he had left me a brief message on my cell phone to check on me, but no one else had called. Not even Thorn. Right now, I wanted so badly for him to comfort me. For him to hold me close and reassure me that no matter what happened tomorrow, he'd still love me.

A knock on the front door drew me back into my conversation with Aggie. "I have to go. Someone's at the door."

I slowly walked over to the foyer, trying to catch the scent of my visitor. My nose immediately told me it wasn't Thorn, but another friend: Heidi. I beckoned her inside.

"What are you doing out in these parts?" I asked her.

She came in and sat down in my living room. The mermaid glanced at the fireplace, where I had a small fire going. "I came to see you one last time."

With everything I had, I managed to walk to the opposite love seat without showing my injury. "What are you talking about?" But then I remembered what she'd said at group therapy. "Are you sure you want to go back? It doesn't seem like you're ready for that."

She laughed softly, her red curls bouncing. At the top of her head, I noticed, her roots were white. I leaned forward to get a better view, and she pursed her lips at me.

"Yes, my roots are showing," she snapped.

"All this time I thought you were a natural redhead."

"I'm not." She rolled her eyes. "And I bet neither are most of the redheads in NYC these days. Anyway, this is what happens to mermaids when they stay out of the water."

My mouth formed an O, then I said, "So, have you actually gotten in the water yet?"

"I went with Eren to put my feet in to prepare."

"Eren—that's the man we saw in Maine?"

She nodded and continued to stare at the fire.

"You said at therapy that he's your best friend. Did he come to tell you that you had to go home?"

"Yeah."

From the length of silence that followed, it appeared

I'd have to keep prying information from her. "What happened?"

"I'm not just your average truck-driving, bartending mermaid who likes roughnecks." Her face brightened for a moment. "I'm a member of the Royal Court of the Atlantic Coast."

"A princess?" As in a fairy-tale princess who's also a truck-driving, bartending mermaid?

"Oh, nothing that fancy. My dad's a high-ranking general. He's like the equivalent of a duke or something."

I nodded and encouraged her to continue.

"Eren's one of my father's men. He was the one who left me that message at the gas station."

"So he's the one who killed all those imps. He didn't leave a trace of his presence other than the note."

"He's the best of the best at what he does. I wish he'd fail once in a while so I wouldn't have to go back." She bumped her head on the back of the couch. "The note said it was time for me to go home to call everyone to arms."

I frowned. "Don't most armies have multiple generals? Why do they need you?"

"My father's dead." She said the words without any emotion. Maybe that's what broke my heart the most for her.

I swallowed hard and stared at the floor. When I couldn't bring myself to speak, I took in the view of my boxes. "I'm so sorry, Heidi."

"I barely remember the last conversation I had with him before I left." She smiled briefly through her pain. "He'd always been on a mission of some kind."

"So you were alone a lot?" After all the time we'd been in therapy together, I didn't know much about her past.

"Children are left to fend for themselves at a young age where I'm from. Your mother gives birth to you, and then you go live with the rest of the children born at the same time. Everyone either lives or dies by learning to be strong and choosing to make the right decisions. I was part of a pod with other highborn merpeople. We found a place to grow up protected from the darker things that lurked in the deep."

My imagination built a picture for me of the ocean with Heidi inside it. She'd frolic with the fish and be carefree.

"Many of the highborn in my pod died from creatures you'll never see on land. The ocean's a cruel and vicious place compared to the safety of land."

Okay, I take it back. No frolicking.

Heidi continued. "When I came of age, it was time for me to start thinking about looking for a mate. My father urged me to join the army so I could learn fighting skills and catch the eye of a suitable male." She grinned devilishly. "There were plenty to choose from, and most of them were the bad boys my father liked to train. As I worked through training, I came to bond as a lifelong friend with my pod mate Eren. He wasn't like the others. He followed orders without questioning them. He was—dependable. I came to find that honorable about him.

"While we were resting from a training mission once, Eren took me to a grotto he'd thought was interesting. None of the other soldiers liked him much since they thought he was a brownnoser, so he spent a lot of time alone.

"We traveled for hours, until we entered a cave off an underwater mountain." She shivered and then closed her eyes.

"Everything went perfectly until we were separated. It

shouldn't have been a problem. I was a mermaid, and I could easily search for a path outside. But I never found one." Her breathing quickened and then broke as she said, "For hours I searched in the darkness, and then suddenly the water shook as an underwater earthquake hit. The cave I was in collapsed."

I knew where this story was going and I didn't want her to finish, but she appeared to need to get it out.

"Even though I'm nearly one hundred years old—just barely into adulthood—I've seen the deepest part of the ocean, touched the warmest of vents, next to underwater mountains taller than Mt. Everest. But I'd never been trapped all alone in a place that dark and cold in my life. I could move, I could breathe—but I was all alone, and no one came to me when I called. For the longest time I thought I was *dead*. Eren didn't come when I needed him."

I swallowed painfully as her tears flowed.

"Time passed. I don't know how long. But when I woke up, I found myself floating along a current heading up the coast, toward Canada. Somehow I'd escaped the cave."

"What happened after that?"

Heidi's face paled even further. "I washed ashore in Boston, and I haven't entered the ocean since."

"But what about your home? Your father? Didn't anyone come looking for you?"

She shrugged. "My family doesn't work the way yours does. We don't band together to help someone unless that person is of value to the merfolk. No one except someone's mate cares what they do with themselves."

Heidi said it matter-of-factly, but to me it came off as cold. The ocean was definitely more of a sink-or-swim kind of place than I'd want to live in.

"So why do they care about you now?" I asked.

"I'm the heir to my house. There are things my father was supposed to do that I must now accomplish. Or many people will die."

"Are you ready to go home?"

Her sigh came out slightly choked. "No, I'm not."

I stood, wobbling a bit before I managed to sit down next to her.

"I envy what you have," was all she said. "Sometimes I wish I'd been born on land. With a family like yours, who cared for me and protected me."

Most of them cared for me—and that was more than I'd ever need. But I was perfectly glad to share my babushka. She seemed to always have enough love for anyone.

Slowly, I reached behind my neck and undid the clasp on the seashell necklace. She gave me an evil eye when I placed it around her neck.

"What are you doing? That was a gift."

"Right now, you need it more than I do."

Her eyes darkened. "You offend me by giving this back—"

"And you offend me by not *taking* it back," I said gently.

Her face immediately softened, and she sat a bit straighter. Her fingers traced a line over the shell's most prominent ridge, like I always did. From her smile I knew the truth: Its magic would work *only* on mermaids.

"I don't know if I can do this," Heidi said.

"You can and you will. Weren't you the one who told me home's the place we always have to return to someday?" I wrapped my arm around her shoulders. Her head leaned in to rest on mine. "Tomorrow's a big day for both of us."

"Yes, it is," she said quietly.

"You'll do just fine, and come back in no time."

"You make it sound so easy."

I snorted. "It will be, 'cause I'll come find your sorry butt if you don't bring me my necklace back."

Chapter 26

As I walked down the first part of the course, I wondered if a cell phone call to Mike's Supernatural Drunk Bus would be my best move. I had to be boozed up and out of my mind to be here with my injury.

After my talk with Heidi last night, I should've felt fired up and ready to go. She had to take a step toward what she feared the most. Why couldn't I do the same?

The course's location was never revealed to the candidates. After walking it with the others, I was glad they hadn't told us. Whoever planned this trial had smoked from a cheap crack pipe and then passed it around asking for bright suggestions on how to scare the piss out of people.

Out of the six candidates, I appeared the least anxious. But, well, after everything I'd been through to get my family's honor back, it was either join the pack or leave so I wouldn't have to witness Erica parading around with Thorn's ring on her finger. Today I was here to finish the job. Whether I made it or not, at least I might get my respect back.

I took in the scene. It resembled a boot camp obstacle course. The serene scene, if you could call it that, included a wall to scale, a tire run, horizontal ladder rungs, and a frozen moat to swing across. Snow covered the ground, except for on the low crawl, where chunks of frozen mud and branches had collected. Filthy and disgusting, by my standards.

And what the hell was up with the wall the size of a small mountain? In terms of upper-body strength, I had zip. *Don't think about that. Think about victory. After everything you've endured, you'll go home as a respected member of the South Toms River pack. A position you can hold and not have Thorn in your life.* The Stravinskys already treated me like family, other than Auntie Yelena, but underneath it all, I wanted the pack to give me the respect I truly deserved. If I could survive touching this stuff without thinking about all the germs. Hell, that was what drugs were for. And with the amount of mellow purple pills I'd popped, most normal folks would have been stripped naked in the snowdrifts making snow angels.

The trials would begin at twilight, after the divorces. In my opinion, it's a bit much to make the candidates suffer after a couple dukes it out as if the obstacle course were a California courtroom. Werewolves should mate for life, but I guess if the couple hated each other, then why suffer for it? From what I've heard and witnessed, the Atkinses needed a divorce. They fought constantly, about everything—including the Atlantic Ocean—while I'd shopped at the grocery store.

"You're an idiot," Jillian Atkins had spat. "I told you the Mariana Trench is in the Indian Ocean."

"Oh, shut up," her husband said. "You always have to be right. I'd bet my ears it's in the middle of the Atlantic. I watched a program about it on the Discovery Channel."

They had the kind of arguments where all you could do was try to look away from the pending train wreck. Of course, I didn't intervene to tell them they were both wrong. They weren't in my therapy group, after all.

The divorce ceremony should only last about twenty

minutes, then the other candidates and I would be initiated into the pack by Farley. Who had somehow managed to live this long without dying from being an asshole.

After an introduction to the course, the candidates separated to head home to rest for three hours. I didn't bother to rest at the cottage. Instead, I sat in my car with a large lunch from Archie's and my last exchange with Nick on my mind. He'd come by early this morning to check on me.

"Are you sure you want to do this?" he asked. "You're still weak."

"I thought I could let it go. But I can't." Instead of looking at his face, I watched the way the wind whipped the lapel of his black coat. When I finally braved a glance at his face, he avoided my gaze, and I suspected he knew my feelings hadn't changed—even with Thorn's marriage approaching fast.

We didn't talk about whether I'd see him as more than a friend after the trials either. Maybe after I'd healed I'd be strong enough to think about the future and what I wanted to do. Maybe I wouldn't. I had a lot of thinking to do once I got past the trials today.

"You've given me a lot to think about—especially in terms of healing others," Nick said.

"I've given you that much practice, huh?"

His smile raised my spirits. "I've made the decision to enter medical school, under Dr. Frank's tutelage."

My mouth dropped. "That's a big decision."

"I need something new to occupy my time. A long-term goal instead of working at a pawnshop." He shrugged and appeared thoughtful. "Doing the same thing year in, year out won't give me a sense of accomplishment."

"You'll do great. And if you need help editing research papers, I'm pretty handy with a red pencil."

"I'll definitely keep you in mind." He reached into his

pocket and palmed something. Then he slowly opened my hand and placed two rose petals there. Bright red and freshly plucked. My skin tingled from where they lay.

With my other hand, I traced along the edge of the petals. "Is this from the rose you gave me? The one to protect my property?"

"Yeah. The magic still lingers there." Our gazes locked briefly. "It'll always be there."

As part of our first therapy exercise together—for me to go into an antiques store without buying anything—Nick had to give me the rose these petals came from. It had been so beautiful.

I managed to nod and thanked him for the gift. He'd never fully explained what powers the rose held, but ever since I received it, I'd kept some of its petals tucked away within my coat. Even though I'd told Nick we weren't meant to be together, he would always be with me. Forever my friend.

The adrenaline rush of waiting for the trials to start surged through my veins. Underneath it, doubt and apprehension tried to break free. But I refused to let those feelings overwhelm me.

Instead, I focused on what I was about to start. I gathered together with the other candidates so I could hear an introductory spiel from Rex. My luck just kept getting better and better.

"Good evening, candidates," Rex said. He frowned at me and shook his head. I gave him my screw-you look and then stared straight ahead. "You have the ten-mile run first. Those who complete it will be rewarded points. Anyone with times below the expected minimum will be disqualified as unworthy."

He paced back and forth between us in a lousy attempt at intimidation. "After the run, you'll encounter the most difficult obstacle course on the eastern sea-board. We don't allow cowards to enter. In our pack, only the strong prevail. The weak go rogue."

Oh, come on. Can you jack off to your glory speech another time?

(I zoned out for a few minutes but then paid attention again when he talked about the scoring system.) "Those with the lowest scores after the obstacle course will be eliminated. The final trial is the ranking showdown." He grinned. "My personal favorite. The candidates left will prove themselves worthy before the alpha by mak-ing their enemy submit. We want to see strength and char-acter added to our ranks. Not some pussy-whipped morons who can't defend a perimeter. You will have or-ders, and we expect them followed. You've got two min-utes to get ready before the run."

I checked out the competition. As the only woman, my odds weren't great. All of these werewolves had lived as rogue wolves at one time or another in places outside my territory. I recognized two of them. One was Ian, the mechanic who worked on Aunt Vera's car. He was a good man and wanted a fresh start in town with his small family. The other one I recognized, Sean, had arrived in town a little over a year ago. He had drifted here from Arizona and worked odd jobs until he'd se-cured a position at the mill. The other three candidates eyed me with disdain. To them, I was an easy way to gain points and achieve a higher rank.

Ian nodded in my direction. "You ready?"

Not really. "As ready as I'll ever be."

"I can keep a good pace if you need a running part-ner."

I smiled. "No need. I couldn't prepare for the rest of this course, but I did train for the run."

He chuckled. "Well, then I expect you'll be running circles around me."

Aggie and my family waited at the starting line, along with the rest of the South Toms River werewolves. Far behind the crowd, I spied Thorn standing next to his father. Bundled up for the cold, Old Farley leaned against his cane and watched us with his beady eyes.

"Let's go, Nat!" Aggie cheered.

The sun hung low in the sky as Rex raised a flag to signal the beginning of the trials. My heart nearly exploded in my chest as I waited. The frost in the air created gusts of mist with every breath. As I watched the flag hold steady in the air, I psyched myself up. Flared my nostrils. Allowed adrenaline to fill my blood. I could survive a ten-mile run in the middle of winter. Even with an injured leg. This was what I wanted.

The flag flew down with a *whoosh*, and we all sped ahead as fast as we could—in the snow. The path hadn't been carved out for us; only flags marked our route. Whatever happened to global warming, with all this powdery white? I plowed through the snow in my light boots, trying to think only of the course, to empty my mind. Does that ever work? The forest was quiet, except for my heavy breathing and the sounds of boots thumping through the snowdrifts. I had dressed appropriately, of course, but that didn't prevent the film of sweat across my brow under my cap. Aggie had warned me earlier to wear warm yet light clothing. Thankfully, my father had supplied me with some of my uncle's work clothes from his automotive repair shop. The garment was clean, and now I had something with movement and that would ensure my hairless rear end wouldn't freeze as I battled through the snow.

The three candidates I didn't know managed to sprint to the front. Sean was about five hundred feet ahead of me, while Ian had slowed down to run next to me.

"Come on, Natalya," he belted out. "You need to

move them legs, girl. You can't let those guys set the pace."

I grunted in response.

Ian resumed his faster pace, then doubled back to push me forward.

"All right, all right," I said. There went the idea of pacing myself to protect my leg.

"Hike them legs up! There you go," Ian panted.

After half a minute, we passed Sean.

"Move it, Sean!" Ian yelled. "You got to show them pups ahead who's boss."

Panting, Sean barely yelled out, "I couldn't train with the hours I got to work."

At the pace Ian the Taskmaster set, I couldn't catch my breath. My lungs burned, but with his sturdy legs and army-built voice urging me on, we rounded the corner and spotted the first of the other three ahead.

"We can pass him. In your head, keep seeing yourself passing him." Over and over again he spouted his mantra as we approached the man in a red snowsuit. The snow began to clear a bit as we approached a thicket of trees, and as we bounded over a log, we noticed another competitor ahead of us, trying to trudge through a heavy patch of snow.

I pointed to a log on the left. "There!" We went around the patch and, with a celebratory war cry, passed the wolf in red. The work was almost done. We had two runners behind us. Of course, my bad leg picked the perfect time to have sharp pains.

I tripped in an attempt to grab my thigh. "Ack!"

"Damn it, woman! Quit whining and ignore it."

"Oh, that's easy for you to say. You're in shape!"

"Yeah, right. I was shot three times in Vietnam, had the butt of a gun shoved into my face at the Alamo, and now I have a pissant werewolf complaining about leg pain. Move it, woman!"

As best as I could, I plowed ahead with him . . . and, finally, the finish line was in sight. I couldn't help but laugh as Ian shoved me forward so I'd finish with a time slightly ahead of his own.

I turned to him and punched his shoulder. "Thanks. For yelling at me."

Ian shrugged, grinning. "I don't get to do it often." He walked over to a friend waiting with hot coffee. I didn't have to wait long before Aggie and my father came to my side. My best friend pushed a mug of hot coffee into my hands.

"Drink it."

I took a sip and choked on the strength of the alcohol. "What the hell is in this?"

"Oh, it's just Irish coffee. A little bit of whiskey should keep you warm *and* wake you up."

"Wake me up? Is this before or after I pass out from inebriation?" I shook my head and shoved the cup into her hands. "You should tell people what's in stuff before they drink it. I can't have alcohol—I'm on enough anti-anxiety medication to calm a herd of horses in line at the glue factory."

Aggie rolled her eyes as my father chuckled. "Fine! I'll go get the drink made for the pups."

I scowled at her as she stalked away.

"How are you holding up?" Dad asked.

"As well as I can. Thanks to Ian over there." I wished I could tell my dad I was in pain already, but he looked so proud of me.

Dad nodded and patted my back. "Ian's a good man."

We stood side by side, and he didn't stop me when I leaned against him for a bit to focus on forgetting the persistent pain in my leg. My dad was also a good man—even with the past he had. No one could change that in my mind.

"Dad?" A question tickled the back of my throat.

"Yes?" He looked at me.

"How do you endure all the things that have happened to you without breaking? Without becoming an animal?" Some of what Roscoe had said about Dad went through my head. As I'd grown up, Dad had never exuded all the bad things Roscoe and even Luther had said about him. But it was hard to deny the truth: Perhaps a killing machine lived within my father. It was rather hard, though, to look up at him and think that. I much preferred to focus on moments like this.

Dad sighed. "I've roamed the earth for almost a century, daughter. I've been broken many times in the past." He paused. "Seen and done many things I wish I hadn't. But I still have my heart. And within my heart I have unrelenting love for my family. For my children. The wolf within can't change that."

Dad tilted my chin up. "You'll always be my daughter. And as such, you have what it takes to be part of the pack again. I know it."

I nodded and tried to fight the emotions that threatened to overflow. Before I could ask Dad more questions, Rex announced it was time for the obstacle course.

"All right, candidates! Let's head on over."

The course was less than a mile long. I'd learned from my father that every year the pack gathered together for more than a week to create the obstacle course. How they managed to accomplish this feat during the winter left me baffled. Maybe they kept warm and toiled drinking Aggie's Irish coffee.

Tired and in pain, I joined the other candidates at the startling line. The urge to limp was strong, but I kept it at bay. By this point, the sun had disappeared and only the winter moonlight cast a glow against the snow. The wintery breaths of the other werewolves filled the air as we waited. The other candidates's hunger to complete the trials hit my gut.

"Based on your final finishes we have the following point values: 100 for Sean Smith, 200 for David Fields, 300 for Ian Denton, 400 for Natalya Stravinsky, and finally 500 points for Heath and Kyle Reynolds, due to a tied finish."

The current standings left me eager to begin. I had a few people behind me, but then, the obstacle course and the standoff didn't bode well for my entering the pack. I glanced at the Reynoldses.

We all lined up at the starting point. I could hear Aggie cheering for me from the sideline. She held a mug and took a sip. I figured it was some of her coffee—I sure hoped she didn't drink too much. The last thing I needed was a drunk cheering squad. Before Rex threw down the flag, I caught Thorn's eye. From his position on the hill above me, our gazes locked for a half second.

He pumped his fist in the air and mouthed, "C'mon, Nat." Erica noticed our exchange and marched over to him. Before I could witness their conversation, Rex threw down the flag. Fresh out of the starting gate, I ran ahead of the men through the snow, toward the tire run. The snow had been cleared here, and I used my few seconds' lead time to plow through the tire run. Then I encountered the horizontal bars. Shit! I tried swinging from rung to rung, hoping my meager upper-body strength would hold me up. I watched in despair as everyone passed me.

"Move it, Natalya. It's just a bunch of bars!" Ian barked.

To make matters even worse, when I was only halfway done I fell from the bars, into the soggy mix of mud and snow. My bad leg took the brunt of my fall. The werewolf who oversaw this portion of the course told me to return to the start. "Go on, it's the rules."

With bared teeth, I limped back. I tried to ignore the fact that the other candidates had already moved on to the low crawl, while I used my weakening arms to head across.

The man overseeing the bars took pity on me and yelled, "Move faster. Grabbing each rung on its own takes longer."

I took his advice and immediately felt the bite of wood in my palms. I felt at least two splinters but ignored them—and persevered. No pain, no gain.

When I reached the end of the bars, my chest was heaving and I stumbled to the low crawl. I wanted to rest and alleviate the burning sensation in my shoulders, but by then, the men had completed the next obstacle. And with calming drugs or not, I had to overcome the worse thing imaginable: I now had to crawl through dirty snow—some of it partially melted into a dark, gooey soup. The men had already stirred through it, and my mind recoiled at the thought of what their clothes looked like.

A panic attempted to settle in my chest, but I took a deep breath and lay down. Maybe if I channeled my inner wolf, it would convince me I was rolling within the mother forest. *Yeah, right.* The sweet scent of fresh snow mingled with mud and I knew my deep thinking wasn't working worth shit. I couldn't close my eyes as I crawled forward, but I could mumble, "Oh, that's so gross." A whimper settled in the back of my throat. "Happy place. Happy place. I'm in a happy place."

Twenty feet later, I emerged from the low crawl to see the rope climb in the distance. Fifteen feet high with bright yellow rope hanging from the top, the wall was an imposing structure.

Ignoring the mud caking my arms, I grabbed the rope and made it about three feet before I knew I couldn't ascend any farther.

This particular section had a woman to oversee it, Mrs. Pearce. She chuckled and then offered a conspiratorial grin. "You know, no one ever said you couldn't use the trellis to get up."

I nodded to her and quickly ascended via the support beams. Using this method, I caught up with the trailing candidate Sean.

He peered down as I ascended and laughed. "Hell, I should've done that."

A hint of a smile broke out on my face, but it turned to horror when he suddenly lost his hold and plunged to the ground. Everything around us stopped for a moment—except for the snowflakes falling around him.

I was frozen in place as others raced to Sean and swarmed around him like excited worker bees. The snow darkened around his leg, where a bit of bone protruded from his pants. Not a simple break. It seemed so hauntingly similar to mine. Sean groaned and glanced my way as the chaos ensued around us. The rapid beating of my heart drowned out the noises of the men helping Sean.

His lips moved, and he mumbled faintly, "What the hell are you doing, Nat? Get going."

I looked up and once again focused on climbing.

Ten minutes later, I huffed and puffed to finish the course. The balance beam and moat swing weren't so bad. I clenched and unclenched my fists. The slow-healing blisters and burns would sting for a while. But they didn't compare to the burning sensation in my leg. Like Nick had warned me, his healing magic had only gone so far.

I watched a few members of the pack carry Sean away. Should I have felt fright or sadness when he fell? Due to his fall, I'd survived this round. I would advance to the next round, but what would that mean for the family he had to support?

Wet, dirty, and near exhaustion, I lumbered over to where the rest of the finalists were gathered around Rex.

Earlier, I'd seen Erica speaking with him. Why did she need to jump off her evil broomstick to bring malevolence and destruction to those around her?

"Looks like Sean has to bow out until next year, guys. Also, David Fields's scores won't qualify him for the next round so he's out too," Rex said.

I sighed. In the distance, I watched David down a beer one of his friends threw at him—glad that wasn't me. I'd scraped past elimination so far.

"We've already assigned the pairings. Ian, you and Heath will face off." Then he smiled at Kyle, a man far bigger than me. "Kyle, you and Natalya will fight."

I glanced at Heath. The Reynolds brothers were solid men, but Kyle was the larger and stronger of the two. I smelled the stench of a Rex/Erica conspiracy.

For the final trial, the entire pack formed a large circle, with a gap for Old Farley to watch from the side. He sat in a worn lawn chair and peered at us with his beady eyes. When I glanced his way, he scowled even more than usual and took a swig from his Thermos.

First up were Ian and Heath. I wanted to show my support for Ian, but I had my own problems about to bust loose. As I assessed the two combatants, I suspected everyone would expect the younger werewolf to have an advantage over a man like Ian. But after a few unsuccessful charges and swings, Heath learned the hard way that Ian had combat training.

Especially after Ian's fist connected with Heath's nose and knocked him back five feet. His legs flipped over his head and he landed on the snow with a wet *plop*. I could've sworn it was Ian getting back at the dude who hit him with the butt of his gun at the Alamo.

Around me, werewolves cheered and yelled as blood was spilled. Under normal circumstances, I would've turned away. Carnage wasn't my style, yet the wolf lingered under my skin and forced me to watch.

Heath's brother picked him up and carried him off to the side, where Pearl waited to check the participants. When Kyle returned to our waiting area, he had nothing but fury and anger in his eyes. Waves of aggression poured from him, leaving me quaking from my toes to my knees. Six feet and five inches of solid werewolf stood between me and my entrance into the pack. But this wasn't one of the werewolves who'd take pity on me, as Ian had on the course. From the way Kyle was rubbing his knuckles, he meant business. I was his final test, and he meant to pass.

How the heck could I beat him with a bad leg? But then again—no one knew about my leg, unless Erica had blabbed. Which was most likely the case, during that chat she'd had with Rex.

Rex urged Kyle and me forward to the center of the circle. He sneered at me, "You know the rules. First one to tap out or be knocked out loses." He glanced at Kyle. "Good luck."

As Rex backed away, I wished I knew how to fight properly. It wasn't as if I couldn't fight—like a girl, of course, but I could also unleash my claws with speed and agility. Unfortunately, none of those things mattered when brute strength was snapping your neck.

We faced each other, neither moving. Then Old Farley tapped his cane once on the ground, and Kyle charged.

In the distance, I heard Aggie yell, "Rip his ass a new one, Nat!"

As he raced toward me, I wondered if I could replicate Ian's moves. After Kyle slammed me into the snow and knocked the back of my head against a rock, I realized I lacked such knowledge. Once on the ground, Kyle raised his fists like a mad ape and hit me squarely on my forehead.

Now, it's said the forehead is the hardest part of the body. I would like to testify that this might be true, but

Kyle wasn't the one moaning in pain after the hit. Stars danced in front of my eyes for a half second. Then I formed a fist with one of my hands and struck him in his happy place—hard.

Like any man not wearing a cup, Kyle sputtered and used his hands to protect his package. Using the opportunity, I extracted my claws and raked them across his chest. The deep gouges bled heavily as he rolled off me, spurting curses.

"Get up, Nat!" Aggie screamed. "That's it. Get him!" I tried to rise, and weaved. My head throbbed. This time was far worse than my head's introduction to the dump truck's dashboard. The sky and ground blended into one before separating again. Damn, he'd hit me hard. But I couldn't just stand here, I had to make another move. I had to reach the end.

Unfortunately, I had come to this realization too late. Kyle had recovered quickly and now snatched the back of my neck. With a rough yank, he sent me face-first into the snow. I took in a mouthful of powdery white, then he raised my head again for a brief moment before pushing it back into the snow.

From that point, he pinned my face into the snow as I continued to thrash. I opened my mouth. Tried to turn my head to the side, while my lungs begged for air. No escape. All I had to do was tap out. Surrender. But as my hands clawed at his arms, the drive to release the wolf and win lost out. The efforts I'd made to decide to do this—even with the pain—were a waste. The moon debt I'd fulfilled for my family. I didn't want them to be for nothing. But the odds were too great. My failure was assured.

I tapped Kyle's shoulder—and sealed my fate in the same second.

When he released my head, I turned it to the side and took in a deep breath, which became spurts of wet coughs.

Through my haze, I heard Rex yell, "Kyle's the winner!" Rex slapped the other man's back to congratulate him. I rose on unsteady arms to sit Indian style in the snow. The sounds of cheering and disappointment blended into a strange cacophony around me. *I'd failed.*

Emptiness and sadness stabbed into my beaten torso. Aggie walked over to me and draped a blanket over my shoulders as Old Farley spoke. "Now that we have our entrants into the pack, Ian Denton and Kyle Reynolds, we can move on to our final task for the night." Thorn's father offered a rare smile to his son. "On this night, marriages are both severed and created." The pack leader beckoned Erica forward. I couldn't look at them anymore and, sagging into myself, wrapped the blanket closer. Not as protection from the chill in the air, that didn't matter anymore, but as a—albeit flimsy—cushion of comfort for my sadness.

"You okay, Nat?" Aggie brushed the back of her hand against my cheek. "Don't answer that. I know you're not. I'm so sorry."

I didn't shift to look at her face. Nor did I search for my parents. Tears welled in my eyes, and I wiped a bit of blood off my forehead. I never should have attempted this in my condition. If I'd remained at home, I could have spent my New Year without the headache from hell or palms that throbbed.

I couldn't look at Thorn and Erica. I refused to look at them. But it was like a car crash; I had to watch. For one final time I'd take in Thorn before he belonged to another. To my surprise, he was staring at me. Unwavering. His gaze reflected my pain, both the mental and physical. Then he said something that silenced the crowd and robbed me of my remaining breath.

"Don't joke with me, son," Old Farley grated.

Thorn repeated his words. Much more slowly this time. "I refuse to do it."

Erica's shoulders trembled, and she glanced from Farley to her father and then to Thorn. Did he refuse the pairing? Or did he refuse to fulfill his legacy as alpha male of the pack?

Erica took a step forward, her voice shaky. "What are you saying, Thorn?"

"You heard me quite clearly, father. I *refuse* to live with the decision you made." He chuckled and bit his lower lip. "I'd already changed my mind a long time ago."

Erica rolled her eyes. "What kind of bullshit is this? The pack needs a leader. Not a second-best replacement."

Will crossed his arms and glared at Erica.

"No offense, Will, but if you would've been the first choice, your father would have appointed you."

Will growled, "Plenty offense taken. And now I know why you don't have a say."

She thrust her manicured index finger in Will's direction. "I will be the alpha female of this pack." Her gaze returned to Thorn. "Baby, now, think about this. The pack needs the investments from my family." Her hands reached for him, but she pulled back when he flinched. "This isn't the time for you to turn into a lovesick pup. Is she worth more than your pack?"

My gaze flitted to the ground, and I wished I could ignore what words would come. He'd place the pack before me. That was our way. To make any other decision would be selfish.

From Thorn, I heard a heavy sigh. "Yes, she is." A long pause. "I refuse to live without her. She's meant to be my mate."

Erica flung her hands in the air and spit out a string of curses. "Do you think I'll allow you to ruin this night for me—fuck this!" Erica leaped in my direction, but before she could claw my eyes out, Aggie tackled her.

And what a sight Aggie made. She took a generous piece of Erica's golden mane and used it to fling her backward. When Erica attempted to tear at Aggie's face, my best friend slammed her fist square across the other woman's chin. Suddenly Erica's father was there, pulling his snapping and hissing daughter away from Aggie, while my father wrapped his bearlike arms around her.

"That's enough, everyone!" Thorn thundered. "I will not renounce my choice."

But Erica still wouldn't be denied her moment. With blood trailing down the side of her delicate mouth, she sputtered in my direction, "You. Me. On my family's honor, a challenge. A fight to the death. For the position of alpha female."

A curtain of seriousness passed over everyone. The silence ended when Aggie whispered, "Oh, fuck."

Chapter 27

M*ost* folks who have been challenged to the death wear white-powdered wigs and sip wine with their pinky fingers extended in the air. They swung around and pointed their ancient pistols in duels to take out their rivals. On a cold wintry day in South Toms River, New Jersey, I wondered if I'd meet my maker on this night, sans the flamboyant drama.

Challenges to fights to the death among werewolves weren't a casual "Ha! You challenged me to a death by battle." During this kind of fight, someone had to die, kaput, that was all she wrote. And for that reason, I froze on the ground, staring at my hands as my heart skipped a beat—twice.

When I looked up at Thorn, I thought I was looking at a ghost. His pale face illustrated his fear. He was concerned I might not survive.

I almost expected him to intervene, he even took a step forward, but I put my palm up to stop him. This was my fight to finish.

That didn't prevent Aggie and my mother from stumbling toward me. Mom begged, with tears wetting her cheeks, "Let me stand in her place. You don't need to do this, Natalya." Then she reached to grab at Erica's father. "I beseech you. Don't allow this to happen."

But Mom's words fell on deaf ears. Tradition was tradition. And among the pack, even my mother held tight to the Code. Among all the excited chatter, I tried to ignore the soft cries of my grandmother. In between sobs, she murmured the Lord's Prayer in Russian.

Aggie pulled me up and whispered, "You and I both know you can't walk away from this. I can create a diversion, though, and you can run away—"

Through my layers of pain, I smiled at my friend. If this was the end, I would end my life on a high note. Thorn had chosen me. *Me.* And even if Erica ended my life, she couldn't take back the words he'd spoken in front of everyone. "Thank you, Aggie. For everything."

I shifted my gaze to Erica. "I accept your challenge for the position of alpha female for the South Toms River pack." Weariness tugged at my shoulders, and my leg throbbed painfully, but I tried to stand tall.

Farley ambled forward on his cane. He barked, "Apparently we have a real fight coming." He assessed both of us, his frown shifting into a malicious grin. "About time I saw some real blood spilled tonight."

Erica stood at the edge of the circle with an air of fury marring her perfect features. The debutante had been washed away. Now only the ugly ice queen remained.

"You ladies know the rules. Both of you fight until we have a victor and the loser is dead. No one," he eyed Aggie, "is allowed to intervene."

Aggie lowered her head and shrunk back.

Erica's mouth formed a snarl. She rushed to unbutton her coat. Fiery and hungry to fight, she tossed it to the ground. The whole time she did this preening, I slowly unzipped my coat. I mean, who in their right mind should be in a hurry for an ass-beating?

The wolf within me hungered for this final confrontation. A chance to set things right had always been desired. But I was in control now. And this type of thought brought me both joy and self-confidence. I refused to surrender to the bloodlust.

"Oh, come on, bitch!" She paced back and forth, panting gusts of air that formed a fog around her. "Don't think by going so slow you'll get me to change my mind about tearing your throat out."

How ladylike. From the way she behaved, I doubt the local Girl Scout troop leader would use her as a mentor. Not with that potty mouth. As she stared me down with rising fury, I continued at my own pace, my gaze never leaving her. By the time I discarded my coat, a growl rose in her throat as she surrendered to her wolf and hunched over for the transformation. But I didn't give her a chance to start. I leaped toward her, swinging.

Erica reacted quickly to my move and slid out of the way. For my quick-thinking, I was rewarded with a vicious jab to my face. Her other hand swiped down my shoulder gouging my left arm. I stumbled away, but she wasn't done with me. She pounced and grabbed a fistful of my hair. Pain coursed through my scalp. Raw and vicious. Then she slammed my head into the snow. Again and again. The spittle from her growls fell on my face as she continued ramming the back of my head into the earth.

Since I'd recently fought with Kyle, the black spots so close to the surface returned. *Thud! What the hell are you doing? Kick this crazy bitch!*

I drew my legs in and thrust upward. The movement sent Erica flying into the crowd. She crashed into a few werewolves, who pushed her back into the circle with glee. Woozy, I could barely make out their yellow glowing eyes. Their excited growls. They wanted to see more blood.

The snow continued to fall and cast a strange scene as Erica came for me again, her blonde hair bouncing as she plowed into me with her claws extended. I used her momentum and propelled her again into the onlookers.

Deep in the crowd, Becky cackled, "Kill her, Erica!"

My moment of recovery didn't last long. She jumped on my back and viciously clawed at my ribs. From the way she feverishly swiped and scraped at my clothes, she wanted to rip my body in two.

Then she played dirty and slammed her fist right into the place she'd hit with the crowbar.

I wish I could say I took the blow quietly—that I didn't scream out and cower before her, but I did. I might've even blacked out for a second there.

Aggie continued to roar from the crowd. "Natalya, damn it, fight!"

Lights danced in my vision, but I managed to thrust the back of my head into her chin. The sensation jarred my skull, but the effect jolted her enough for me to free myself. I scrambled to the other side of the circle. The blood from my arm dampened my coveralls and trailed down my side. The healing process was much too slow in human form, but I had to use the advantage, since Erica, as a more dominant female, was stronger in wolf form. I couldn't allow her to change. Before she could initiate the transformation process again, I ignored my leg and ran full speed and rammed into her hunched body. She sidestepped my movement, caught me, and slammed me into the bitterly cold snow. Erica pounced again, this time wrapping her hands around my throat. Her legs held mine subdued, and all I could do was stare her down while she choked me.

"Your life belongs to me," she whispered. "In your death, I will live on." Her eyes, once blue and regal, became amber. She said more words, but I missed them as she faded away. Everything went numb except the sensation of her blood dripping on my face. "And as you die by my hand you'll know it was I who killed you. It was me who flooded your little piece-of-shit house."

Give up, whispered the wolf. *Play dead. Set me free.*

Erica giggled, sweet and melodic. "It wasn't too hard to release the locks on one of the levies. And watch the water spill forth."

My flailing arms ceased while I faded again. I heard the cries of my grandmother begging Erica to let me live. The nonchalant snort from my aunt Yelena. My brother had attempted to intervene as I laid still. *Slow your heartbeat. Calm yourself. Slow down.*

The spell that Grandma had taught me flowed through my head and emerged from my lips. No matter how much she'd beaten me down she couldn't take away the fire I had within. The spell calmed me and helped suppress the wolf that never surrendered. The wolf wanted to fight, but now wasn't the time. Soon my chance would come. Nick was right, if I believed enough, the magic was there waiting for me.

As expected, Erica shook my shoulders. When I didn't twitch, she stood to scream out, "I win!" She kicked my side, the force propelling me onto my belly. With wide, staring eyes, I watched my blood turn the snow crimson. I breathed into the snow once and then no more. Let her gloat. "Let me go to her," Alex snarled. "If she's dead, it shouldn't matter."

Not far away, I spied Thorn with his fists clenched. He hadn't intervened—there was no sorrow on his face. From the way his gaze bore into mine, he probably knew what I was about to do next.

The roar of the crowd dulled the sounds of my heartbeat. Erica would never see me coming. I set the wolf free. Unchained the vengeful animal within. Rage over the flood that had occurred a few months ago and ruined my belongings. All my precious ornaments. All the cleaning my family had done on my property. All those new memories I had due to the flood. I should thank her for bringing my family together—after I beat the living shit out of her. I slammed into her back. With my left hand wrapped around her golden mane, I lifted her head up and belted her face with the other. Again and again.

The stunned crowd fell silent to see Lazarus had risen from the dead. The change enveloped me. Fur sprouted along my back. The bloodlust filled my vision with crimson. Soon enough the hissing from my bruised throat turned into grunts as I gave into the fury. *Must. Kill. Her.*

But then I stopped.

The landscape around me turned white again. The all-consuming anger left as quickly as it had come. It took me a moment to realize I'd won this time. My gaze went to my hand, which held a thick portion of her hair. I dropped it. My opponent gasped in wet breaths, but didn't stir.

Somehow, I found my voice. "I refuse to lower myself to treat you as you've treated me."

Everyone, except Thorn, stared with wide eyes. My mother and aunts huddled together with handkerchiefs over their faces, drying their damp cheeks. They'd mourned too soon.

Even Auntie Yelena, who'd cheered—for Erica—had been silenced.

Farley finally spoke. "Kill her, Natalya. End this now."

I didn't waver. "No."

Every head bowed before Farley except two—Thorn's and mine. "No? You defy me?"

"If you want her to die, you come kill her." With my entire body yearning for me to rest on the bitterly cold snow, I stood my ground with a straight back.

Farley nodded to Rex and Will. "Finish this, now! A challenge has been made. According to the Code, the challenge must be completed."

Before they touched Erica, Thorn stepped in front of us. "That's enough." He growled deep in his throat. "It's over!"

"Thorn! Stand down." Farley's withered body shook with anger. Erica's father seethed as well. Their deal had been broken—in front of everyone. Farley poked his cane at Rex and Will. "This has gone on long enough."

Thorn thundered, "The alpha female has been chosen by me and, as my father decreed five months ago, I am the new alpha male." He shifted his gaze to his father. "Unless you want to stand before me and contest *your* decision." A battle of wills ensued as father and son stared each other down. In all my years, I'd never witnessed a fight for the position of alpha. Whines and growls of anger accompanied the tension in the air. But it was the elderly wolf Farley who backed down and bowed his head.

"We had an arrangement—" Erica's father cried.

"Oh, shut up!" Aggie pushed him into a snowdrift. He attempted to stand, to snap at her, but Will jumped between them. "It's over, Blake. Go get your daughter. She needs medical care." Erica's father rose, but his gaze never left Aggie's as he walked backward to where I guarded his daughter.

When he got close, I stepped back so he could pick her up and cradle her in his arms. Becky approached, with her eyes averted, and wrapped Erica's coat around her still body.

In one fell swoop, the cold air and my injuries gripped me in a savage vise. I clung to Thorn's back as my legs became warm custard.

"Nat!"

"No!" I ground my teeth together as the chill bit into the soles of my feet. "Don't turn around. This is my time. My moment. Don't take it away by babying me."

"Still the same stubborn Nat. You do realize you're

bleeding all over the place." He chuckled and placed his hand over mine to make sure I didn't let go.

"No shit, Captain Obvious."

When Erica's father carried her away, I took an unsteady step to reach for my shoes. Thorn grabbed them for me. Gently he placed my coat over my shoulders.

"You want to try to put them on?"

I grunted—even that hurt my ribs. "Bending over right now isn't a good idea."

My limp was painfully obvious, but I managed to walk through the crowd with my head high. What happened next was something I wasn't sure how to take in.

In between the shouts of congrats from the pack, I noticed that no one made direct eye contact with me. Every man, woman, and child lowered their head when I passed. The whole scene felt surreal.

But then I stopped before Auntie Yelena. Proud Auntie Yelena Torchinovich. Our gazes locked for a moment, and I could almost hear her virulent words, "They *tolerate* you since they pity you."

This time I didn't back down—I didn't turn away. After everything I'd been through, she could take me down with a single flick. But tonight I'd been pushed over the edge and survived. No one could take away my victory.

Auntie Yelena trembled, and then slowly turned to gaze at the forest ground, exposing her long neck. Thin fingers pushed her coat down to further expose her collarbone. Her acquiescence to me was complete.

The whole time, Thorn didn't speak or look my way.

At the edge of the crowd, I found my parents waiting. They quickly surrounded me in a hug. My knees buckled again, but Mom and Dad held me up without the others noticing. Grandma reached between them to sprinkle kisses along my forehead.

I managed to whisper, "Thank you, babushka."

"No worries; you rest for now." She blew me another kiss then hugged for my brother.

I thought my father would offer to carry me to a car so they could take me to the healer's house, but instead he took Thorn's hand and extended mine to him.

"She's yours to take care of now." He gave Thorn a stern look that melded into a grin. "Be careful, though, if she's like her mother you may need to keep her busy in the kitchen."

I rolled my eyes as Mom swatted Dad's arm.

Thorn kissed my forehead, and I winced. Every step to his SUV was pure torture until he set me down on the passenger's seat. Instead of closing the door after me, he stopped and stared.

"Did you doubt me?" he asked.

I didn't hesitate. "Yeah, I kinda did, but that doesn't matter now. I know the truth about my heart."

"What's that?"

A smile snuck on my face. "You never lost it. You just *kept* it."

With that wide grin of his, he shut my door then moved around the car and climbed into the driver's seat. Once the car was started, he set the heater on full blast. "Looks like I have some work ahead to patch you up." He took my hands and rubbed the palms. "I want to make everything right between us. We got a lot of talking to do."

Yeah, we had many conversations ahead of us. But then again, didn't all relationships have baggage—or in my case, baggage in the form of boxes? "We'll figure things out, but there is something I need to make clear right now."

"What's that?"

I took a deep breath. Right after I won the fight I knew I'd need to say this. "I'm not completely ready yet to be alpha female. And after a night like tonight, I don't know if I'll ever be ready."

With a slight smile, he set out to reassure me, whispering, "You won't ever need to do anything you don't want to, not anymore."

I returned his smile. "Thank you for understanding."

As I settled into the seat and turned my head to look at Thorn more directly, I knew pain still loomed in the future. He still had a blackened wound on his soul that would eventually eat away at him, and even though I now had him back, I knew our time together would be all too brief. All because of me.

Dark thoughts threatened to creep further into me, but I pushed them away. I'd won a major victory tonight. Thorn was all mine, and I planned to have it that way. If I kept my wits about me and quickly found a solution to his problem, I could keep him forever.

And I *would* find a way to save him. One thing I knew for sure was that the Stravinskys never backed down when it came to family.

As Thorn pulled out of the parking lot, he smiled and tapped the steering wheel to Creedence Clearwater Revival belting out "Midnight Special." "I know you're tired and all, but I have an important question to ask you," he said. "How the hell do we live with my stuff and your ornaments?"

I snorted—and it even hurt to do that. "Oh, we'll make it work. You'll make room after you see this adorable red and green bra and panties set I've been dying to show you."

He appeared somewhat satisfied with my response and flashed me a wide grin. "I think with those kinds of terms, I'm more than willing to find some space."

EXPLORE THE WORLDS OF DEL REY AND SPECTRA.

Get the news about your favorite authors.
Read excerpts from hot new titles.
Follow our author and editor blogs.
Connect and chat with other readers.

Visit us on the web:
www.Suvudu.com

Like us on Facebook:
www.Facebook.com/DelReySpectra

Follow us on Twitter:
@DelReySpectra

For mobile updates:
Text DELREY to 72636.
Two messages monthly. Standard message rates apply.

DEL REY SPECTRA